T0285215

THE NUDE

THE NUDE

A Novel

C. Michelle Lindley

ATRIA BOOKS

New York   London   Toronto   Sydney   New Delhi

An Imprint of Simon & Schuster, LLC
1230 Avenue of the Americas
New York, NY 10020

First Atria Books hardcover edition June 2024

ATRIA B O O K S and colophon are trademarks of Simon & Schuster, LLC

Simon & Schuster: Celebrating 100 Years of Publishing in 2024

For information about special discounts for bulk purchases, please contact Simon & Schuster Special Sales at 1-866-506-1949 or business@simonandschuster.com.

The Simon & Schuster Speakers Bureau can bring authors to your live event. For more information or to book an event, contact the Simon & Schuster Speakers Bureau at 1-866-248-3049 or visit our website at www.simonspeakers.com.

Interior design by Jill Putorti

Manufactured in the United States of America

1 3 5 7 9 10 8 6 4 2

Library of Congress Cataloging-in-Publication Data
Names: Lindley, C. Michelle, author.
Title: The nude / a novel by C. Michelle Lindley.
Description: First Atria Books hardcover edition. | New York : Atria Books, 2024.
Identifiers: LCCN 2023032959 | ISBN 9781668032954 (hardcover) |
ISBN 9781668032961 (paperback) | ISBN 9781668032978 (ebook)
Subjects: BISAC: FICTION / Literary | FICTION / Feminist | LCGFT: Novels.
Classification: LCC PS3612.I532749 N83 2024 | DDC 813/.6--dc23/eng/20231031
LC record available at https://lccn.loc.gov/2023032959

ISBN 978-1-6680-3295-4
ISBN 978-1-6680-3297-8 (ebook)

For Logan

Seeing is pleasure, but not knowledge.
—Elizabeth Bowen

THE NUDE

1

When a Greek fisherman caught a woman's body in his net—a marble statue, around five feet tall, missing two arms—I was working for a museum in Los Angeles on the other side of the world. After the discovery, a group of men hauled the figure to the island's only museum, cleaned her, and kept her on a metal table in a climate-controlled room near the back of the building. It was there, somewhere in southern Greece, on a windy day in April, where I first saw her.

"Doctor Clarke," the local antiquities dealer, a man named Alec, said. "What do you think?"

We were standing on opposite ends of the table where she lay, the only living people in the room, his eyes darting from me to her, her to me. I specialized in female statues of the Hellenistic Mediterranean, and though I was a curator for one of the most respected institutions in the states, whenever a colleague or patron called me Doctor, I did not immediately register myself as the object of their address, and in the ensuing blip of silence, an overwhelming self-consciousness would turn my tongue to stone.

What did I think? Pentelic marble, head tilted back, a stretched neck. If the statue should have cracked anywhere, it would have been there, but that delicate neck defied its own vulnerability. She was completely nude, with a rift on her right breast, a smooth abdomen, and censored vulva.

Minor depressions carved into both sides of her hips. She might have been holding something in her left hand—a mirror, likely—based on the way her chin pointed slightly upward, as though she were studying a reflection of something—or someone—behind her.

I tried mentioning this possibility to Alec in Greek, but upon hearing me, he appeared shocked, offended. I repeated myself, quieter, and with a questioning lilt. He shook his head. In English, I apologized. I told him my Greek was rusty. He waved his hand as if to say, it's nothing.

He offered me a pair of white cotton gloves and I began inspecting the statue's every bend and fold, casually measuring proportions, lightly tracing areas of abrasion. Both her arms had snapped off at nearly identical points. It wasn't uncommon for figures to be found without limbs, noses, genitalia, but usually, the breaks were uneven. Hers appeared, somehow, purposeful. Which isn't to say the fissures seemed inauthentic—just, rare. Each new vantage point conjured more questions, more ways of seeing. Her hunched posture insinuated a self-consciousness, while her curved torso and bent knee invited the eye to travel down, then back up again, suggesting either an indifference to possible observers—or else, an invitation. I bent to her level, my eyeline meeting the top of her head, where ropes of wavy hair twisted into a crown, curls like limpets around her temple.

Meanwhile, Alec circled the room's perimeter, the edges of his wrinkled khaki shorts skimming each hairy kneecap, his black socks pouring into white tennis shoes. On his left ring finger, he wore a thin silver band.

In English, he asked if I had been to Greece before, and in Greek, I said I'd been to Athens.

"Athens," he said. "Alone?"

"Yes," I lied, hiding my hesitation, "alone."

I stood and glanced out the single clerestory window, where I could see nothing but a stone wall covered in pink-blooming cacti. I'd noticed the size of the room—no more than a ten by ten—but it was only then that I allowed myself to feel its smallness.

"My cousin," Alec said. "Your—" He searched for the word. "Translator. Here soon."

"Yes, great," I said, thanking him, and though I certainly did need a translator, I resented this stranger's disbelief in my abilities.

As I walked around, the statue's pupil-less eyes followed me. I couldn't decide if her expression was desireful or agonized. Likely, it was both. Her features had remained in decent shape and, when eyed from certain angles, glitzed with traces of red and gold paint. That any pigment had remained was highly unusual for a figure so ancient. Elsewhere, she was either poorly sculpted or else decayed: the ears, for example, pockmarked and peppered with limonite; the feet, hewn without detail, except for the toes, of course, which curled under, as though in a perennial pre-orgasmic state. When viewed holistically, these mismatched conditions gave her beauty a patina of unease. I'd never seen anything like her.

A few moments later, someone walked through the door and a gust of cold air hit me in the back of the neck. I turned. The translator came to me piece by piece: bouncy dark hair, a long-lensed camera in his right hand, swim trunks, a white poplin shirt open slightly to expose a rose-tinged tan. His features were impeccable. The kind of face I fell for in my youth, but tended to avoid now, the soft, feminine shapes too familiar—though he was a couple of years younger than me, I guessed. Early thirties.

I had come straight to the museum from the airport in my usual, conservative work attire: anemic blouse and slacks, closed-toe pumps. Hair pulled into a neutral ponytail. My luggage—an ugly shade of purple, the kind of monstrous bag someone usually reserves for backpacking—leaned up against the wall in the corner. To get through the long plane ride, I'd knocked myself out with a careful concoction of pills, which meant that I had not brushed my teeth or reapplied antiperspirant in over sixteen hours. When I shook the translator's hand, I offered a close-lipped smile, trying to maintain eye contact as a way to show a dominance unfelt. He introduced himself as Niko Yorgos and began taking photographs of the statue.

"I thought you were the translator?"

He picked the camera up and said, "Budget cuts."

As Niko walked around the room, he relayed unprompted information about himself (he grew up in Athens, but disliked the pace) and tried to gather knowledge about me (he asked where in California I was from and I said, "Northern," and then he said, "Los Angeles?" And I said, "I'm not *from there*, from there. I've just been living there"). He asked how I was liking the island (good, though I had just arrived). After some time, he returned to my upbringing and said, "You know, my wife, she spent many years in Los Angeles. Is that not a miniature world?" He got closer to the statue's nose and pressed the shutter. Though I knew little about this man, his having a wife seemed odd. I couldn't exactly place why.

"It's a big city," I said.

At the thought of discussing my life back home, I turned away and refocused on the statue. I noticed something about the positioning of her body: her chest and shoulders were slightly turned inward, which made me consider the possibility she had come in a pair.

"What do you think of her?" I asked Niko.

"Well, Doctor," he said, as though reading my mind, "I think she looks lonely."

Soon, Alec suggested we take a walk around the museum. He wanted to show me the architecture and some other prized items, which were mostly chipped vases, and various clay figurines. Alec was the leading purveyor of terra-cotta vases around the Cyclades Islands and so, the nude was an atypical sell for him. I'd never handled a deal this large, or this risky either, at least, not on my own. A few months previous, I'd attended an antiquities sale in Switzerland in the hopes of acquiring a promising vase, but it turned out to be worthless. I'd watched my colleague Madison purchase a femur-sized figurine last year in London, and even though I was the one who helped him with the appraisal, I'd received no recognition. Not that I'd put up a fight or complained to anyone after the fact. I was still trying to showcase commendable sportsmanship, prove I worked well with others.

Alec's tour was quick, as the museum wasn't large, mostly underground, and with various parts closed for repair. When we passed by the front, I grabbed a brochure with a Spedos figurine on the cover. After a few minutes, we walked down to the lowest level, where an entire wing was cordoned off. I wondered what was inside but didn't feel comfortable enough to ask. Alec quickly led us out to a small, overgrown garden, where he began a lecture about the museum's history. Above us hung a swollen mid-day sun, and despite the heavy wind, it felt unbearably pleasant. The more Alec talked, the less I understood, but I followed along, feigning engagement. Every so often, someone would walk into the garden and wander around with their brochures and coffees. The island draft—warm and wicked—threatened to blow everything out of their hands.

Niko said hot wind came up from the south and caused the locals to believe the earth's passions had the power to change their personalities. He called it the siroccos effect. "It offers people an excuse to act out of character." But, he said, the sirocco had come early this year. His shirt, white and blank as a canvas, rippled as he rolled up the sleeves.

"Perhaps it's a by-product of the impending apocalypse," I said.

He nodded. "Y2K." He nodded again. "Are you ready?"

A loud group of Westerners—four or five college-aged men dressed in sagging jeans and American labels—ambled inside the garden, their loud conversation supervening ours. As they walked around in total disregard of the property, I felt a shift in the air, or else in myself, the distinct foreignness of my own presence projected back at me. I watched Niko to see how he would react, but he only eyed the young men with an unconcerned, passive expression. Alec, on the other hand, stared at them like a scorned and impatient father. A minute gruelled into two, and finally, the party lost interest and swaggered back inside, leaving behind only an echo of their arrogance, a sound I feared I wouldn't shake, but then, as though there'd been no disruption at all, Alec began orating again, quickly losing himself in his performance, and so, I turned back to Niko, pleased to see that he was smiling at me, waiting still, on my answer.

"I've been ready," I said. "You?"

He laughed but did not reply.

Alec instructed us to move on, and Niko walked alongside me, his hands poised behind his back. He smelled charged, moneyed, or else gorged on luck, as he leaned in unguardedly, whispering into my neck, "I think you make my cousin nervous." I regarded him again. This time, he struck me as especially masculine. Algorithmic. I stood straighter, churning my head for a rebuttal: something presumptuous, yet lighthearted. But nothing came in time.

Once we reentered the room, Niko insisted the two of them take me to lunch. I didn't want to go. I'd have rather stayed with the figure, to whom I already felt a sense of allegiance, but I knew what William would say back home. Gaining trust with sellers was vital; curation was nothing if not a business built on relationships. Unfortunately, I'd had an eye for sculptures, but not for people. *If you are to fail,* William had warned me once, *your tendency toward coldness will be to blame.* What I couldn't say was that I did not feel cold, I felt attached to too much, all the time.

Alec and Niko invited a woman named Melia and another man named Thomas, both of whom had worked at the museum for years, though I wasn't sure of their positions and did not feel energetic enough to manage conversations with more than two people at one time. Thomas was somewhere in his forties, and I hoped I wouldn't have to correspond with him much. With his designer denim and clean, leather shoes, he emitted an air of quiet self-importance. Melia, on the other hand, was just quiet.

We all walked up the marble steps, and into the cobblestoned town, where the air had cooled a few degrees since my initial arrival.

Seeing as I planned to leave for my rental after our meal, Niko insisted on carrying my bag. Every time I caught sight of its color in the corner of my vision, its youthfulness irritated me. How unbecoming it appeared amongst the contours of the ancient architecture, the stooped timeworn trees. On top of that, it seemed as though Niko was struggling with the bag's weight, and though I wanted to take it off his hands, I worried the suggestion would paint me as a person incapable of trusting others. Which, for the most part, I was.

As we plodded along—the roads narrow, mazelike, at times, dangerously steep—we passed several churches and small shops, bleach-white buildings, and more cats than I could count, most of them immobile and unperturbed by commotion, their ears pulled back, eyes squinted shut. The air smelled of salt and tar. Bells reverberated; bay laurels rustled somewhere behind us on the hillside. The blend of sensations had a calming, alchemic effect on my mood, and I tried to personify this by smiling when passersby looked our way, though I was often hindered by a rolling ankle, as cracks in the stones kept taking hold of my heels. Every time I almost fell, Niko reached for my arm, and every time, I politely thanked him and retracted. After what seemed like miles, but was likely only minutes, the pleasantry wore itself out, and the balls of my feet pulsed with pain. I began counting down the hours until I could be alone, prostrate, and anonymous in an impersonal hotel bed.

We came across a café, in the middle of the town square, with bright blue umbrellas and white plastic chairs. Under a yellow awning out front, Niko and I sat on one side, facing the square and its central fountain, while everyone else squeezed on the other. This all happened without my input, which I wouldn't have given anyway. Niko handed me a cigarette, and though I didn't smoke, I took it and thanked him. He offered me a light, and then I said, "No, sorry. I don't smoke."

"Why did you take the cigarette?"

I examined it and considered. "I don't know," I said. We laughed. Already, we had our own little jokes. I couldn't stand how unprofessional he was making me feel.

The sun dropped behind a mountain and the table ordered a round of ouzo. "To your time in Greece," Niko said, facing me, lifting his glass, a thin shadow garroting his neck. The table toasted and the drink tasted like licorice. Niko asked if he could take a group photo of myself, Alec, Melia, and Thomas. Not wanting to ostracize myself, I obliged, sitting straighter and smiling without teeth. As soon as the shutter clicked, I regretted saying yes to the photograph and was sure it would be unforgiving. When the waiter reappeared, I ordered like a philistine: white wine and a salad, and then Niko scoffed and reordered for me. At first, this perturbed me; it was a clear undermine. But once the food arrived—a plate of stuffed grape leaves, sodden with oil, curled calamari, sautéed wild greens—I forgave him. We finished the meal with Lokmas, balls of fried dough drenched in simple syrup, and freddo espressos. Mostly, Melia and Thomas talked to Alec, and Alec to them. For their inattention, I was grateful.

I turned to Niko and asked when he would develop the photographs he took. He said he'd have them to me right away. We digressed. He said he knew a man who photographed Gustave Courbet's painting *L'Origine du Monde*, a close-up view of a woman's nude torso wrapped in white sheets, legs open, revealing her genitals. "Are you familiar?" he asked. I said of course I was. "Right," he said. "My apologies." He went on. Apparently, the man sold photographs of the art to tourists on the street, passing them off as originals. I said that was unethical because the photos were not the real piece of art, and he said, "If the customers were happy with the reproductions, then does the reality of it matter?"

"Plato said mimesis was a corruption of the soul."

"Is it not true, that much of the Grecian objects with which you work, is it not true that they are Roman replications?"

"Well, sure, but those were born out of admiration. Roman citizens were feeling this—this desire for Greek culture. They wanted a piece of it for themselves. Something they could display in their homes with pride."

"And this is a deviation from my example, how?"

We lapsed into a silence, his confidence clouding my thoughts. But then, off my look, he held up his hands. "Of course. I am no expert."

By the time we were done, it was four pm, though it felt like three in the morning.

On our way out, Niko said something about his wife, whom he hadn't mentioned all lunch, but whom I'd thought about whenever he nodded or smiled—suspiciously eager—at my comments. He said she was a photographer. A better one than him. A real one. He said she had received some acclaim, a few years back, for a series of self-portraits. He likened her early work to Cindy Sherman if Cindy Sherman had an interest in the naked form. I nodded along, my curiosity waxing. Alec, Melia, and Thomas said goodbye and walked off, leaving Niko and me alone, a cavalcade of shiny bicycles whizzing past us, car horns blaring. Someone around the corner yelled; a glass shattered.

"Are you married, Doctor?"

I told him I was not. Usually, I'd have bristled at such personal questions, but I found myself softened by his sincerity, his directness. Or else, by the ouzo.

"It is probably better. For your line of work? Lots of travel."

"I suppose," I said.

He told me his wife was working on a new project, and then, curiously, he paused, as though waiting for me to inquire.

"What kind of project?"

He hesitated, then said he wasn't at liberty to discuss. He said his wife had a strong sense of self and of what she needed as a person, as an artist, and what she needed most of all, right now, was privacy, because there was no freedom without privacy. I had a feeling he didn't know what the project was either, and I didn't understand why he'd brought it up in the first place. Maybe he thought I'd be able to illuminate or validate something for him, and though I wanted to be helpful, or at least appear helpful, outside of some required classes, I'd known shamefully little about contemporary art. Over the years, I'd pared my focus down to certain, sacred aesthetic truths—geometric patterns and cool, objective faces; the movement of a body, caught in marble. But I couldn't let him know this, and risk not living up to the person I thought he wanted me to be, so I said nothing.

He dropped his head, and in newfound shyness, slipped his hands in his pockets, kicked away a small rock. "In most simple terms," he said, "she is interested in vacancies."

I said the project sounded interesting, because it was the only thing to say about a pitch so vague.

When he looked back up, I felt penetrated.

The wind began moving the other way, or else we had shifted without my noticing. A piece of dust flew in my eye, and I tried to feign indifference as Niko said he'd like to walk me to my hotel. I thanked him and said no; my feet were tired, and I wanted to take a cab. Truthfully, I'd wanted some quiet. He asked how long I was in town for. I said I didn't know. I mentioned that I'd be taking a break at some point to deliver a lecture in Athens, but he didn't respond to that information, and instead asked how long acquisitions usually took. I told him it depended on many factors, but likely, no more than a week or so. This seemed to disappoint him.

"Well," I said. "It was nice to meet you, Niko Yorgos." He moved in closer for a hug, but I intercepted with a handshake, and once I noticed his discomfort at the interaction, I wished I'd had more to drink.

I managed to find a cab quickly. American music boomed from the driver's speakers, a hit from the previous year, the melody slow and dull. A photograph had been taped on the dashboard—a little girl with her front teeth missing. The cabdriver's daughter, years ago, I assumed. He told me his name was Dimitri. All men exhausted me, but I found older men, anyone from my stepfather's age upward, especially draining, as I often tried too hard to impress them. Thankfully, this man seemed unimpressible, with his balding pate and puffy hands. When we got going, the labyrinthine streets opened up like mouths. I felt feverish. My limbs, my neck, rubbery. I rolled down the window. The middle of town bumbled with noise, with people, clusters of shadows fuzzy in the waning light, coteries of teenage girls perched on railings, watching. Their sinuous, informal posture reminiscent of the statue's. Dimitri turned away from them, onto a residential street where fuchsia flowers laced the sides of homes. An iron chair dragged across stone. A mother called for her child. A wind chime blew. I suspected Dimitri was taking me on the longest route, but I didn't mind. I was either delirious or content, but perhaps I'd never been able to tell the difference. I stuck my hand out and reached toward the architecture, toward something concrete, the smooth curves of the statue's body flashing before me, taking hold. "Be care," said Dimitri, instructing me to pull my arm back inside, and I relented, but not before I allowed myself a few more seconds of freedom as I closed my eyes, and reached again, one inch farther, a breath held in my chest, the tepid air slapping my palm.

2

William's assistant Sandra had booked the rental through an agency, and I'd had no way of surveying the property before arriving, so I wasn't sure what to expect. To find it, I had to walk down a narrow street that I'd at first thought was nothing but an alleyway until Dimitri assured me, twice, verbally, and then once with a delicate push forward. I craned my neck. Balconies jutted from the building; wild plants grew over iron railings. Open windows gave way to cerulean blue, grass green, apricot orange shutters—so bright they seemed, almost, to glow.

As I hauled my luggage toward the entrance, Dimitri asked for the fare. I searched my wallet and couldn't find any euros, though I remembered procuring some at the airport, the weight of them in my hand. I apologized profusely, my breath quickening. I asked if he took the dollar. He shook his head, and I worried I'd upset him. I said I was good for it, if he came back. He handed me a business card, printed with checkered yellow and black. His taxi was number twenty-six. "Me, I will find you," he said. He didn't mention when.

I made it inside, where a child stood at a walnut-wood front desk with headphones on, bobbing his head. The lobby was less of a lobby and more of a dim, oblong room with a water cooler, a pile of plastic bags containing other plastic bags, and a mop left damp in the middle of the entryway. As I approached the kid behind the desk, he eyed my luggage. I set it down, then pushed the bag behind my leg. I told him my name and handed him my passport, which he smirked at and then photocopied twice. He gave me a set of rusted keys, a tie-dyed rabbit foot attached, then took me outside, where we walked up several flights of concrete stairs.

My room was on the corner of the second-to-top floor, and though it did face the water, another building obfuscated the view, so I had a direct line of vision into another woman's space, which meant that she, too, could see into mine. The idea of this made me uneasy, but what could I do? Her studio looked like the mirror image of my rental—our bathrooms and kitchenettes on opposite sides. Unlike me, she didn't have a terrace. Mine faced the street, iron rails lined with plants: sharp succulents in belly-shaped terra-cotta pots, olive trees, a cluster of bear's-breeches sprouting from a watering can. I turned my head and squinted. Up the stone walls ran a wilted vine of bougainvillea. There was a café across the way, and beyond the café, a pharmacy with a broken, neon green plus sign missing its top so that it looked like a squat, uppercase T. Between buildings, multiple strings of light—the bulbs as big as oranges—hung.

When the boy left, I kept the window open and thought I'd take a nap for twenty, thirty minutes. Anything longer would distress my already fragile circadian rhythm. I slipped into the twin bed with its crinkled sheets and floral comforter and fell asleep quickly to the sound of wind soughing through the linen curtains, the faint smell of garbage and sugar and sea. I dreamed of my little sister Margaret pulling herself out of the pool water and twisting her neck like a rag, tongue out. I dreamed of a room full of male statues, each with a mouthful of bees. I dreamed of Margaret's eyes gushing with honey.

I woke to the familiar, pulsing beat of an oncoming migraine, unaware of how long I'd been out, displaced by the change in light, by my dreams. I almost never dreamed of Margaret.

The clock on the side table flashed numbers: *88:88*, their brightness worsening my headache.

I decided I'd run to the pharmacy for extra-strength ibuprofen to get ahold of the pain before it took hold of me. With the possibility of a promotion ahead, and against the unflappability of Madison, I promised myself I'd cut back on my prescriptions, though I'd already taken two—three—on the plane ride over.

I grabbed a sweatshirt from my alma mater and walked down the stairs and out the lobby, where the front desk child now sat with a backward cap, reading a comic book, a silver Discman in his lap. He waved at me but did not look up.

The sun had already begun disappearing behind the horizon; the sky twisted from pale blue to wistful violet. Whenever I blinked and opened my eyes, the world appeared a little duller. This alarmed me, though I tried not to let it. The last thing I needed was a migraine aura. Hippocrates was the first to describe the phenomenon in writing—noting a glare that shone before him, superseded by a violent throb in his right temple. Then again, he also believed that a womb could wander upward toward the throat like a blood-thirsty animal, block a woman's airflow, and therefore, choke her to death. At the museum, we had a collection of ancient amulets said to hold headache-breaking spells. I sometimes spent my lunch break staring at their inscriptions, tracing with my mind's eye the lines, the curves of the characters. But in their presence, I'd never felt anything other than an untenable, uncertain dread.

None of my colleagues knew the extent of my afflictions, and if I ever endured an attack on the clock, I'd take a pill and wait it out in my office, tell someone I was in the middle of a substantial research project, as I tried to will away the floaters, the blurring zigzags. I'd experienced total blindness twice in my life—the first time after Margaret died, and I couldn't see anything but vague colors for a few hours, and again, when Julian and I married. In the latter case, I'd lost my vision for days. I lived in constant fear of another episode, certain the next would last longer and preclude me from hiding the condition at work—everything I'd cultivated, unraveled in a literal blink.

3

When I got to the pharmacy, I pulled the door, pushed it, put my face against the warm glass. At first, I didn't see anyone inside, and then appeared the shadows of a group of men sitting around a plastic table. I couldn't make out what they were doing, but they waved me off and said they were closed, so I moved on in the hopes of finding another location. Walking through town felt like walking through someone else's warped idea of the island, my headache washing everything in a tint of the unreal. A large gray dog with black ears—husky-like—seemed to be trailing me, but every time I turned around, he stopped, sat down, clicked his jaw shut, and stared at my face through shrewd eyes. I had the odd sensation he recognized me, or that I reminded him of someone. Elsewhere, it seemed oddly desolate. A silver-painted man stood stoically in front of some hat shop, eager to collect coins from guilty tourists, though no tourists were around. Except for me. If I counted. Hot pain seared the base of my skull, and the air felt dry and distended, pushing on my lungs. I could smell the aromas of several restaurants either opening or closing—garlic, onion, disinfectant—and hear, in the distance, the acoustic strum of a guitar. I moved toward the music, stepping over a red sandal, flipped upside down in the middle of the street, the strap torn violently from its sole. Eventually, the music stopped, but I didn't notice when.

I made it to a busier street where locals sat outside with newspapers, smoke and dust in the balmy atmosphere, soft chatter and silent babies on laps. I waded in and out of couples holding hands, lighting cigarettes, but could see only their silhouettes, their faces vacuous.

At one point, I thought I heard someone say my name, and turned around to find no one there but that same gray dog—or was it the same dog? I was fairly certain. Wasn't I? I knew I wasn't far from the rental. Before meeting Julian, I'd always thought I had a decent sense of direction, but he never trusted my assuredness, said I'd rather kill him than look at a map (once, after a wrong turn at night, I almost drove us off the Pacific Coast Highway). Presently, I felt a similar stubbornness—a blister forming on my heel. I turned around to look for the dog, but he was gone, and the sky had darkened once again. Had I walked in a complete circle? I heard the water to my left and followed the sound, and then, finally I saw something familiar: bleary bulbs hanging between buildings. A green neon T. The sight of them like the breaking of a days-long fever.

My headache relentless now, I prayed the boy at the front desk wouldn't notice and ask what was wrong or if he could help—*was* anything wrong? *could* he help?—but as I walked inside, cooled by a charitable gust of AC, I knew I'd worried for nothing. Head down and away from me, he didn't even blink.

Once up the stairs and inside the room, I reached for my pills. Since my stepfather Henry began treatment on me, I'd been on and off, though mostly on, a variety of medications: benzodiazepines for anxiety, methysergide for preventive purposes, even antipsychotics. If it promised to quiet the percussive echoes of pain, I'd swallowed dutifully, hopeful as ever that its specific chemistry would make me whole. But benzodiazepines had always been my favorite. Even though lately, I'd required more and more of them to achieve any ounce of effectiveness, they numbed me to the dreadful, nettled textures of existence in a way nothing else ever had.

I took one—stopping for a moment to gape at my dwindling stash—and when that didn't blunt me quickly enough, I took another, and afterward, fell into bed, shoes on, dizzy with weariness, relief. I slipped into a deep sleep, my aches dissolving. This time, I did not dream.

4

I woke in the middle of the night. It was two pm back home. Soon, I'd have to call William. He'd need to know that I'd gotten in all right, that I'd seen the statue, that she was everything we'd hoped her to be. But I didn't feel settled enough to speak with him, didn't feel I could yet impress him with my assessment. I needed more time. To calm myself, I ran a bath.

The bathroom's terrazzo floors thermal under my feet, I undressed and plunked into the tub, draped my leg over the side and shaved, immediately nicking myself on the ridged bone of my shin. Blood leaked out fast, alarmingly so. When I put my leg under, the carnage—a red tendril—disappeared into clear water. I dipped my head beneath the faucet, scrubbed my scalp. Once I got out, I took a pill and then twisted a towel around my wet hair and wrapped one around my chest before falling back onto the bed, weary to the bone and completely still. I took a deep breath in and held it behind the nose. Often, before one-on-one meetings with William, I'd shut and lock the door to my office, turn out the lights, lie on the floor, and perform a similar breathing exercise. Afterward, I'd peek through the glass of William's office and try to decipher his mood. Knowing never changed his reactions, but the foresight afforded me a temporary sense of agency, of control.

A few weeks prior, William had been promoted to Director of the trust, and the antiquities department was feeling pressure to fill his spot. They wanted a new, younger face—fresh blood. And who better to choose his own successor than the man who had built the department himself? Everyone knew it was between two assistant curators: me and Madison. William's favorites. Madison was a distant relative of a prominent donor and younger than me by several months. Though I'd never heard William call Madison *kiddo*, a condescending nickname he'd ascribed to only me. Both Madison and I had been working for William the same amount of time, and both of us were offered this trip—actually, at first, William suggested we go together, but Madison's wife had gone into early labor. *Everyone understands*, I told him in the hallway between our offices, trying to hide my smile, *family first*. Until then, the promotion might have been going in Madison's favor—he had the connections, the pedigree—but in that moment, the score evened itself out, and now, as William had reminded me before I left, it was all but mine to lose.

An ambulance's siren pealed through the streets, and the unfamiliar, European bleat of it, the blue flashing lights, jolted me from the bed and brought me closer to the phone, which was poorly affixed to the wall. International calls weren't going through, though I tried several times before giving up. My panic crested, and against my will, collapsed into frustration. I threw on some clothes, took a calling card from my wallet, and went outside to find a pay phone.

The streets were blank, the air filled with the smell of burnt firework powder, the sound of errant car honks, motorcycles. One came out of nowhere and almost hit me. I yelled out an apology. A few blocks away, I found a booth and went inside. The wind shield was dingy and cracked, the number buttons greasy and warm to the touch, as though someone had just been there.

"Hello," I said.

"Hello?"

"William, it's Elizabeth."

"Elizabeth? Elizabeth who?" he said, laughing.

Already, the interaction left me drained.

"Got you. Hi, Elizabeth."

"You got me," I said, adding a compensatory, "ha-ha." I heard someone on the other end of the line, out of earshot. I wondered what conversations my coworkers were having in my absence. There were only two women who worked on the curation side of things—me and a retired professor, whose interest was in The Baroque. As for those in my department, I wondered what they thought about me being here; if they preferred Madison take the helm; if they believed he'd already inherited it, been prepared for it in a way I hadn't—though I was not so deluded as to think that I'd been rewarded on merit alone—the difference was that I, unlike Madison, had been caught somewhere I didn't belong.

"Pardon the interruption," William said into the line. "Now. Tell me everything, kiddo."

I relayed my initial thoughts. ("It's one of a kind," I said, "and the marble is in excellent condition.") He asked if it was Parian and I said no, I thought it was Pentelic, which he and I both agreed was unusual, unless the figure had been created nearer to Athens than we'd originally assumed. I told him about the potential mirror. The crown of hair. The flecks of gold paint. He applauded my efforts. ("Good instincts. Is it strong enough to anchor the new space?")

Along with a staffing change, the museum was set to undergo extensive structural renovations: seventy thousand square feet dedicated to Hellenistic art, from Alexander the Great's death to the Roman Empire's birth. Under my direction, I envisioned an experience of chronological timing, a narrative of beginning to end, encircled by topiary, lauded by scholars and casual admirers alike. The statue was the perfect object to fill a gap in the museum's oeuvre. She would be featured prominently. People would travel from all over to see her.

"It's going to be even more influential than we imagined," I told William, citing the Riace bronzes, discovered in Southern Italy in the early seventies. Their display was such a cultural event that their image crossed over the art history milieu and into the general consciousness. At one point, the pair's likeness was even printed on postage stamps.

"I'll fax you the photographs when I've got them," I said, "along with some notes."

"When?"

"Soon. Very soon."

"Good," he said. I heard his thin lips smack together. He might have been eating. He was always eating. "Let's move quick on this. We don't want anyone sniffing around."

It was an unfathomable kind of luck, finding the statue in such good condition. It seemed unlikely it had been submerged long, and yet we would be able to claim the provenance as international because it'd been found far enough away from the Greek border—at least, according to Alec. And who were we to dispute his word? On this technicality, Greece did not have ownership. Although, somewhere down the line, those in power could claim the figure illegally exported *before* it'd been discovered, and therefore, ask for it back. But we'd deal with that when the time came, if it ever came at all.

"Just remember to act in good faith," William said.

The phrase had become something of an internal joke in our department, shorthand for the show of it all, for our acquisition policies—if you could even call them policies—the ways in which we believed our commitments to art rose above the so-called laws. Work a few days in the business and you start to see the paint peeling back. I'd witnessed a few indiscretions firsthand: under-the-table kickbacks, flying families on the trustees' dime, allowing high-profile friends to claim tax breaks. William had faked paperwork—or looked the other way when a dealer had—but only when desperate, only when he was sure the benefits would outweigh the risks, when he knew bringing something valuable to the public took precedence over everything else. At first, I questioned his methods, the ethics they presented, the lack of protocol, but every time we unveiled a new piece of art, and I saw its earthly beauty through the eyes of our patrons, I could justify almost any sin. Nothing on which a mind might sway lives free of indiscretion.

"Elizabeth?"

"Right," I said, forcing myself to smile. "Good faith."

The truth was every institution behaved improperly, it was more a matter of who did it best.

"And one last thing. It won't kill you to be extra friendly, would it? Show some warmth. Do what you can to speed this along?"

"Consider it done," I said, my best attempt at assurance.

I heard a soft chortle in the background. A mumble. Someone's voice—"Ask if she's got any of those low-cut numbers," it said. "That should do it." By instinct, I prepared to get ahead of the joke by offering a light, easygoing laugh, and a coy rebuttal that I would likely regret for the rest of my life, but before William returned to the line, the time ran out. I hung up and stared at the receiver. A woman with a screaming child walked by the booth, trying to coo it back to sleep.

5

When I first met William, I was fresh out of graduate school, twenty-seven years old with a PhD, but no real experience—I'd graduated college early, shy of twenty-one, and went straight into a doctorate program. My last semester, a professor had told one of my male peers William was hiring, and I'd overheard him. William had an impressive résumé, one of the most esteemed in the industry. He'd become the head curator of the department in the late sixties. I knew he was tough, and I knew he'd trained the best curators in the country—they called him Wily Willy. He'd rub your neck if you seemed tense, then ignore you for days at a time, forget your name. He'd hand you a hundred-dollar bill for lunch, but as an outspoken agnostic, if you used *BC/AD* instead of *BCE/CE*, he'd humiliate you in front of everyone. Still, to a select few, he had his moments of brilliance, of generosity. He was exactly the kind of man from whom I'd sought approval.

That afternoon, I cold-called William's secretary, explained my credentials, said I would fax my résumé over. She seemed unimpressed. She must have received so many calls like mine, but there was something about me William took interest in. A few days after, I got an interview.

The museum was clean and slick and expensive. As I walked through the halls, I imagined the envy of my classmates. They would have killed for this. I let that fuel me.

At the front desk, I greeted William's young secretary, Sandra. She was pretty and kind but seemed suspicious of me. "What is the name again?"

Immediately, I wanted her on my side.

"Elizabeth. Clarke."

"I've always loved that name," she said. "Elizabeth."

When she rose from her desk, her stomach protruded. I admired her bump. She was one of those women who carried everything in her belly.

"Congratulations," I said. She gave me a meek smile. She probably hoped for her body to go unnoticed. She led me to William and opened the door into his office. It had rounded vaults and ceiling-high windows. A whitewashed bookshelf without books, populated instead with a collection of pottery shards. And on his desk, a shock of yellow daisies.

His handshake was a death grip, and his palm, a little sweaty. That he might have been nervous comforted me greatly. It spoke to some complex anxiety that I felt only I could see or understand. It gave me an in. He placed his hands on his desk and maintained eye contact throughout the interview. He said my credentials had been sufficient, but what had set me apart was my cover letter, wherein I discussed the prototypical Greek female nude, the *Aphrodite of Knidos*.

The original sculpture hadn't survived, but the *Knidia* was the first full-sized statue of a goddess's unclothed—and therefore human—form. This, four centuries after the first disrobed male. Hundreds of imitations were created in her likeness—the bend in the stomach, the slight hunch—after she was destroyed in a fire in the fifth century CE. That original statue became legendary. According to an old tale, an admirer once fell in love with her, spent days of his life visiting her shrine, until one evening, he hid at the temple until everyone left. The next morning, she was found defiled, a mark across her thigh: evidence of his uncontrollable lust. He was exiled. He couldn't have her. So he went mad, jumped off a cliff, and impaled himself on a rock. I saw a copy in the Vatican once, right out of college. I was so overcome that I sat down on the floor and zeroed in on her, afraid to miss something, afraid to move. Cooled by the icy, marble tile below me, I felt like I was in the presence of real *Beauty*, real *Art*, a slice of history bigger, more important than I'd ever be, and I truly believed, however naïvely, this kind of *Beauty*, this kind of *Art* had the power to alter me in all the ways I'd needed to be altered. For hours, I stayed there, fixating on the statue, every so often getting up and sitting back down on a different side, completely unaware of my other surroundings. By her, I wrote in my letter to William, I had felt consumed. I had felt, for the first time, bodiless.

William said my words had provoked something dormant inside him, and that he'd culled me from a stack of applicants. It was not lost on me that *culled* meant both "selected" and "destroyed."

I felt we had a good rapport, even though, when he looked at me, he looked either at my neck or past my ear. I wondered if he was a drunk; he seemed like the type. Whiny eyes and a mild case of rhinophyma. This simplified our relationship for me. I liked being around venerable men with bad skin. They made me feel shiny and untouched.

He got up from his chair and shook my hand to confirm the end of our meeting, his grip looser than the first time; he'd softened to me already. I saw on his desk the framed article of his profile in the *Los Angeles Times*, and then, the photographs of his daughters. They angled toward him. A pair of white-blond twins, and one girl with dark hair. The twins wore matching black dresses with Peter Pan collars like subjects in a Diane Arbus. I said, "Your daughters?" He told me their names and said he'd adopted the darker-haired girl. She had a larger photo than the twins, an aureate frame, the specialness of which made me uneasy. I said they were all lovely. He liked that. I said I had a sister. He liked that too.

He asked if I wanted children. I said, "Not any time soon." Which was a lie. I wasn't sure I'd wanted them at all. To mother seemed—at once—too public, too private an act.

"Good," he said. "Smart." He picked my left hand up and searched for a ring. "But you are married."

I let him hold on as I said, yes, yes I was.

"That's a beautiful blouse," he said. It was deep blue and silk. "What color would you call it?" I thought for a moment.

"Somewhere between lapis and royal."

"Are you a tetrachromat?" he asked. "It's when—"

"I know what it is," I cut him off, though in a friendly manner.

"Very good," he said. "Are you?"

"I like to think yes," I said.

"And where are your weaknesses?"

"You'll never find them."

"We'll see about that," he said.

He told me I had a strong presence, and I knew the job was mine. On the way back home, I rolled the windows down and listened to the susurration of the hot Los Angeles air, overwhelmed with gratitude. I knew I wasn't special or more deserving than anyone else, but I loved nothing more than being made to feel special, especially by someone like William, who had heard me, my words, my ideas, and deemed them worthy. It was such a small thing, but then again, it was comprehensive. By his attention, I felt fed. Alive. Moony about the future, about who I could become under William's direction, his care. I'd failed at a lot of things, but my career was not going to be one of them.

When I got home and relayed the good news to Julian, he was unable to hide his disappointment. He was jittery, fidgety, said he'd been worried about it all day. The museum's name was too big. "Couldn't you work for a smaller one? Couldn't you be a professor? Get summers off? This is all a bit sudden for us, isn't it?"

For us? It had nothing to do with him. From the beginning, he'd known about my ambitions, my priorities, and I was about to reiterate this point, until his face grew serious. "Do you think," he said, "this man—what's his name—has a thing for you or something?" At that, I let his words go. Not because I was afraid of standing up to Julian, but because—even if his question circled around some unseemly truth that I myself had wondered about—I'd found his disillusionment shamefully uninspired. If this was the worst of what he thought of me, I decided I could live with it.

For the most part, I didn't hate working for William. He was up-front about his ugliness. In a room full of men, he referred to *Aphrodite*'s breasts as knockers. I was flattered by how he didn't better himself in front of me. He didn't expect me to be a saint either. Perhaps I should have been troubled by this, but I wasn't—and that's what he'd really seen in me during our first interview, that I would do almost anything for his acceptance. Regardless, in those eager, early days, I felt William viewed me as one of his own, someone with whom he could really work. The others didn't seem to agree. I was rarely invited to any post-work drinks or unofficial celebratory dinners, despite doing everything I could to appear willing.

Once, at a holiday party, I had a few glasses of champagne and confessed to William that when I was a teenager, my sister had died.

He leaned into me, scotch on the rocks rumbling in his hands. "So, you had two sisters?"

"Right," I said, not having the energy to clarify. What did the truth matter in the face of death? "I had two." The declaration felt so easy, feathering out of my mouth.

"I could sense you had lost someone," he said. "You have that look."

He told me he'd lost his mother when he was nine. Car accident. She was a drunk. "I'm so sorry," I said.

I thought I watched a tear roll off his cheek and drop into his glass, but even in the moment, it seemed dreamlike, too perfect to be true. I put my hand on his obtuse shoulder. An instrumental version of "Baby, It's Cold Outside" played above us and the AC in the corner rattled. It'd been seventy-eight degrees that day. "There, there," I said. I felt huge.

After that, he kept a closer eye on me, often called me into his office, stood close to me, and christened me his protégé. I registered the warmth of his attention, clocked it as impure, unfair—to whom, I didn't know—and reveled in it anyway. Whenever I walked out his doors, I could feel his gaze rolling down my spine and onto my ass like sunshine. It wasn't apparent to anyone but us, and for a while, he never crossed the line; rather, he teetered on it with blithe privilege. I understood my role. I understood that—at least for a little while—my body was an asset and an affront, a creation made for everyone else's eyes and opinions but my own. I understood that there would come a time when I'd walk into a room and fade into the wall, when my presence would no longer grant me access to certain things. I feared this more than I was ever willing to admit.

6

After the call, I settled into a spotty, uncooperative sleep. Sometime later—I couldn't be sure when—I woke to a banging at my door. Groggy, I rolled out of bed and assumed it was the boy from downstairs or someone coming by to clean. Instead, in the hallway stood a man. With his hair fixed into a gelled swoop and metal-rimmed glasses, it took me a moment to recognize him as Niko, and another moment to see the person to his right: a young, long-limbed woman of about twenty-five. Niko leaned forward, kissed me on the cheek, and reflexively, I receded into the room. In my braless state, I felt naked. I was wearing some old shirt, maybe an ex-boyfriend's or Julian's, the material thinned from too much use. Through it, you could see everything. I crossed my arms and lifted my eyes to the young woman's face, then back toward the two steaming coffees she held in her hands.

"This is my wife, Theo," said Niko.

"Oh. Right. Theo the photographer," I said, feeling unsure, disoriented by her sudden presence. Yesterday, she was nothing but a few offhand comments, and now, here she was, brought to life.

"Nice to meet you," I said. But she said nothing, her reticence an admonishment of my own pathological politeness, as she reached through the door and handed me a coffee, a fervid, unidentifiable glance passing between us. When I went for the drink, I remembered how uncovered I was, and pulled my arm back too quickly, which caused the coffee to spill. Hot liquid slipped down the sides of the cup and onto my wrist, scorching my skin. Neither she nor Niko seemed to notice, silence quickening between the three of us like an endless, unglittering void. In a panic, I took a sip.

"It's a surprise to see you here," I said, trying to sound unbothered. My tongue, my wrist, burning with pain.

"I tried to call early this morning," Niko said. "You did not pick up."

"I must've slept through it," I said. "I got sick." I snuck another peek at Theo. She was pretty. Small boned with expressive, wide-set eyes, and a sharp but delicate chin, which gave way into a lean, Modigliani neck, around which a camera hung.

"Oh," Niko said. "I am apologetic to hear this."

"Nothing contagious. Jet lag, I think. Yeah. Do you two want to come in or—?"

"No, no," Niko said, shaking his head. "We should get going."

"Going?"

"To the museum," Niko said. "That fisherman. He, the fisherman, found something else. By the grace of God."

I told them I'd like to change, and could they give me a minute and meet me downstairs in the lobby? In a hurry, I put on a bra and brushed my hair, tied it back, applied lip balm with haphazard speed. I was uncertain about the correct amount of effort to put into my appearance. Too little and I risked coming across careless, too much and they'd see me as vain. Either way, I couldn't keep them waiting. I took several large sips of the coffee, reapplied the lip balm, then hurried down the steps and found the two of them outside. Theo was sitting on a dusty curb, tying on a pair of retro roller skates, hair falling over her shoulder.

She took one foot out and removed a pebble from her sock, then slipped the sock back on with childlike placidity. Her feet seemed too big for her body, a fact that endeared her to me further. A moment later, she looked back and caught me studying her. Instinctually, I tried to avert my gaze, but the way she returned my stare—furrowing her thin brows and cocking her small head ever so slightly—confirmed that my interest was not only welcome, but reciprocated.

"Doctor," Niko said. "Are you prepared?"

A red bicycle leaned against Niko. It appeared overloved, the seat cushion bursting open, the insides protruding like a cotton tongue. He asked me to get on the back, like I used to ask Margaret to do when we were children, rolling up and down those big hills, bending like birds of prey over the handlebars, arms stretched wide.

I hesitated.

"I can get a cab."

Niko frowned. "But it is less fun."

I asked how long it would take.

Theo answered for him, "Not long."

"Do you have an extra helmet?" I said.

"No need. I am an excellent driver."

It was almost noon, the sun high in the sky, its warmth seeping through my skin as sweat gathered on the insides of my elbows. I sat on the seat as Niko stood on the pedals, my arms roped around his lean chest. The streets were busy as Niko veered in and out of small crowds, avoiding a cat, a dog—a child. Another dog. A large gray dog. A large gray dog with black ears. He gaped at me and barked as we passed, his ombre gums wet with saliva.

"That dog," I said into Niko's ear. "He was trailing me last night."

Niko yelled back, "What?" But I didn't press the matter. He followed Theo through town: café after café, white umbrellas hovering over square tables. Dried octopi strung like laundry between buildings, their suckers puckering and tentacles curled. Shop owners placed fresh produce in bins outside their storefronts: viridescent quince fruits, marbled eggplants, papery nubs of garlic. The streets smelled of fresh bread, gasoline, grilled fish. Gnats flew into my eyes, caught on my lip balm, tasted like rust. We came upon the water, the bright blue nearly blinding, wooden groins scattered on the sand like teeth. Up on a ledge, a plein air painter stared at a blank canvas. The bike bounced rhythmically over dips in the road. My body tensed with fear, excitement. Harder, I squeezed my arms around Niko, though all the while, I couldn't stop myself from focusing on his wife. And yet the more confidently she glided through those streets, the wind blowing her hair up in theatric waves, moving with such control, such ease, the more unbearable she became to watch.

7

In time, we arrived at the museum. Niko's tires crunched over the graveled path. He hit the brakes with such suddenness that I nearly fell off. As I disembarked, he turned around and placed his hand on my hip for assistance, but when I flinched at his touch, he pulled away quickly and looked off into the distance, toward anything but me. We laid the bike next to Theo, who had found a cast iron bench under a tree dripping with bloated figs. She kept her skates on and pulled a book out of her bag, the title Greek, the pages dog-eared. The wind blew harder; a piece of fruit fell and dropped by her heel, then rolled away.

Niko ushered me toward the museum's entrance, where families sat staggered around on benches and curbs, teachers handing children cellophaned sandwiches. Alec was waiting for us in a pale blue turtleneck and faded jeans, staring at his feet, twisting his wedding ring. He looked up; his forehead glistened.

"Good," he said.

We stomped down the stairs and entered the white-walled room, where a marble arm rested on a small table, soft light cascading over the wrist. The statue was against the wall, gowned in its sheet. The air redolent of talc and dust, and desiccated in silence. Alec came in and shut the door behind him. Turning his back to me, he said something to Niko in a pleading tone. In a way I could not yet explain, the scene felt choreographed, rehearsed.

Niko and I walked closer to the object. "It is incredible," Niko said. "Do you not think?" His voice quivered like a child's as he blinked at me in anticipation.

Like the statue, the arm's marble was clearly Pentelic, a material composed of calcite and quartz, opaquer than some of its counterparts, suffused with golden tones, and fine-grained. For a moment I lost myself in its softness, its creaminess, its mimicking of real skin. But something was off. The appendage seemed too pristine, the marble nearly unblemished.

"And they found it where?" I asked.

"In the ocean," said Niko.

"Today?"

Niko looked to Alec, who nodded.

"This morning, Doctor," Niko said. "Is something the matter?"

"It's already been treated? Desalinated?"

Niko and Alec said nothing.

I crouched down to observe it closer. It seemed a fit for my statue—the carving styles were identical, it was the correct size, and I could sense that its hand had been holding an object, which I still supposed was a mirror— but the men were lying. Or at least, Alec was. I wanted to think Niko was innocent, that he would not deceive me so bluntly, so casually.

Either way, the arm had not been found underwater, or at least not recently. Unlike the statue, the arm had undergone a crude restoration. Probably, it had been looted and passed around from seller to seller, inexpertly repaired somewhere in the process.

As I stood there—nodding my head and pretending to be impressed by the discovery—I felt my skin flush. I couldn't decide if Alec thought I was an idiot or if he was testing me, seeing how much I could stand. If he was lying about this, what other truths might he find elastic? Still, I had to be careful with my questions, couldn't show suspicion or even hesitation. A hundred other curators would look the other way, and if I interrogated Alec too harshly, I would lose his trust, and therefore the sale.

The door opened and Thomas from the day before tiptoed in, appearing moved by the discovery, as though it were divine. I realized then that he might have been the owner of the museum. Was he aware of what Alec was doing? He acknowledged me only with a glance, his posture rigid.

I knew I needed to say something reassuring, but I didn't know how to begin. My eyes scudded toward the figure, reposed under its sheet, eliciting in me a pang of guilt, like I'd been complicit in this deception. In its current state, the arm would cheapen the statue's allure. Against her, it would look like a joke—a worthless facsimile. Though I wasn't sure anyone else would agree—especially William, the board. It went without saying that the more of something the museum had, the better; museumgoers mistaking wholeness for worth, as though it could ever be so simple.

"Doctor," said Niko. "Are you feeling acceptably?"

I resented him for asking. In fact, I resented all three of the men, standing there like a row of soldiers, their expectant eyes taking me in, repeatedly. Their faces appearing like geometric shapes, equations I could not understand. My own face felt strange too. Hollow. Predatory. I swallowed too loudly and cleared my throat. The noise reverberated between the walls. I cleared it again.

Niko stepped forward, put his hand on my shoulder, and suddenly, the room's corners went dark, leaving only a small prism of light in front of me. I blinked and everything returned to normal, but another second in there and I was sure the dark corners would return, and then would come the pain, a drumline at my temples, and I would embarrass myself— maybe faint, or worse, cry. A collective nightmare, for a room full of men. I leaned back and felt Niko's arm fall away. I told him I needed a minute to step out. "Please, let everyone know," I said, mustering all the pleasantry I could, as though they weren't right there, as though I couldn't feel their collective breath, damp on my neck.

Down the hall, I found a bathroom, locked the door, and ran the water. When I looked in the hazy mirror, I was shocked to see how normal I appeared, how composed. I held on to the sink and tried to assign numbers to my breathing. In for six, hold for six, out for six. I thought of the statue, the unreadability of her expression—those searching, pupil-less eyes. What had they seen, I wondered, when they looked at me?

A knock on the door. I yelled, "Just a minute," washed my hands, and left, grateful to find an absent hallway.

I snuck out the museum's back entrance, and ambled down some steps, my palm gripping the railing, my mouth tight. The air smelled restless and chalky, like wet stone, and I was surprised to find that the sun had lowered significantly. Hadn't I been inside less than twenty minutes? I felt pushed away from reality, abandoned by it.

Once I made it down the stairs, I leaned against a wall and pressed my palms to my eyes. I'd staved off the pain. If it wasn't coming by then, it wouldn't come at all. But I didn't know how I would go back in there and save face, and I felt, even more so than back home, acutely aware of my aloneness—and then, to my left, I heard someone fumble around.

Theo had dropped her packet of cigarettes. She picked them up and rolled over in her skates, then pulled a cigarette out and pointed it in my direction. I glanced at her long arms, remembering how they swayed as she moved through the streets. How she flew.

"Oh, I don't," I said. "Sorry."

She shrugged, placed the cigarette in her mouth and sparked the end, gliding closer before she leaned against the wall, all her weight on her back, her thin hips forward, one skate pressed up in brake position. Smoke twisted out her flared nostrils. She asked me if I thought the museum was prepared for an earthquake. I said I didn't know. I glanced around to see if anyone was looking for me. My eyes watered.

"The island is in a complicated tectonic zone," she said, casually.

"Aren't you a photographer?"

"Who told you that?"

"Your husband."

She shook her head in a dismissive way that both intrigued and irritated me. I suspected no one had ever let her know that she risked coming across as impolite. Or else they had, and better—she hadn't cared. I wondered how old she was really. The age Margaret would have been? A flash of resentment passed through me.

"There are quakes all the time," she went on, "but most people don't feel them because of how low they are on the Richter scale." She exhaled. "But I've got to tell you. I've been having nightmares about the big ones." She told me about the quake in '56, the seven pointer that triggered a tsunami, killing at least a hundred people, and the one in '94: western

Greece, a six point two. No one died during that one. But last year, there was a six point three on Crete that left four dead, fifty injured, and a few, still unfound. She was supposed to be there, but she'd left the day before. Gotten lucky, she said. Tempted fate.

I remembered what Niko had said about her project. *She is interested in vacancies.*

"And now, there's another big one coming. I can feel it, and it's going to be bad and it's going to ruin structures, monuments. You heard of what happened in Mexico? A Mérida mural, completely destroyed. Sometimes I think it's God's punishment for the institutionalization of art."

"Why would God," I wondered out loud, emboldened, perhaps, by her odd monologue, by my desire to bide time, to not go back inside, "have any stake in the institutionalization of art?"

"That's the thing people always get wrong. Even God picks sides," she said, then without taking a breath, flicked her eyes at me. "How come you aren't in your meeting?"

I thought about lying, but instead, I told her it had gotten too hot in there and I'd felt a little woozy and needed some air.

"Oh, it's the jet lag," she said, with a smirk. "It makes me wild too." For a moment, I worried she would share something intimate about her life, which would then prompt me to share something intimate about mine. Instead, she turned to face me, her shoulder against the wall now. "You should let me shoot you. Have you ever posed before?"

I thought: All the time. All the time I am posing.

But I told her no; I told her cameras made me feel trapped. Which was something I did not often reveal.

"Niko told me you only do self-portraits," I said.

She laughed. "That's reductive."

I tried to steal a glance at her face, but I was too nervous of being caught, found out. My heartbeat stuttered up my chest; I felt it in my neck. My eyes cast downward, fluttered toward Theo's legs, the tension of her calf muscles, flexed. I wondered if the statue had been molded after a real woman. Most nude figures from her epoch were an ode to *The Knidian Aphrodite*. But this statue seemed too strange, too idiosyncratic, to have been created after the likeness of the *Knidia*— who herself was said to be modeled after a woman named Phryne, an ancient Greek courtisan best known for her trial in Athens, where she was charged for impiety, and nearly sentenced to death—until, that is, her lawyer saw an opportunity. As the legend goes, Phryne was on the cusp of losing the trial, when at the last minute, her lawyer turned to his client, undid her cloak, and revealed Phryne's breasts to a jury of men. Apparently, they were so breathtaking, so close—it might be said—to the *Knidia's* in shape and form, that Phryne was acquitted on the basis of their beauty. Though this was not the only version of the story that existed. In the version I preferred, it was Phryne's idea to remove the cloak.

"So," said Theo.

"So," I said. "What are you working on now?"

"Something new. It's more—how should I explain it—more performance oriented than what I'm used to."

Just then, Niko's voice boomed out into the air, calling for me from around the corner. Theo put her cigarette out on the ground, and I winced when I saw how it littered the museum's faultless, green property. At my eyeing of it, she kicked the butt away and then said quietly, "I'll cover for you." I considered thanking her, but it felt like too much of an admission.

Back inside, by some miracle, I composed myself and played along as I'd needed to, telling everyone this was a marvelous find and I was so pleased and I'd be making a call to my supervisor soon, and on I spewed, my face now fresh, my cheeks sore from smiling. These were how important meetings went: you exchanged enough words with one another until all parties involved seemed happy or else bored, until one brave person stood and unsubtly checked his watch. How exalted I'd felt during these little productions, but how empty they left me later, when all the formidable men in the room would leave without shaking my hand, reminding me that my presence had been merely ornamental. Now, at the helm, all these faces waited for me to call time. I could have drawn it out, but I didn't have the energy, or maybe the wherewithal. Either way, I made a joke about getting them more money for this new discovery—which Alec laughed at, perhaps a little too excitedly—and then, I thanked them. Not too much to make me seem desperate, but enough to make them feel good about our impending correspondences. Tomorrow would be Saturday, and I would have time to think, to take a break. To get myself right again.

Once outside, I didn't see Theo anywhere, and I was relieved, but disappointed too. I wasn't sure if my curiosity about her had been born of true interest or something else, but as I walked back to the rental, I thought about her nonetheless, about the seriousness with which she discussed tectonic plates, the demandingness of her tone. The way her eyes had eased onto mine. The unnatural frankness of their regard.

As I wandered along, I thought about trying to hail a cab, but it seemed unlikely I'd find one. Maybe the fresh air would be good, a welcome balm. I passed a man on an ATV, a cigar hanging limply from his mouth, his shirt open and flapping in the wind. He moved at a comically slow pace, and when he got closer, waved like he knew me, but then, retracted his hand and frowned. I passed a lone goat grazing, flies fluttering around its head. Did it belong to someone? Cyprus and pine trees whooshed on either side of me, reaching for each other's branches. I felt criminally out of touch. So exhausted I'd landed on the other side of fatigue: bones laced with a brittle kind of energy, eyes dry and wide. A few feet down the road, a swarm of honeybees formed into a frothy, sparkling mouth, turned toward me, and laughed.

When I got back to the rental, the kid was not at his desk and my room door was left open a crack. The sink tap dribbled. I thought perhaps cleaners had come by—but did this rental have any? I hadn't seen anything of that nature. The bed was unmade, nothing altered. I'd probably left the door open myself. I let it go and made a gritty instant coffee, then seized a notepad and pen and sat down in the middle of my bed to compile thoughts about the statue, the newfound arm. It was expected that I would share this information with William, who would then show it to the board—a group of old-money men with severely chapped lips and several useless degrees from the top Ivies—so they could sign off on the purchase. Usually, though, I would have written everything down right away. How had I let time slip away, so easily? I took a pill and waited for the effects to sink in, counting to one hundred and then back again. Roaming across the floorboards, until the croaks quieted, until the walls fell away. At that point, I returned to the work, feeling alert again and pleasantly blank, the empty page below me, gleaming with possibility.

Name, I wrote. *To be determined.*

Date created: Contrapposto stance suggests Praxiteles influence, 4th century BCE.

Physical dimensions: Sixty inches tall.

Origin: To be determined.

Subject: Divine, as evidenced by complete nudity, I noted. Then again, I wondered, was it possible that she'd been intentionally mortal? And not in the way of Phryne-as-Aphrodite but in the way of a real female citizen? As far as I'd known, such subjects didn't exist in her time period. Did they? I continued. *Possible drapery in hand not ruled out. Or else mirror? Posture is suggestive, inviting (pre-ablution stance?).*

Material/condition: Marble, probably Pentelic, with few iron stains, small indents around ears, surviving traces of pigment, suggesting polychromy. Severed near the shoulder on both sides. One arm, detached and heavily restored.

As soon as I wrote it, I erased the last sentence. I would keep the information to myself until I understood the object further, the intentions of its belated presentation.

Discovered: Off the Mediterranean coast, international waters. April 1999.

8

The next morning, I slept late, a little too long thanks to the extra pill I'd taken in the middle of the night. If I kept going through them at this rate, I'd run out before my trip was over, but I tried not to think of that. I got up, made coffee, took my notes out, and pored over them. I read and reread what I'd written, sometimes practicing the way I might describe things to William. I didn't add much—every time I tried, my ideas felt blurry at best, rudimentary at worst. I needed to return to the museum, this time with a clearer head. I needed the photos Niko had taken. Proof to back up my thoughts. As I closed the notebook in defeat, the museum's brochure slipped out of the pages and fell onto the floor. I stalled before picking it up, surprised by its heft, the female Spedos on the cover pixelated and glossy. *The most routine model,* read the translation, *a product of the era of biggest prosperity, is the so-called Spedos type. Representing a female with her arms folded under her chest, where there is nakedness, such as the pubic cavity.* I held the brochure in my hand and thought about the phrase *pubic cavity*, repeating it in my head over and over, mindlessly tracing the edges of the paper, until I felt a burning on my pointer finger, and jerked away, placing the wound closer to my eyes for observation, coaxing the dry, thin cut for blood. But nothing rose to the surface. Just a fatted, microscopic ache. I tucked the brochure back into my notes and opened the one book I'd brought with me: a study on

Classical and Hellenistic portraiture. The prose was dense, and I could hardly concentrate, the words doubled over on themselves, each letter like a mirrored reflection. Eventually, a noise outside my window distracted me. I looked out. Someone on the roof—a child, I presumed— threw rocks onto the ground, and I sat there, sucking on my finger to tire the pain, as I watched the stones fall like hail.

In the late morning, the front desk kid knocked on my door holding a plate of feta cheese bathed in olive oil. Did he bring a plate of fresh cheese to all visitors? At the sight of it, I felt guilty. But also, hungry. I let him in.

Soundlessly, he slogged over to the small kitchen table and sat the plate down. He asked if I spoke Greek and I said sort of. I asked if he spoke English and he said yes. His name was Baz, and with his hat off, I noticed his benign eyes and pierced ear, his large canine teeth, the color of amber. He might have been around thirteen, fourteen, but small for his age. He beheld my mess, zeroing in on the notes. I hoped he would say something about them so I would have to explain and perhaps in that explanation I would arrive at some helpful conclusion. But he didn't say a word. I asked him why he wasn't in school, and he reminded me it was Saturday. He showed me his Discman, which had no CD inside. I asked where his CDs were, and he shrugged. After that, we had nothing to discuss, so I offered him some of the feta and we sat at the small kitchen table, eating in silence. The cheese was salty, crumbly, warm—like it had just been made.

"We have sheep. Goat," he said. "Up in the—" He pointed behind us.

"Mountains?"

He nodded. "Do you like?"

I nodded.

"What is good," he said, "is to put." He stuck his palms out and turned them horizontally, one on top of the other, to mimic bread. "Inside."

"A grilled cheese."

He thought for a moment. "No."

He thought again. "Yes."

Margaret had left a half-eaten grilled cheese on her nightstand the evening before she died. Her bite marks fresh, an intaglio sculpture of her tiny teeth. Henry—doleful and weak as I'd ever seen him—cleaned around the sandwich for days, weeks, but it started to mold at the edges and gather ants. He left it out as long as time would allow. At first, I loved watching him struggle—and then, I hated it, his sudden subservience. How small he had become, under the tyranny of grief.

I had the urge to share this anecdote with Baz. I knew he wouldn't understand, but at least then, I would have said it aloud.

"Well," I said. "I should get back to work."

He seemed morose. Then he asked me for a cigarette. When I said no, he asked if I had any weed. When I said no, he went back downstairs, dejected, with the empty plate. Instead of returning to my notes, I watered the plants on the terrace, brushed my teeth, flossed twice, and refolded my clothes. Back home, all I ever wanted to do was work. But now, I couldn't seem to get started. It was easy to blame the island. The lack of clocks, of communication, the off-season heat. The night-thrum of insects, the meaty scent of charcoal. The tree branches lashing my window every time the wind blew, which was, for the most part, always. Every detail had taken on the quality of impasto: dense, abundant, distorted.

In the early evening, I got a call from Niko. He wanted to know how I was doing—how I was feeling, actually. I gripped the phone and told him I was fine. In my head, I made up some lie about how hard I'd been working—but he hadn't called to discuss business. He said he and Theo were eating dinner at his favorite restaurant that night. "It is off the beaten path. No tourist is allowed." I imagined myself sharing an authentic meal with them, Theo asking me questions about art, about life, my responses effortless and moving, nimble, and humorous.

I said, "Aren't I a tourist?"

He laughed, too easily. "Join us." He said, "It will clear all ailments."

I sensed a restlessness in his plea. I thought about their apartment together, overcome with the spontaneity of young romance: a coiled-up comforter, thigh-high piles of books and records. Bent, bespoke silver-ware.

"And after," he said. "We can show you an exceptional place."

"A what place?"

"An exceptional one. Only if you are equipped to take part in the activity, Doctor."

I heard a shuffle. On the other end of the line, I perceived a presence, another breath. I focused on trying to act natural, laid-back.

"Yeah, all right, we'll see," I said.

In the background, Theo laughed. Blood shot to my scalp. The phone felt warmer, a muffled noise filled my ear, and then a second later, her voice.

"Elizabeth?" it said.

"Yeah, yes? Hi?"

"You should come to dinner." Surprising me, she appended, "Please."

And with that, I could do nothing but agree. I was sure they both knew I would.

Niko gave me the restaurant's address and I looked it up on the map the rental had left for guests. It was about a ten-minute walk. I ruffled through the contents in my luggage. An outfit that appeared easy—that's what I needed but didn't have. Everything too structured: pencil skirts, blazers, starchy slacks in various dark blues, grays, and blacks; items that discouraged projection; items that made of my body a pleading blankness.

I didn't really know what kind of clothing I liked outside of work. Even on the rare occasions Julian and I went out to dinner, I stuck with what I knew. *You don't have to go all the way up to your neck,* Julian used to tell me, popping my top button loose and declaring, *It's like you're afraid to let people know that you're a woman.* Not that he'd dressed any better himself. Ill-fitting jeans. T-shirts with stains on them. I hated how superficial I could become inside a relationship. How much I cared what people thought of him, and therefore us, and therefore, me.

I decided on something simple, something I reserved only for sleep: a black, satin slip dress. It was revealing, unsupportive, evoked the kind of boldness I lacked, and back home, I'd have never worn it in public. But I enjoyed how it hung on me, its uncomplicated elegance. I nabbed a light jacket and shrugged it over my shoulders, then took it off and draped it over my arm. I went into the bathroom and stood in front of the mirror, wondering what Julian would think. For a second, I saw a flash of myself sitting in the middle of our living room floor with a broken glass in my hand, a few drops of blood on the carpet below. The way he looked at me, like I'd done it on purpose, like he was not scared for me, but *of* me.

I shook my head to let it go, surveyed myself once more in the mirror. That the slip did nothing to hide my bra straps seemed uncouth, but the thought of leaving the rental without support made me queasy, preemptively sore. I stalled, sure I'd change my mind about the dress. I never did.

As I walked outside, a rush of adrenaline moved my feet from cobblestone to cobblestone—it had been years since I'd shown this much skin, but amongst the crowded streets, I felt anonymous, invisible. I could have been anyone, or no one at all, parading through the teeming heat, the air lush with the smell of overripe apricots, yeast. Sound flickered from building to building—the swish of a broom, the hiss of an espresso machine, the mumble of a handheld radio. A mosquito landed on my hand, and I slapped it off. In every shop window I passed, I searched for my reflection but never stopped long enough to find it.

I tried to plan what I would say to Theo and Niko, but I had no way to know the types of questions they would ask, the kinds of charades I'd have to keep up. For this reason, I struggled to make new friends: too much unknown, too much to get wrong, and why should Theo want to listen to what I had to say? She probably thought I was trivial and boring and too serious, and I wondered if I felt threatened by the truth of this perception, or else pleasantly challenged to prove it wrong.

Deep in these thoughts, I got lost on the way to the restaurant, passing the same church twice before I realized I had already come down that road. But this time, I saw something new, a small fountain tucked away in between buildings, its plinth choked in dead branches. I strolled closer and surveyed the stone figure—a woman perched on a rock, holding a large vase on her shoulder, from which water poured and poppled. Her one breast exposed, the other concealed in modeled cloth. Usually, a single exposed breast signified an act of violence against a mortal woman—rape by some divine creature. *Leda and the Swan*, for instance. I thought, specifically, of the rendering from the 300s BCE, where Leda's peplos covers only the left side of her chest, the cloth sculpted in waves. On the other side, a swan nestles into her abdomen, its feathers softly etched.

But this statue seemed disconnected from that history. Its body bore no details: no nipples, no belly button. Her knees and elbows, creamily wrinkleless, her face rendered warmly. A pert nose, eyes dreamy and downturned, lids half-open. I stepped closer and craned my neck. The marble had cracked around the figure's thigh, and in this space, the cactus had made a home. I touched my finger on one of the needles and pressed, but it didn't break skin. My eyes traced her back, landing on the thickness of her neck, the delicate ornament of her hair, swept up into a bun—pulled a little too tight, but full of purpose. The bridge of her nose protruded forward. A transgression of her femininity, a refusal of the ideal.

I envisioned someone else on the other end of the road, studying me, as I studied her.

9

When I arrived, the restaurant didn't appear open; all its windows blacked out. It didn't have a sign, but a faint cross, made of ash, was stamped on the front door. I leaned against the wall and waited. Ten minutes later, I heard laughter coming from the alleyway to my left, and then, I saw the two of them, evening rays flaring the backs of their heads. They were wearing matching clothes: all white, linen, and soft, but hardness lurked behind both of their eyes, a pinkish tint to their cheeks, too much time spent under the sun. A latte-colored stain in the center of Niko's shirt. Theo's black bra, a shadow under her blouse. Had she meant to show it off? Such contradictions, such imperfections, only added to their Dionysian charm; they didn't have time to be faultless. I imagined their lives hinged on unbridled desire, on impulse. But if the occasion called for it, they could be balanced too. Grounded.

When they got closer, I wasn't sure if we were going to hug or shake hands, or if I should make the first move. Gripping on to the jacket I still held in my arms, I said hello and nodded my head forward in a way I immediately regretted. Theo nodded back, smiling, as Niko handed me a white envelope. "Photographs of your lady," he said. I thanked him and felt the photographs' heat. I wanted to open the envelope and look, but I also wanted to stay present, here, with them.

"After you," Niko said, ushering Theo in and then me. Neither of them touched me, and for that, I felt a transient sadness—until Niko's hand made contact with my elbow, his fingers soft and warm. He pulled me back ever so discreetly, whispering into my ear, "My wife seems quite fond of you. You made a real impression?" It was then that I became reacquainted with my near nakedness, the forced intimacy of my chosen dress. As I watched Niko's hand let go, it hurt to see so much of my own skin, bare and needy as an unanswered invitation.

We walked through a tiny restaurant and out to a patio with wrought iron tables and chairs. White tablecloths cloaked the tables, glasses upside down, one set of vinegar and olive oil per table. Fragrant jasmine hung heavily from an overhead trellis. After we sat, more people arrived; babble imbued the air, the clink of glasses and silverware, the click of a lighter. The waiter came by with three laminated menus, but Niko ushered him off. He said we didn't need them and ordered us a bottle of wine. I eyed the waiter. He eyed me back. There was a chill in the air, but not a disagreeable one. The night moved both fast and slow. Every time Niko poured me a new glass of wine, the contents would disappear in a flash, but the purl of the dark liquid pouring from a carafe would fill my ears for what felt like minutes.

Niko and Theo slipped in and out of Greek, the language's Indo-European patterns capering between their mouths, the thoughtless volley of a shared world, a shared life. Sometimes Niko would translate for me. Other times, not. Still, I acted engaged, nodded along, tried to smile, appear pensive when appropriate. They discussed all the different reds as each hit our table. "Full-bodied," they'd say. "Weighty." I drank everything, though I wasn't much of a drinker, preferring the dull, predictable hum of medication over anything else. I noticed other people were clapping loudly to get the waiter's attention. But not us. When the waiter resurfaced, Niko ordered in one breathless monologue. "We eat in what you might dub family-style," he said, his face unapologetic. "Is this acceptable with you, Doctor?"

I said, "Yes, sure."

When Niko got up to use the restroom, the waiter materialized again with a pitcher of water in his hand. Theo covered the top of her glass, which appeared to irritate the waiter, so I held mine up and let him fill it as Theo and I both watched in silence.

Once the waiter left us alone, Theo observed me, her placid expression unsettling. She cleared her throat and began to speak: "You know the white church with the fountain in front of it, in the center of town?"

I said I did. Niko and I had been near it during our first lunch. Though, as I sat there before her, I could not recall the specifics of the architecture, or the specifics of anything I'd seen or experienced on the island up until that point, and though I didn't know what to make of this, as I waited for her to speak, I felt a sentimentality, a stumbling toward some alternate understanding of my place in the world. I wished I could fly overhead and see myself as I felt then: a chrysalis, on the verge—as if novelty could cast such a meaningful change, as if it could be so painless.

"Well, I was in there a few weeks ago when this woman came in and sat down in the pew behind me."

Theo stopped, put her hands on the table, leaned forward, then leaned back, and placed her hands again onto her lap. For a moment, she closed her eyes, and I looked at her, directly, prolongedly, for the first time. My eyes found her mouth, the corners downturned in gloomy concentration, and the frosted contours of her transparent eyelids, a single teal vein running along the breadth of each. To say she was beautiful would have been to miss the point. The point was that her beauty overwhelmed me and every time I stared too deeply at her, or thought too much about the ethics of having so much of one thing, my earlier excitement faded, and I began to feel less and less like a person, and more and more like some indistinct animal, hazy and immaterial, and let loose in the wild.

"All of a sudden, this woman," said Theo, "she, she started to sob—and I mean really, really sob. Hysterically. I didn't turn around because I didn't want to, I don't know, embarrass her? I was planning to get up and leave her be, give her some space. That's what I would want."

A man and a woman walked by, arm in arm. Theo smiled at them, sat up straighter. Somewhere behind us, a plate dropped and shattered.

"But right when I was getting ready to go," Theo said, "I felt this tap on my shoulder, so I turned around, and there she was. Her face six inches away from mine—very close, oddly close. And I saw that she was a nun."

That makes sense, I thought. You were in a church.

"She must have seen that I had a camera, this woman, this nun, even though I was carrying a small one that day, a point-and-shoot, the kind you keep in your pocket, you know?"

"Maybe she'd seen you around before? Taking pictures, I mean," I said, though I had no idea what her camera had to do with anything.

"Maybe," Theo said quickly, and I felt sorry for butting in.

"Because then," Theo went on, "she asked me to take her photograph. Of course, I didn't want to tell a nun no. Especially in a church."

I nodded, trying not to appear too invested as I reclined back on my chair. It wobbled and caused me to nearly fall. Theo didn't notice.

"So, I got my camera, and we both slid out of our pews and stood in the middle of the church."

"Nobody else was inside?"

"Nobody else was inside."

The waiter returned and said something under his breath to Theo. She moved her hand in dismissal, like I'd seen her do the day before—but kinder this time. Then she smiled—a little coyly—and he left. There was so much freedom, so much finesse, in the way she allowed people into her space, and then equally, and without much effort, escorted them out.

"Sorry," I said, apologizing for the waiter's interruption. "Go on."

"And that's when I saw that her habit, from the chest down, was drenched—and she reeked, I mean, *reeked* of alcohol. Did I mention that?"

I shook my head no. In a quieter tone, she continued, "And then I saw, I saw that she was holding a match—and a matchbox. She told me she wanted to set herself on fire and she wanted me to capture it."

"Capture what?"

"The moment she went up in flames."

I pushed my neck back and mouthed, *Wow.* I took a sip of my weighty red wine, self-conscious of how loudly I'd swallowed.

"I kept telling her, 'No, I'm not going to do that. And please, don't set yourself on fire.' But she just looked at me—really deeply, still holding the match and the box. She said she'd needed proof. She was acting like she—"

I waited, unable to move now. My hand stuck on the stem of the wineglass.

"What?"

"Like she wanted to give it to someone. A lover, I presumed."

"I didn't think nuns had lovers."

"Well, I said 'OK, yes.' I said, 'I'll photograph you.'"

"And you did?"

"No. God, no. I called her bluff. I lifted my camera up to my eye"—
here, Theo mimed the action—"and I asked her if she was ready."

Theo sat back in her chair, her face wholly unreadable.

"And?" I said.

She looked off into the distance. "She said she was, and then with
this—"

The waiter strolled by, and Theo stopped talking. She watched him.
Then resumed. "With this huge sigh of relief, she threw the unlit match
on the ground."

Niko returned from the restroom then. He pulled out his chair, the
screech of which made me shudder. When he sat down, his eyes yoked
mine. I laughed out of discomfort and touched the straps of my dress,
making sure they were still in place.

"After all that," Theo said, leaning back in her chair one last time. "She
just left. Performance, over."

Niko looked between the two of us.

"Performance? Is this about the protestors?"

"Protestors?" I said.

"Theo is friendly with them," said Niko.

"Friendly," repeated Theo, with a certain playfulness that sought to
end the matter. "I'll show you friendly."

Niko apologized for keeping us waiting as he draped a serviette over
his lap. He told us he'd been locked into a conversation with the chef,
an old friend of his. I wondered how often Niko and Theo had come
here together, how many meals they'd shared at this establishment. How
many others they'd brought with them. I couldn't have been the first. In
due course, we moved on from the chef and his dying mother, and as the
minutes ticked by, as my empty stomach filled with wine, I took a more
active approach to our conversations—the NATO bombing of Yugoslavia,
political extremism, the evils of large corporations—offering mild, intoxicated opinions. But every so often, when my brain manifested a share-

able thought, Theo's story about the nun would re-enter my mind, and I'd become distracted, obsessed with untangling her intention. Had she shared the story with me to gauge my reaction? Because she thought I'd understand? Over the years, I too had considered inflicting catastrophic self-harm. But I didn't want to *die* die. Not really, no. Death was too theatric, too finite. I just wanted to not *live* anymore, to take a little break, perhaps one long nap, and come back eventually, bright-eyed, inspirited. Made anew.

Finally, the waiter arrived with plates of food balanced on his forearms. Careful and exact, he placed a bowl of something orange and soupy, swimming with snails, in the middle of the table, and next to it, a buttery langoustine, and next to that, a flaky white fish over a bed of oiled purslane greens, and lastly, a phyllo-wrapped block of feta cheese webbed with truffle honey.

Theo pulled the snails toward her and began eating completely unselfconsciously, as though she were alone. Tendrils of hair fell into her face, dribbles landed on her chin unbeautifully, and she wiped them with the back of her hand, hunched over the bowl. She consumed like a child, lips parted open, wild tongue licking leftover sauce. After a few moments, she turned—her fork in mid-air—and looked at me as though she were surprised to find I'd still been there. "Here," she said, thrusting the fork toward me with her long arms, like I was her baby now and she the adult. Without thinking, I moved my mouth toward the snail, wrapped my lips around the meat, and scraped it off with my teeth. I rolled it around in my cheeks, chewing slowly. It tasted like olive oil, like sage, like wet earth. Niko pushed the langoustine near me. "Bon appétit," he said, and eyed me as I took a bite. It was like a mouthful of spume from the Mediterranean: buttery, and ripe with salt. I took another bite, another, another, nearly choked. I moved on to the fish and the purslane greens: they were delicate, oily, citric. Soon, my hands found the phyllo feta, the truffle honey. I spooned out a piece and held it to my nose. The scent was musky, floral; it ran down my throat and back up into my brain. Behind us, a woman laughed so hard, it sounded like a scream.

After we were done, Theo and Niko shared a cigarette out front. When Theo's heel got caught in the groove between cobblestones, she teetered and clutched Niko's shoulder. She was drunker than I'd thought. After dinner, she'd taken her hair down and then, with seemingly little care, nestled it back on top of her head. Baby hairs smudged the edges of her temples like graphite on paper. She flicked ash onto the ground and whispered something to Niko, which I should have found insolent, but instead found exciting. He nodded and gave a soft, fleeting laugh. I realized then that they might have been talking about me.

Theo hiccupped. Her wide eyes plumbed me with a stare. "Elizabeth," she said. "Have you been to Greece before?" It wasn't until then that I noticed we hadn't discussed the statue at all during our meal. Had I even thought of her, once?

I told Theo I'd been to Athens. She frowned and then, I saw two of her. To recenter myself, I closed my eyes, and when I opened them, the world appeared a little duller, a little darker. I panicked, before I realized the streetlight above us had gone out. I smiled at Theo. She smiled back. "I'm glad you chose to come here," she said, as though I'd had a choice.

"Actually, I'll be going back to Athens in a few days. I'm speaking at the university." I waited for Theo to look impressed. Instead, she hiccupped again. My chest warmed. I felt silly for having mentioned it.

"They are more than adequate photographs," Niko said, gesturing toward the envelope in my hand, his eyes sleepy and unfocused, "I hope you will find."

"Niko believes he has captured the statue's true nature," Theo added, lightly touching the tip of his pinky with her own. "What is it you told me? About your obligation to the essence?"

"I did my best. We cannot all be geniuses like Theo," said Niko. He put his hands in his pockets and rocked on his heels, his attention floating elsewhere. Theo cast a glance at him, then me.

"Do you think it is possible," she said, "that the statue is complicit?"

"In what way?" I asked.

"In several ways. Her passivity. Her self-consciousness maybe. Her unfreedom."

"Unfreedom," I repeated, nodding slowly, hoping to appear contemplative, or at least respectably sober. I thought about how Hesiod described the first created woman as the "beautiful evil," the root of life and suffering. Complicit for merely existing. But what did Theo know of the statue, and whether it was passive, or self-conscious—or free?

"Now, shall we go get another drink?" said Niko. "Doctor? What is your opinion? I have got somewhere special in mind."

"The place you mentioned?" I said.

Theo turned to Niko. "She knows?"

Was her tone one of happiness, or was I too desperate to read it any other way?

The place was exclusive. You had to call ahead and make a reservation, but the number changed every other week. Even the location. I pictured myself entering some hazy, aspatial establishment, alongside the two of them. A hundred sets of haunted, pretentious eyes, trying to calculate the angles of our dynamic. The thought made me feel restless, flighty—and a little dumb too, though out of helplessness rather than intellect, for I doubted my ability to say no to either of them, to forge a believable excuse.

"Last time," said Niko, his face flushed from the wine, his features suddenly, queasily boyish, "we sat next to an American actress."

I opened my mouth to ask *who*, but Theo stopped me. "Don't take the bait," she said, shaking her head. In what appeared to be a rebuttal—amusement on the surface, but aggression just below it—Niko smiled and hooked his arms around his wife's waist, pulling her closer to him, and in effect, me. As they embraced, her soft temple now resting on the knob of his hard shoulder, the borders between them collapsing, he told me about a friend of theirs, an internationally acclaimed journalist turned documentarian. But I was barely listening, my focus on Theo. Through the side of her mouth, a stream of smoke escaped. She smelled vineal.

"Have you heard of him?" said Niko's voice.

"Heard of who?"

"Our friend. Leon Demir," replied Niko. "He will be present." Niko went on, mentioning something about Greek and Turkish politics that went over my head, something about the kind of film Leon used, and then, about Leon being from money. Lots of money. Theo wasn't listening either. Her eyes drifted off and into the night like a clairvoyant's.

"Oh right," I lied, "it sounds familiar actually." I pointed to the cigarette in Theo's hand. "May I?"

She handed it to me, the paper damp with her spit. Niko watched with a knowingness but said nothing. I inhaled too hard, tried to stifle a cough.

"We will be taking a car," Niko said.

Could he drive? He seemed in no condition. But at that point, I'd been provoked.

10

At first, the streets were busy. An accident had caused a holdup in traffic. I leaned my head against the cool window; my mouth tasted of garlic and metal. We came upon a policeman waving at us to go around. I scanned the space between Theo and Niko. Up ahead, in the middle of the street, lay a body covered in a white tarpaulin, a motorbike on its side, the driver's shoe a few feet from his spread-out hand. The sight nauseated me, and I held my breath until we passed it, the scene dissipating behind us.

Soon, we were out of the stone streets, somewhere new, driving on an incline, up a mountain dashed with elm trees, deep olive groves. We drove past two drunk men fighting on the side of the road, grabbing each other by the neck. They were so close it seemed carnal. I turned my head back and continued to watch as they receded behind me, falling onto the ground, one on top of the other. My legs shook.

I leaned forward. "Are we close?"

Niko's eyes found mine in the rearview mirror. "We are close," he said. He had one hand on the steering wheel; the other gripped Theo's knee and moved up her thigh, centimeter by centimeter. Their affection pressurized the air. My ears popped. I closed my eyes and saw Theo, undressed and on her back, yielding to Niko's weight. In my vision, it was broad daylight, and they were on the floor, in their living room or someone else's, windows wide open, the sun lighting up their skin.

The farther we got, the darker the road became, but every so often, the clouds would disperse, the moon would irradiate the mountain's sides, and I'd catch a glimpse of the inky water, which gleamed like it'd been varnished. I thought about all the things in that water, still unfound. I thought about the statue. Her expression: that inattentive, opaline gaze. I fingered the edge of the envelope, hoping it might quell my uncertainties; how much I wanted to open it, take the photographs out and spread them before me, see her again. But to do so in front of Niko and Theo would have felt wrong, the moment too personal for their collective, benevolent gaze.

After another ten minutes or so, we pulled off the main road and rumbled down a narrow side street. We passed a bridled mule, sauntering along, aloof and alone. Shirts and dish towels hung up in front yards, swollen in the breeze. Theo rolled down the window and stuck her head out, her back arched, her face toward the sky. I watched every pole we passed, anxious about what kind of violence could occur, if Niko veered too far to the right. Once it began to rain, Theo moved her head back inside, and took her hair down again. Thin, thoughtless fingers ran through it, as she laughed at something Niko said, something about a storm. From down the road, I heard a little girl's voice, fast and light, and then a splash. Wasn't it too late for children to be outside, playing? I felt a vague, second-hand terror for them, their possible punishment.

When we arrived, Niko tried to parallel park, but failed; each time, whopping the curb with his tires. Theo crawled over the console and sat on his lap. They pushed the seat back as she manuevered the wheel, his face lost in her hair, the two of them coalescing into a whole. I pictured him getting choked by her strands, gasping for help. A muted pain stalked the right side of my temple, paused in waiting.

When we got out, Theo told me to leave the envelope in the car. "You don't want to get those wet, do you?" she said. Though leaving them unattended made me uneasy, I acquiesced. Under the misty sky, the three of us ambled down an unlit road until we came across a normal, unassuming home, in front of which stood a white wooden gate. An intercom spoke at us. Theo spoke back.

"Oenotropae?" she said.

A tiny voice replied, "Nai."

The gate clicked open.

I didn't have a good feeling about where we were headed, but I ascribed that discomfort to social unease, to my distaste for crowded places.

We walked down a dark passageway, the air damp and loamy, and then through a panel door. For a while, we walked down a steep set of black stairs, Theo in front of Niko, me trailing them both, though I couldn't see either, could barely see the step in front of me.

At the bottom, we turned a corner and entered a dim, drafty room. We seemed so far belowground I was expecting a cave, stalactites hanging above. Instead, a chandelier refracted muted light onto a concrete floor. A dark-wooded bar—lined with unlit votive candles—stretched across the right wall, which was made of black brick. Three bartenders, all of whom appeared fragile and uninterested, moped from corner to corner. On the other side of the space, several tables clustered together, framed by empty, high-backed wooden chairs. Here and there, people drank sullenly in shadowed groups.

Over the speaker, a man's voice began to sing, soft and lullaby-like. The beat dropped, and the song turned flighty and techno. Theo said something I didn't register. I draped my jacket over a velvet stool, and then I missed its weight, so I took it back and clutched it in front of my stomach, feeling both too covered, and not covered enough. She said something again.

My body bent to hers.

"Sorry?"

"To drink?" she said. "What would you like?"

I told her anything would do and sat on the stool, which squeaked under my body weight and swiveled easily. I couldn't figure out where to focus. Mostly, I watched a juvenile bartender with Prussian blue hair smile at Theo and fill toy-sized glasses with what looked like watered-down milk. He handed the drinks to us as a phone rang, the noise a startling perforation. He left, showing off the opposite side of his head, which was half-shorn and dyed a light fuchsia. The phone was hidden behind some tall, amber-colored bottles. He picked up the receiver, held it to his ear, opened his eyes wider a few times, narrowed them, nodded once, said yes, no, and then slammed the phone back down. It seemed the same kind of phone as the one back in my rental: dull, anachronistic.

I caught sight of my empty drink and didn't remember taking the shot. A coolness cut through the air as the bartender returned to collect our glasses. Behind him, a sconce on the wall flickered. I stared at the light, then turned back and blinked at Theo, who had said something again that I hadn't caught. Lucent floaters drifted over her face, into my line of vision. When I blinked again, they dispersed. Though I still felt the threat of an ache. If I'd wanted to leave, how would I? I had no idea where I was. Around me, I could sense the shapes of people, but not the warmth of them.

Theo leaned toward me. "Can I tell you something?" She was so close, I could feel the heat from her mouth.

"Of course," I said.

She leaned back. The heat escaped me.

"I was hypnotized the other day. Willingly, of course. For smoking," she said, as she pulled a cigarette out from her back pocket and hung it in her mouth. "Obviously, it didn't work," she added, lighting the end, and inhaling with unmistakable flair. She seemed, at once, entirely unaware of her allure, and entirely too alert to it.

"What were you trying to fix?"

"A small thing," she said, shrugging. "Death anxiety."

"Oh?"

"But I need to quit these first." She extended her hand, squished the cigarette between pointer finger and thumb, and squinted at it like an anthropologist. "Before I can really deal with the fear, that is. Seems backward though, doesn't it?" She thought for a moment. "Thing is, I'm not really afraid of death. I'm afraid of being trapped. And cigarettes make me feel—untrapped. You see?"

After a moment of silence, she signaled the waiter for another. I scanned him again. He had the full cheeks of someone who had yet to be disappointed.

"How do you stand it?" she said. "Western museums are fluttering with death. Wall-to-wall, I imagine."

"Preservation isn't death," I said.

"Everything frozen in time. What is more deathlike than that?"

The waiter slid two shots toward us. She thanked him and took hers, and then I took mine, the citric burn of alcohol scudding across the width of my tongue, mothering me. I looked at her, and for a moment, forgetting where I was, who I was, I told her I'd been hypnotized before.

"What for?" she asked.

"Headaches," I said, surprising myself with the truth. The half-truth.

In the late seventies, Henry started using hypnosis techniques in his practice. He thought entering an altered state would help me improve my *response formations*, citing my mind as the origin of my bodily pain. I saw us then: me, sitting on the green velvet lounge in his office, him, stooped on his little, wooden chair. His voice, *imagine your anguish as a certain color*, meanwhile, a giant baroque painting of Margaret—oil on canvas, moody, masculine strokes hovering on the wall—*and now*, his voice again (weightless, sharp), *obliterate that color with your mind*.

I told Theo all this, but didn't mention the portrait of Margaret, or how my psychiatrist moonlit as my stepfather. I didn't think anyone would ever understand. The ways it so obviously defied a code of ethics, why my mother had let it occur. It was a different time then. Henry was a soft-spoken extremist, a left-wing Lacanian, a self-described forward thinker. That he bent the rules did not bother my mother—if she was even aware of the rules in the first place, so desperate she was to cater to Henry, to lose herself in him.

"So did it work?" she asked.

"No, of course not."

"Maybe you chose the wrong color. Which did you go with? Don't tell me. I would have chosen red. Or chartreuse." She paused. "I think," she said, plucking her words carefully now, an affect which seemed incongruent with what I'd known of her, what I'd thought I'd known. "I think my husband believes that you'll be a good influence on me."

"A good influence?" I repeated. "You discussed me?" As I heard myself speak, my voice sounded static, a distant recording. I watched her eyes fall to my neckline.

"I like your dress," she said, pressing her cigarette into a tray until it burned out. "Is it vintage?"

"Oh," I said. "No, I don't know."

At her smile, my misgivings began to dissolve, replaced instead by the thrill of cool air on my bare skin, by the charge of her attention. I wondered if I could become the kind of woman who, when forced to confront the aliveness of her body, does not choose obliteration.

A moment later, I felt a tap on my shoulder.

"This is our dear friend, Doctor Elizabeth Clarke," said Niko's voice. I turned around to find an exceptionally tall man with mussed hair, wearing an orange batik shirt and a pair of mirrored sunglasses, peering down at me. He extended his hand.

"Leon," he said. "Pleasure." I tried to see him, but all I could see was my face reflected at me in miniature. I rose to shake his hand, but he said, "Please. Sit." I obeyed. His words were clipped, his accent Germanic.

As they both stood over Theo and me, Niko told Leon about my line of work. He praised me far more than I was comfortable with, extolling my résumé as though it were a paragon of virtue, when I knew all too well that I'd accomplished most everything through a mix of unhealthy stubbornness and inexplicable luck. Theo swiveled her stool to completely face them. She angled back, elbows propped on the bar, her eyes blankly scanning Leon, like he was an apparition or an annoyance or both. I remained in half-swiveled purgatory, facing neither the bar nor them. I wondered how well Theo and Niko knew Leon. He seemed at least ten years older than them. Was he Niko's friend? Or Theo's? Or had Theo and Niko been together so long that there was no delineation between whose friend was whose?

Leon scooted himself between me and Theo and ordered four shots. I could see his classic handsomeness—sharp jawline, high cheekbones, groomed eyebrows. When he handed me my drink, I put the libation up to my nose, the liquid like sweet turpentine. Passively, I hoped one of us would choke so we'd all have to leave. "It's souma," Leon said, then to me, directly, "made from figs. Powerful aphrodisiacs. Did you know?"

"Nah, I don't buy that," Theo said. She took the shot in one gulp, slammed it back on the bar, and leaned forward, elbows on her thighs. "No reliable evidence suggests food increases the libido."

"Well," Leon said, pondering for a moment. "What about the act. Of eating itself? The carnality . . ." He trailed off, removed his sunglasses, and cleaned them with his shirt, two pink indents marking either side of his nose.

"Eating can be sensual," Theo said, reclining again. "I'll give you that."

Leon smiled. "It is mimetic. Of sex."

"It is not," Theo scoffed. She thought for a moment. "Perhaps oral, but Leon, that's a bit of a stretch, no?"

Leon turned to me. "Doctor Elizabeth Clarke. Your thoughts?"

"I don't know. I can only speak to the etymology," I said.

"Ah," said Leon. "Mrs. Encyclopedia. Go on then."

"Well, when Cronos castrated his father, he dropped his, well, his genitals into the sea." Leon's attention was a distraction. So too was the noise of the bar. The liquor. I couldn't think. All eloquence out of reach, I felt myself diminish. "Right and so, then, Aphrodite emerged from the foam. And—"

Theo interrupted. "Aphrodite, aphrodisiac," she said, laughing, sort of madly. Her eyes moved away and off into the distance. "Of course," she said. "Of course, Aphrodite was supposedly created from a cock and a cock alone."

The song changed and momentarily muffled us, axing the aphrodisiac debate. That I hadn't been able to make a salient point bothered me, but as the minutes passed, I had to let it go. Soon, revelers began to arrive in groups. More women than men. Everyone thin and young and serious, standing against stone walls in silky slips the color of coins, or else dressed in reflective leather jackets, necklaces threaded with cowrie shells.

Leon continued to observe me; I sensed it even when I turned away, like a frequency only I could hear. Are all of us born with the ability to feel a man's stare? I pretended to be oblivious but knew it wouldn't matter. He seemed the kind of man who wouldn't give up, who'd tell you point-blank, *I want to sleep with you.* Maybe he'd use the word *fuck* to see if you squirmed. Or maybe his skills were sharper, more sinister. Maybe he was the kind of man who made you believe the idea of sex had been yours *No, you pursued me.* I appreciated men who were honest about their toxicity. I slept with many who weren't. Those were the kinds you really had to watch.

Out of the corner of my eye, I spotted Niko's leaving. Theo got up and followed him. Before I could do anything, Leon sat on Theo's stool and leaned closer, resting his chin on his hand in an almost apologetic posture. "So," he said, "you've come to take our property, have you?"

My spine lit up.

"We are acquiring it in a legitimate fashion."

"This is what they all say."

"You've met with many curators, then?"

"Tell me. How does your institution get the money, Doctor?"

"I don't deal with the money," I said, presupposing he would mistake my coyness for ignorance, which would, in turn, allow me to feel some semblance of control over our conversation. But inevitably, he spoke again. "It is inextricably linked," he said, into the air. "The art. The money."

I turned toward him. His glasses were back on. I had no idea when he'd done that, but the effect of seeing myself in them was even more unsettling the second time around.

"Why all the curiosity?" I asked.

"Perhaps I have an interest. Perhaps you are looking at a future donor." I couldn't tell if he was serious.

"It is kismet that we've met," he said. "Do you think?"

I shrugged. He ordered another round of shots. We clinked glasses, and swallowed at the same time, a discomforting pause stretching between us.

A few moments later, Niko returned.

"Where's Theo?" I asked.

He ignored me, lifted his finger for the waiter's attention. Leon excused himself, leaving Niko and me alone.

"Please, let me get this one," I said, reaching for my jacket, my wallet, which, I realized then, was missing from its pocket.

"No, Doctor, I insist."

Again, I searched the jacket. "This is very unlike me," I said, glancing around the bar, idiotically, like it might help. "I must have left it—"

He placed his hand over mine with solicitude and squeezed. "It is OK," he said, then pulled a wad of cash out of his pocket and planted it on the bar.

When we got our drinks, Niko tasted his with care. "Real Greeks don't drink ouzo," he said. Glassy-eyed, he surveyed the bartenders, staring at the blue-haired one for a while, something restrained in his expression. I told him what Leon had said. "I am not surprised," said Niko. Leon had funded some of Theo's art before. We spent a few moments searching for the English term, *deep pockets*. When we arrived at the understanding, I could see in his face relief. Joy for such a miniscule win. I wondered if that made him simple or kind. He cleared his throat.

"But she has not been working much. You know how it is."

What exactly did he think I knew? I waited for him to go on. He pointed to his head, and under his breath, said, "She has been unwell." He turned away and rimmed the top of his glass with his finger.

"Has she?" I asked, carefully, afraid I'd spook him out of telling me all the things I longed to be told.

He turned back to me, and then, as though realizing the weight of what he'd shared, buckled.

"Oh, no. I should not have. It is nothing. Please, say nothing."

I told him not to worry, I had no business discussing Theo with anyone. I wanted to say, *I am good at keeping secrets. I am the best I've ever known.*

He thanked me and said, sloppily now, "It is a dangerous performance, this intimacy."

Someone bumped into Niko, which caused him to spill his drink, distracting us from our conversation. The bartender handed him a napkin and said something I couldn't translate. Niko wiped his shirt, nodded, and rotated his head up, examining the ceiling. "The storm is not over," he said. "We will need to be careful on roads back."

Suddenly, Theo came up behind Niko, yoked her arms around his neck, and pulled him to her. She seemed much lighter, blurrier than she'd been only a few minutes before. A piece of hair fell in front of her face, and I picked up my hand, with a rushed, cursory movement, like I was going to fix it for her, like I'd fixed it for her a thousand times already. This evinced something inside of me—an unmerited, terrifying tenderness—that I did not recognize as my own.

Niko held on to Theo's arms with a desperate grip. It was not a worrisome gesture, but now that I'd been aware of his concerns, it carried more weight. A moment later, he turned his head toward his wife and began talking to her in a whisper. She replied, speaking into his ear, and there it was again: that private language. I ached to listen. How could they so easily tune the world out? What a skill that would be. What a salvation.

Afraid I was the soberest of us three, and therefore, would be the one tasked with driving us back down that winding road, I asked the bartender if they had coffee. I thought it could help my headache too—which had settled in now, a steady pulse rapping at my forehead. He examined me with vacant eyes. "Uh, like Nescafé?" he said. I nodded with enthusiasm.

"No," he said, shaking his head. "Do not have."

Theo chimed in, "Do you need a pick-me-up?" I told her yes, in sincerity, I was tired and could use something. I told her I'd lost my wallet, and had she seen it? With enviable confidence, she said it would turn up. She leaned over the bar and hushed something into the bartender's ear. He held up his pointer finger, and left, routing his way toward another area, into one of the closed-off rooms. It seemed like he was gone for a long while, while Theo, Niko, and I waited. Soon, Leon joined us again. His eyes anchored on mine, delicate and pleading and alive with assumptions. When the bartender returned, he slipped a tiny, clear bag in Theo's hand. It was all laughably indiscreet.

As I stood, the alcohol knocked me back down, benumbed my legs. Leon mumbled something, his words slow and warbled. "Ah, taller than I thought you'd be," he said. When he offered his hand, I told him I didn't need it, and bolted from my seat with indignity. "Have you ever considered modeling?" he said, ambulating beside me. "You know, one does not even have to be all that pretty. Just tall." I was used to men giving me compliments like this. The words rolling out without edges and levitating me into a dumb silence. Should I have been flattered or offended? I understood the tactic—subtly undermine my confidence, wait for me to seek their approval—and yet, I'd still fall for it. I'd lost track of how many times.

11

The four of us passed through the crowd together until we entered a
new room. It was dark, but there was a projection of some video on
the wall. Insects either mating or killing each other, or mating and then
killing each other. There was nothing else inside but a small circular table,
and too many chairs. "Sit," Theo said, not unkindly, and I did, next to her.
Leon settled on the other side. Niko beside him. The table had a sticky
stain in the center, in the shape of a dog's head; I reached for it, then, self-
consciously retracted my hand. The air warmed and a new song started,
which wasn't familiar, but had a familiar quality—like the cover of something I'd heard once or twice, in a different life.

When the activity began, no one tried to hide it, chopping lines with
whatever was near—a pewter butter knife, the flat bottom of a lipstick
tube—rolling a sepia-tinted banknote and crouching over.

A few others flounced into the room, flocking toward us in neat
formations: a short young man with spindly arms, two more shivering
women with British accents. I didn't know if we knew them or not. They
all appeared weightless and fatigued, thick heads of hair, standing around
the table as though afraid to sit still. One of the women turned to another,
her mouth vibrating. "Does the word *scent*," she said, "have a silent c or a
silent s?"

At one point, the woman knelt and handed me a bill. I considered pretending—I could turn a little, knock the coke off the table, and no one would notice. These strangers didn't care what I did; in fact, they probably hoped I'd say no. More for them. But pretending to snort the drugs sounded more exhausting than doing them. Plus, a part of me had always wanted to snort stimulants. During most of high school and college, I'd taken methylphenidate in pill form—legally, of course. Prescribed by Henry to combat the drowsy side effects of the depressants, the antipsychotics. Perhaps that's what interested me in the coke: I could feel Henry's hypocritical judgment. The same man who had put me on pills that made me sick, shaky, angry, numbed, pills that once gave me a mild case of tardive dyskinesia, a neurological movement disorder that caused me to involuntarily stretch my arms and tongue, would have seen this white powder as undignified. And why? Because it didn't come in a prescription bottle? In the end, much of it was the same.

I leaned down and inhaled.

The effect was immediate. My septum felt like it had pared itself from my skin; a bitter taste hit the back of my tongue; a steady buzz stacked in my marrow, new sensations replacing old pain. The woman kneeling beside me was discussing neural correlates of consciousness, but I wasn't listening so much as watching her mouth move. "Cerebellum," it said. "Parallel fibers." The people around the table caught nods from each other like yawns, and the weight of my face pulled me down for another line. Heat crept up my back, and my head swiveled around, independent of my body. The lighting seemed deranged, but lovely too—blue and orange, reminiscent of dusk.

Every few moments, Theo observed me, but only fleetingly. I had the feeling she wanted to say something, but was waiting, calculating when to start. Was it possible that I, too, made her nervous? When the music stopped for a quick moment, she turned to me, and I visualized her focus: a pinprick of light, tunneling straight into the space between my eyes.

She said, "How do you feel?"

"Great," I said.

"Good."

She then wondered if she could ask me something, and I said sure, of course she could. She wanted to know why I'd become an art historian.

Usually, I would pretend to think about my answer to such a question, knitting my brows and looking off into the distance, a sincere—though not sentimental—answer already waiting on the back of my tongue. But with her eyes on me, I could barely think of anything lucid, let alone true. So I repeated something safe. Something I'd heard William say at a conference many years ago. I said I was drawn to antiquities because they provided more questions than answers, because the word *history* derives from the ancient Greek noun *historia*, which means "inquiry," and I liked to be reminded of how much I still had to question, how much I didn't know.

She took what I said, mulled it over for a moment, and then spit it back out.

"That sounds like a line," she said. "No one really wants to be reminded of their ignorance."

My face flushed. I took a sip of something, hoping it would cool me.

"So how much is it going for?" she said. "The figure."

"I can't say."

"You can't or you won't?"

Her tone was brazen, but something in me respected it.

"Both," I said. When Alec had first called William, he'd given him a range between five and seven million. I thought seven was far too high, and though I knew we would pay almost anything, hearing the number out loud only heightened the pressure. The most we had ever spent on any one acquisition was six point five. I worried that William was trying to get a kickback from the sale, something many of us had heard he'd done on the side. But soon, it wouldn't be my problem anymore. Let him have what he wanted. All I cared about was the statue, and I'd do whatever it took to get it.

"But don't you think"—Theo said, stopping halfway to bend over and do a line, her head flicking back in quick abandon—"art should be devoid of commercial interest?"

"I don't think art should or should not be anything."

Her eyes rolled back. I asked if she was OK. She said she was phenomenal as she rubbed her gums, and then repeated what I'd said about art not being anything as though she were tonguing my words around in her mouth again, tasting my thoughts. Maybe she would have interjected her own commentary if she hadn't been out of her mind by then—nodding so hard I thought her neck might snap. At least, her interest in me seemed passionate—even if it was only an effect of the night, the stimulants. For a moment, as the metallic din of other people's chatter blotted out ours, I thought I could see within her, both my future and past and that she'd known me already, not casually, but vitally, perhaps in a former life. But of course, it was only the cocaine causing these thoughts to rise within me, presenting themselves as valid. That, or something else, something Orphic, something in which I usually didn't believe.

"Do you have a family back home?" she asked. "Like children or something?"

I said no and told her that I used to be married, and I appreciated how her demeanor and expression did not change with my admission. Perhaps she had a healthy understanding of loss and I could learn something from her. She queried if the separation was recent—I told her very—and instead of asking why we split, she asked why I'd chosen to be with him in the first place.

"He was kind."

She sneered, her dilated pupils shining, blacker than I thought possible. "I'm sorry." She stopped. "That's all?"

"That's not nothing," I said.

Truth was, I married Julian because I'd never seen him lose his cool and I thought affixing myself to him would be a personal reparation, a way to extinguish my past, or at least keep it entombed. He was all surface level—and in the early days of our union, I adored that about him. We rarely talked about anything real, never experienced the urge to speak about the terrible or divisive. For a long time, I didn't even know if he believed in God.

"Tell me the sex was good."

I smiled in a way that suggested it was. I hadn't wanted her to think I'd stayed in an emotionally and physically unfulfilling relationship—especially when the ardor between her and Niko was so intense it hung around them like a shimmer. More so, I didn't want her to think I was the kind of person for whom pleasure was unimportant.

It was only a partial lie. For most of our relationship, the sex was good, in the sense that it was new, and therefore full of performance. We were still omitting who we really were, what kinds of things we liked. There was a time when I really believed we could build a life on mutual un-knowability, when I really believed it would help us resist the trappings of intimacy, but months passed, years, and something shifted overnight—or else I wasn't around enough to notice the subtle changes—and soon, Julian began having sex with me as though I weren't in the room, as though I was simply a fleshy vessel with which to get himself off, a body of fat deposits and holes. Every so often, to test me, he'd beg me to climb on top, something I could no longer do once I grew tired of faking my confidence, tired of pretending that I was unbothered by my appearance from such an angle—my weak chin, the sagging of my breasts. If he was in a particularly insecure mood, he insisted on keeping the lights on. *Let me look at you*, he'd say, his eyes searing into mine, *like I used to*.

But I wanted to be seen on my own terms, or else not at all. I often thought of Artemis, who'd have rather died than been viewed by mortals, and who, in fact, sicked a pack of wolves on one such voyeur after he caught her bathing naked—or by some accounts, as the ultimate act of revenge, turned the voyeur into a woman instead.

"It's not your fault," said Theo. "I like to think it's never the woman's fault. Even when it is."

"Huh," I said, finding it odd, the way she stretched out the word *woman*, like it was a concept from which she felt removed.

"You know what it's like," she said. "Don't you?"

"Yes," I said, unsure. She had this habit of making me feel I was always a little bit behind, like I'd intruded on a separate conversation.

"We all do what we have to do," she said.

I nodded, feeling vulnerable to say too much, though we were, at that point, insulated by noise, and alongside her, under the dim, anonymous lighting of that room, I felt an uncommon yearning to let myself go, to tell her everything.

But then, she moved on. She began speaking about her field of work, how she'd come here, back to Greece, to start anew. To envelop herself—by which I think she meant her art—in some of the larger, political issues at play. "I'm entering a new phase," she said both unceremoniously and with a hint of Olympian loftiness. As I listened, I avoided staring too directly, but every few seconds when her eyes veered off, I caught a full view of her face. Inside her flesh, she existed so movably, coming alive again and again with something mundane like a sigh, or a laugh, or some other alternate proof of her humanness—a trickle of blood, for instance, running down her philtrum in threadlike strips.

"Your nose," I said. "It's—"

She touched her skin. "Fuck. Why does this always happen?"

When she got up, my eyes found Leon on the other side of the table, his appearance looser than it'd been only minutes ago, a bottle of beer in his hand. He stretched out his columnar legs, proud of their width, their length, proud of how much space his entire body took up, which seemed to color the way he understood himself—or the way I understood how he understood himself. I assumed that many people had told Leon he was brilliant, and so, rather than becoming brilliant, he simply became a person who believed in his own brilliance, and perhaps, for men like him, that was just as good.

He saw me looking and scooted over, robbing Theo of her seat. We exchanged glances.

"I'm a fan of your films," I lied, remembering that Theo and Niko had called him a documentarian.

"Oh no," he said, half grinning. "I like you a little less now."

I disregarded his attempt at sarcasm and asked what he was working on. He said there was one project piquing his interest right now, but he would not discuss it further. He swiveled his knee close to mine and I moved away, not subtly. I felt remorseful for this reaction, as he seemed offended, bouncing his knee, as if to the beat of the music, but not quite. And then, out of nowhere, he said, "Is she Alexandros of Antioch's?"

I turned quickly toward him.

"What did you say?"

I thought I must have misheard him. The name so specific.

"Oh. Look," he said, grinning, "I have surprised you. See. I know more than I let on."

Not willing to play along, I told him the face wasn't indicative of Al-

exandros. "It's not naturalistic enough," I said, "not aloof like de Milo's; its
gaze is"—here I paused, searched for the right word—"focused."

"Interesting," Leon said, though his tone sounded detached, and the
word came out hollow, and pandering.

"What did I miss?" Theo said, sitting back down on the other side of
Leon, her nostrils clean, the skin around them, shiny and pink.

"Leon knows a bit about art," I said.

He pulled his chair closer to mine, farther from Theo's, to bother her,
I supposed. It didn't seem to work, which made his body language more
aggressive. When, a moment later, he brought up her work, she seemed
cagey about it, but he didn't take the hint. A part of me admired this—his
complete lack of care for other people's comfort. He asked if I'd seen her
photos. I said I hadn't. The room contracted in on itself.

"It is about the quotidian. It is Dadaism. Duchampian. It is like: Is this
art?" I looked to Theo, to see what she thought of this description. She
said nothing, only regarded Leon objectively and confusedly, as though he
were speaking a different language.

"Is that wrong?" said Leon. "How would you describe it?"

"I wouldn't," she said.

I tried catching eyes with Niko on the other side of the table, but he
was lost, bobbing his head as a woman chatted at him, loudly. She was
older than the rest of us—pale and delicate, like some phantom out of a
Vermeer portrait, her hair a deadening gray, her accent hard to place, as
though it had been filtered through static radio. She was discussing some
study she'd come across the other week regarding nocturnal orgasms in
women, specifically those diagnosed with psychiatric illnesses. She said
women who were "mentally unwell"—whatever that meant—were ten
times more likely to come in their sleep than women who were "psycho-
logically sound"—whatever that meant too. A few others tuned in to her
diatribe, including Theo and Leon. It sounded like pseudoscience. But
they were all deeply plugged in, their jaws moving in erratic fashion. I
realized mine was doing the same and willed it to stop but was unsure of
my success. As the woman continued, her point seemed to evade us all,
including her. I feared we'd return to the topic of aphrodisiacs any moment now. Instead, she muttered something about a link between mental

anguish and physical pleasure, as in, the more you had of one, the more you could achieve of the other. If you didn't think about it too hard, too deeply, her argument sounded nearly cogent.

"That's all very compelling, Amara," Theo chimed in, ashing a newly lit cigarette. "But doesn't it feel unholy? To care about something as insignificant as wet dreams when the rise of neoliberalism is threatening every aspect of our culture, and therefore, life?" Her voice quivered. We all laughed, but Theo did not. For a moment, her looming sincerity spooked our collective high.

At some point, Leon backed off from me, yet I continued to sense the gore of his stare, which had only become more ratified with time. I wasn't sure if it was worrisome or flattering. Likely, it was both. I knew I'd have reacted differently if he weren't handsome or successful. Yet acknowledging this to myself offered no comfort. I was sure my obsession with beauty was too American, too capitalistic—perhaps fascist—and would eventually be my own demise.

Theo handed me another shot. Time passed, I imagined, but I wasn't aware of it, or how the sun had probably begun to rise outside, brightening the top of the dark sea, and after that last sip of souma, after I laughed so hard I spit it out all over Theo and the both of us could barely breathe, after Leon rubbed cocaine on my dry gums with his calloused finger, after I felt—for the first time in a long time—not happy but not sad either, after that, I remember nothing.

12

The next morning, a storm descended on the island, casting my bed in gray. I woke to a sharp pain on the bottom of my lip and moved my tongue over some split skin. I wasn't sure what the wound was from, or how I'd ended up back here, who gave me a ride, whether I had, God forbid, driven. Despite all the pills I'd mixed over a lifetime, I hadn't ever blacked out—at least not in public, with other people. Colleagues, no less. Trying to remember the night had the queasy, unpleasant quality of trying to assign meaning to a dream.

To my left, a body lay under a comforter. I held my breath and pulled it back to reveal two pillows, stacked on top of each other. Relieved, I swiveled my hips and placed my feet on the floor. My skin smelled unfamiliar, woodsy, masculine. On my body hung a large white T-shirt, one I didn't recognize—a man's, I presumed. Missing bra, missing underwear. I searched for my clothes, found my silk dress draped over a chair. No jacket, no shoes. My feet a little dirty and tender, I stumbled into the bathroom, approached the sink, and leaned over it, the porcelain pressing into the soft spot under my ribs. I looked in the mirror and opened my mouth, as if the answers lurked there. More than anything, my lip stung, but it didn't look so bad. I'd be able to conceal it with makeup. I checked the rest of myself. A small mark—a scratch—branded the side of my neck. Burned when I tried to rub it off with spit.

Faint church bells chimed in the distance—what time was it? When I inhaled through my nose, my nostrils felt lacerated—my brain ablaze. I sat on the edge of the tub—the porcelain cooling my shaking thighs—and pulled up the T-shirt to examine myself. Was I sore between my legs or simply inventing a sensation? I touched the folds—they felt sensitive, raw. In disgust, I dragged myself away from the bathroom and found my pills, thankfully, where I'd left them, under some books and papers in my bag. To look at my notes, to even think of the statue felt wrong. For a second, I caught eyes with the Spedos figurine on the cover of the museum's brochure. It seemed grotesque to me now, with its elongated head, the way its arm folded over its naked stomach, so self-consciously. I popped a pill under my tongue, then went back to bed, pulled the covers up to my face, and waited for my ears to fill with cotton, for my brain to clear out, stagnant water replacing itself with a calm, clean gossamer. I imagined myself fixed in amber, my entire being humming with a stillness, until the stillness made me too conscious of my breathing and blinking, which in turn made me too conscious of my aliveness, and therefore, my body, which, I realized then, was protected by nothing but two thin layers of cotton, one part shirt, one part sheet, and what else? Some air. Space. Whatever the rental was made of. If I left that room, I thought the elements might kill me. If I stayed, I thought the solitude might. Perhaps there was a space in between two fates—like the statue, enduring a life devoid of motion, of choice. Going wherever someone else took you. I was fine. I would be fine. I was lucky. I didn't need to be worried. Or remember the details. Sex had likely occurred—cumbrous, slovenly sex—but it didn't have to be damaging. What good would it do, to let someone else's mistake derail me? A church bell again. *What's done is done,* my mother used to say, sometimes preemptively, resigned to the past before it had even begun. It was probably quick, probably full of miscommunication and confusion. I was too incapacitated to do anything but lie there, looking up, dead eyed, at the other party. The other party. What might they have thought of the interaction? To them, it could have been nothing. Good. I didn't want pity. But would they tell someone? I wouldn't ask anyone what happened. Or say a thing. Speaking was easy. Silence, a skill bestowed upon the strong. Henry used to goad me to scream at him during our sessions. This was after hypnosis didn't work. He was worried I hadn't felt the impact of Margaret's death in my body, that my grief had festered into migraines—and if I let myself shriek in the confines of his office, like some caged, claw-clipped animal, I could be healed. But I would not do that, at least not in front of him, and his sculpted, clinical gaze. By that point, I had become nothing but a concept to him, a theory to prove or disprove. When he was young, Henry's mother had a complete breakdown, stopped speaking, didn't say a word for years. Was sent to a psychiatric hospital at thirty. Electric shock therapy, lithium. She never came home, but she was a genius. This is all I knew about her. That she was highly intelligent and clinically insane. When I wasn't responding to one of Henry's treatments, he'd call me by her name. What seemed petty then now seemed calculated. He wanted to break me. Perhaps to build me up again. Rework his own failed histories. In this way, I can't blame him. We all do what we must, to quiet our ghosts. At various points, I've been both reprimanded and lauded for my reservedness—*just let it out*, Julian used to say. *I know you want to.* And *Elizabeth, your rationale is an asset to this company*—that one was William. *Elizabeth, show me how much you care about this job.* Also William. But I wanted to believe I had outsmarted them. That Henry's mother and I knew something they didn't. Rage was no benchmark for genius. And neither was noise.

I tried to fall asleep to the quiet but couldn't remember how. Which part came first? Did it happen suddenly or with intent? I imagined other people dozing off, hoping it might help, but I could think only of the restless ones. Then I could think only of people doing other things, anything but sleeping: eating, smoking, showering, skipping, masturbating, having sex with intention, perhaps even love—or at least, agreed-upon transactions, monetary or otherwise. I wondered if two people could equally take advantage of each other, if such equilibrium was possible.

The first time I slept with Madison, it happened in the Mesopotamian section, on a Wednesday, after closing, when he and I had stayed late to finish a project. It was the day after I'd turned thirty-three. I'd cheated on every partner I'd ever been with, and though I'd never mixed business with pleasure, my desire for Madison to desire me had become so totalizing that I could no longer ignore it—even if I knew that my want was built on his, and therefore, in some ways, already nullified. Still, I sought him out. His genial laugh and his physical plainness—average height, build, mousy brown shadow of a beard. Unlike my husband, he wasn't golden— he was an alternative I'd never considered, my own private riot against the usual. All workplace relationships were a performance anyway; what did it matter, to add one more layer to ours? At least in this one, I could be in control—or convince myself I was. At first, I didn't tell Madison about Margaret or any of my supposed hardships because I worried he might find my inability to move past things unbecoming. But one night, when I was feeling especially untrusting, I told him my parents were dead just to see his reaction, which was refreshingly nonchalant, which made me want to sleep with him more. It built for weeks, months. The night it finally happened, he bent me over a handrailing, bunched my panty hose down to my ankles, raised up my pencil skirt. The rattle of his belt buckle filled the room and he removed everything but his white shirt and tie. Most of the lights were off, the security for that room was on break, and William had been gone for hours. We'd known where to hide from the camera, where the blind spot was. Madison's hand reached inside my blouse, pointer finger tracing around my nipple, as I focused on a statue in the corner: a male, clay figure with enormous ears and wide eyes, en- cased in glass and bathed in a small floodlight, his mouth in such bad shape it looked like it was screaming, his eyebrows raised, hands clasped together in front of him, a curious, cold mien painted on his face. He was around three feet tall, and only a smattering of his genitals remained. The Mesopotamia phalluses were obscenely large and hardly ever stayed intact. For months after the indiscretion occurred, I'd think of this statue all the time. I'd glance at Julian's face and see the statue's head transposed onto his. I'd have nightmares about him—or maybe just dreams. They weren't particularly scary. Most often, they were benign. The statue and I playing chess—he always won. The statue and I lounging out by the sun, his crumbling hands feeding me overripe fruit. The statue's phallus stuck down my throat—perhaps this one was a little chilling.

As Madison grunted behind me, I told myself I'd never sleep with him again, that it was a fluke, one bad call, that my job was on the line, my marriage, and if I continued down this road, I'd become a self-imploding

cliché. Yet under his divine entitlement, I felt myself immune from consequences, and it was this feeling of freedom, I believe, that kept pulling
me back to him—as excusatory as that sounds. While Madison's ordinary,
sweltering body slammed itself against me that first time in the museum,
I experienced moments of regret, but they were veiled, mostly, by the kind
of self-hatred that presents itself as absolution. Wasn't it a relief to know
that I could be as exploitative as anyone else? At the thought of this,
and without wondering whether Madison had finished, I came, pulled
my panty hose back up, my skirt back down, and soundlessly, walked out.

13

In the early evening, I received a call. Niko was cryptic but told me to meet him at the museum. When I asked when, he said now. Too worried it had something to do with the night previous, I didn't inquire further. I said I'd be right there, though I felt weighed down, uncertain of my bearings, the alcohol still seething in my blood.

The day was nearly over, but nevertheless bright and clear, the air fresh and salted with sea. I wished I could have stopped at an Ouzeri or taverna, sat down in the shade, and nurtured my nausea with a fresh loaf of flour-dusted bread. I pictured another version of me—some unsuspecting tourist stuck in the foreground of the landscape—pleasantly vacant and with nowhere to be as the heather-lined hills rustle behind her.

When I arrived, the museum was desolate, which didn't seem particularly unusual for a Sunday. I slunk down the steps, and for a moment, lost my sense of location amongst the persistent sameness of the halls, until I came across the cordoned-off section and realized I'd gone the wrong way. I turned around. When I reached the right room, I knocked on the door. Silence ensued on the other side. Too aware of my breath's shaky tenor, I opened it, but only a crack.

"Hello?" I said, as I slipped in and edged toward the statue. She was perfectly reposed, and sheeted in white, but something was amiss. Or seemed amiss. Was it in my head? Maybe. I couldn't explain. The room felt ionized with an almost post-coital charge, and the arm, where was the arm? The table where I'd first seen it lay empty.

A minute later, Niko arrived, closing the door behind him carelessly, his floral aftershave strafing the air between us, his torso draped in a light, billowy shirt. I thought of the way he'd sounded last night: slurry and hoarse, tipping his head back as cocaine dripped down his throat.

"Doctor," he said. "I did not see you enter." His voice was smooth now, and his appearance beyond reproach, sharp and well rested, as if he'd just taken the most refreshing nap, and there I stood, unshowered and sore, and further undone by this man's composure, by the certainty of it.

"We have a bit of a situation," he said. At the gravity of his tone, I attempted to smile, unsure if I was doing so for his benefit or mine. It didn't matter. He lowered his head. "The statue has . . ." He paused, inhaled. "Well. There is no other way to disclose. Something has occurred."

He walked over and unveiled her. The sheet let out a gasp, or perhaps I did, but he did not seem to register the noise. I glanced at Niko, then at the statue. Then at him again. He became unrecognizable to me. In fact, I recognized nothing in the room—not the floors, or the walls, not my own body—nothing except the statue, even though her head was no longer visible. From the jaw up, she'd been covered.

"Is that?"

"Adhesive."

If the tape hadn't been so pristine, so deeply black and opaque and glossy, so curiously unusual and unnerving a sight, I might have—what, exactly? The visual eclipsed all thought, all feeling, the taped head refracting back at me, a harsh almost neon light—blinding as sun on water. Each time I tried to speak or move, I found myself not only unwilling but unable. Maybe this was real hypnosis, or close to it: an overthrowing of the system.

The door opened again. Alec sauntered in, pallid and silent. I regarded his expression, the clench of his jaw, the tension of his mouth, a rictus of worry. But he wouldn't look at me. Or Niko. He wouldn't look at anything.

My eyes traveled back to the statue, flitting toward her navel—at which point, I finally saw the arm, balanced on her hips in an insecure position, its hand, its smooth, faultless fingers, reaching toward me. Its perfection even more uncanny, pressed against the complexity of the statue's other stone.

"Have you touched anything?"

"No," said Niko. "Of course not."

I searched for the words, the correct questions. But all I could ask was, "When?"

Niko scratched at his chin, told me he didn't know. Right. He'd been with me. I fought to push the thought away, to remain present, steadfast. I was not going to break, not this time. Niko explained that he and Alec had found the statue earlier that morning, and that they'd been calling me all day. Part of me didn't believe them, that I could sleep through the droll bleat of those incessant rings.

"Did you talk to the police?" I asked. "No police," said Niko. At least, they'd done one thing right. The authorities would have contacted the ministry of culture and messed with the sale—or worse, tried to sell the statue on their own. But why had Alec and Niko been here so early, on a weekend? Was it a foolish act, or a protective one, not to ask? A light-headedness overcame me. I couldn't afford to be implicated.

"Does it all mean something," said Niko, "do you imagine?"

To this, I didn't know how to reply. I rubbed the front of my neck, tender at the spot of the scratch, which, I worried then, Niko had noticed.

"Where were the security guards?" I asked.

Alec let out a sarcastic laugh.

"The guards?" Niko said. "Of course. There is a guard. But she was not in yesterday. Nor is she in today."

"She?"

"It is one guard. Melia. You have met?"

"When will she be in?"

"Melia—is, I do not know. She was not in."

"You said that."

I might have cracked. But only for a moment.

He apologized and I shook my head. I thought then, of security cameras. Was there footage to review? Niko said the cameras hadn't been working since 1997. I asked if we could go through the books. Did visitors need to sign in? Niko gazed downward. Apparently not. I felt emptied—and then, emboldened. I looked at the two of them. They were useless, weak. As softly as I could, I asked Niko to bring me a head-mounted magnifier so I could get a better look at the defacement, wrap my mind around how to proceed. When he returned with one, the lenses were smudged, and instinctually, I wiped them with my shirt, which only smudged them more. "You need better equipment," I said, fueled now by indignation, righteousness, exhaustion. I snapped the magnifier around my skull, and slipped a pair of white gloves over my hands, and then I took a deep breath in, and another, and another, and feeling as though there wasn't enough air in the room to keep us all alive, I held each collected breath inside, tongue fastened to the roof of my mouth, as I reached for the arm, gently lifting the appendage from the cradle of the statue's hips. It was lighter than I imagined, but just as immaculate: polished and glistening like pressed sugar. I handed it to Niko, who swaddled it in fabric, and placed it on the other table in the room, where it had been before. At the thunk of its weight, I allowed myself to exhale.

"And now?" said Niko.

The three of us stood, lingering over the head, which, in contrast to the rest of the statue, now appeared as a negative space, a void. The act of covering, an act of excision. For a moment, the thought exhilarated me. Through the tape, I could see all her concavities, convexities—the outline of her nose, the corkscrew of her hair. I imagined her eyes, her milky, searching eyes, and I held back the instinct to touch, to stick my fingers into the pupils and press. I imagined her mouth, could hear it struggle for air. Or was that my own lack of oxygen? A sharp thought punctured through: what was under the adhesive? Marble: scored, cracked, or else eroded acid. With each passing moment, I saw the acquisition falling through my fingers; Madison moving offices, a dull-toothed grin spread across his face as he sits in William's chair, languid light beating through the ceiling-high windows.

I hunched over and began unpeeling tape from marble, starting at the indent above her right clavicle, slowly rolling the edges inward, my vision exact, focused. Whoever had done this had done it painstakingly. There were no ripples in the adhesive, making of its finish, a reflective, bottomless black. It was, I had to admit, an impressive feat.

"Why do we not scissor it?" said Niko, hovering, his expression pinched.

I told him to give me some space. He apologized and moved, though only a few inches away. We couldn't cut it, I said, because the black tape was too firmly pressed against the material. Marble, in general, is a porous, vulnerable stone. Why expose it to the peril of a blade? My question came out harsher than I intended. Niko retreated, seemingly afraid to refute me. Had he always been this easily intimidated? "Sorry," I said. He said nothing.

Soon, I entered a steady rhythm of unpeeling. As I watched my fingers remove each layer, I began to envision the sculptor's hand in place of my own. Large and calloused, masculine and unyielding. I felt an unfamiliar self-importance, the sensation that I was reaching into some unknowable blank, through time, into the past and future. How much energy must the artist have expelled to chisel this stone into something as recognizable, as quotidian, and surreal, as a woman's face—as her body? How many hours of his life must he have given for this statue to exist, in some inconceivable future? And if he'd used a live model—I thought again, of the *Knidia*, of Phryne—how long had the model stood there, waiting to see herself made? Unlikely that she would have had a choice, in the way she'd be presented, but in the absence of that choice, was it possible that she'd felt—if not liberation—then, at least, relief?

Finally, I arrived at the last strip of tape, casing the statue's mouth. Under the smoothness, I noticed a deviation, a small bump, almost imperceptible to the eye. I unpeeled the tape to find a piece of detritus nestled into the slight split between her lips, the opening no more than a few millimeters wide. I pinched the edge and slipped it out, held it to the light.

"Is that a—?"

Niko stepped closer.

"Doctor, it appears to be an insect wing."

The wing was only an inch or so long, transparent, and oily to the touch; the pattern mosaic-like. Had it been there this whole time?

I stared down the wing's center, rotated it between my thumb and forefinger, when I remembered how, during my first year on the job, I watched our conservators clean a bronze Satyr from Italy, a thousand pounds, shipped via a specially built travel crate, which the team had to unscrew upon arrival, panel by panel. They scanned every inch of the figure with X-rays, unearthing where the bronze had been broken and repaired, new metal mixed with old. An endoscope snaked into the Satyr's mouth discovered a rolled-up train ticket, cocooning a pack of World War II era cigarettes, inside of which lay a single, dusty gem. All these histories, swallowing other histories.

A sudden, loud noise interrupted my thoughts, like a hammering on the roof—but closer, as though inside my head. I stepped back from the table quickly, almost losing my balance, my grip on the wing. For a moment, spots mottled my vision and last night's alcohol ossified in my throat, a pair of hands choking me from the inside.

"Doctor?" Niko said.

I swallowed. "What was that noise?"

"I did not hear. Alec, did you hear a noise?"

Alec grunted.

I considered my reply. The noise was likely nothing, a twist of my imagination, my tired mind. I dropped the twitching wing into Niko's cupped palms. It made no sound.

"What will you do with it?" I said.

"Put it in the bin. What do you mean?"

"No, that's good," I said, "that's right," though I felt sad for the narrative of its small life: cut off from the rest of itself, trapped, and then disposed of.

"What do we do next?" said Niko.

My focus returned to the face, which appeared unharmed, but I wouldn't allow myself to feel relief until I was done cleaning the debris left from the adhesive, starting where the wing had been. It was a delicate vacancy, this space between her lips, made more interesting by its imbalance, how the right side curled upward, more so than the left. As I pressed the applicator around the corner of her nostrils, down her philtrum, and as deep into the mouth as I could go, swishing around for anything else, I felt important again. Immortal. Perhaps a little insane. That everything ended up fine was unbelievable, too good to be true—and then, for the first time since my arrival in that room, reality settled in like a sudden, operatic slap. This was a message, a warning. Why else would someone go to these lengths? I set the applicators beside the statue and—carefully, as if not to wake a sleeping child—backed away. I began formulating plans. I could move out of the rental, stay in this room until the deal was complete, the paperwork done, the figure en route to LA. What else? What would William do? William. I needed to inform William. The safest thing was to get ahead of this. But there was no knowing how he'd react. I hadn't even told him about the arm.

I asked Niko if I could place a call and he told me there was an office with a line down the corridor. I hesitated, felt my vision oscillate, tried to remain present. Rational.

Walking back through the monotonous corridors, I calculated the time in Los Angeles. Morning. He'd be up. Or should I wait? No. I couldn't. It was too much. I wanted this information exorcised from me; I wanted it gone.

The office was tiny as a broom closet with a clerestory window and brown water spots on the ceiling. I picked up the phone and dialed William's home number, nerving myself and resolving to tell him what happened right away, leading with the news, of course, that she was fine. It must have been a prank, I would say, obfuscating certain details, fabricating others, but when he answered, I went cold, cowering instantly under the throaty boom of his voice.

"The Met is hot on our tail," he said, and off he went. Apparently, Alec's paperwork hadn't satisfied our legal team, and someone in New York had gotten word of our find and expressed interest, too. William said he would talk to the lawyers and settle it before his meeting with the board, but that we'd need to move ahead, regardless of their position. He wouldn't let idiotic administrative stuff hold us back. Proof of provenance or not, he said, the statue was ours—we'd gotten there first, and if we made another enemy, we'd deal with them later.

He paused before saying, "You're awfully quiet, Elizabeth. I'm handling it. There's no need to be worried."

"I'm not worried," I said, worriedly. I decided it would be useless to perturb William, and who would say what happened? Alec? The man trying to sell the statue? And what had I wanted anyway? For William to step in, make it better? For him to save me? The idea felt outdated. Silly.

"Good," he said. "Good, good."

We were silent. Then, commotion in the background: traffic, a faint hum of music, a little girl's voice.

"About the lecture," William said. "You're fine to leave tomorrow?"

The lecture. I'd lost track. The change in time had swallowed a day. I thought I'd had another twenty-four hours. Panic began, again, to build.

"It's not too much, is it?" he said. "The acquisition comes first."

I resented the implication that I was overworked, or fragile—even though I was, and we both knew it. But I told him I could leave for a day or two no problem. The words came out so fluidly, I almost believed them too.

"You said yourself that the statue is practically ours, it's just a matter of bureaucracy now," I said. "I trust Alec to not let the Met weasel its way in. He knows the figure is ours."

A branch smacked against the office window. I heard the girl's voice again. He hushed her.

"Do you want to call me back?" I asked.

"Apologies. I'm with my granddaughter. I'm taking her to ballet practice. Or at least," he said, "I am trying." Out of earshot, he whispered, "*Marzella, get in the ve-hic-le now!*"

His attention returned to me. "So, all set then?"

I said yes, absolutely. He said I would leave in the morning and would take one of those hopper planes. He'd have Sandra send over the details. I heard a scream again, and then William's voice, dipping away, "*Oh my lord! What is that?*" And his voice, again, to the receiver, "Elizabeth? Elizabeth?"

"I'm still here."

He hung up. Breathless, I walked back to the room, my fists spooling and unspooling into knots, William's words careening around in my head—*it's not too much, is it?* A night or two away. I could do that. I would have to.

When I told Niko and Alec that I had to go to Athens, tomorrow, Niko ran a hand through his hair in vexation, like I'd just delivered the most confusing news of his life. Alec hung his head, then muttered something to himself in Greek and lifted his clouded eyes at me—in contempt, it seemed, or else I was being paranoid. This wasn't my fault. They knew that, didn't they?

"So," I said. "We are all in understanding. That while I'm away, she must be watched."

They blinked at me, their silence its own kind of hostility.

"At all times," I added.

Niko said they would do their best. For starters, he would add a lock to the door. He looked to Alec, who nodded in agreement.

"Wait." I stepped back, steadied my tone. "What did you say?"

He repeated himself. This time slower.

"There wasn't—sorry." I took a breath. My mind raced, caught on itself. "There wasn't a lock?"

I felt a laugh rise in my chest, involuntary as a hiccup.

"Fine," I said, forcing the laugh back down, vacating myself of emotion, unnecessary, excessive emotion. "Add the lock, and fix the security cameras. And I don't mean later. I mean now. Make the calls now."

"Of course, Doctor," Niko said. "Of course."

I couldn't tell if he was being truthful or conciliatory—it seemed too easy—but I let him make his promises, or else, I let myself believe them. After all, I didn't have a choice. This was our secret now—the three of us.

"And please," I added, trying not to fixate on the space below the statue, where a pile of unpeeled tape coiled like molten skin, "clean up this mess."

Niko and Alec nodded in obedience, and I felt suddenly unfettered, and effective too, ordering these men around, watching them heel to me, their eyes filled with—what was it? Fear, or annoyance?

"Wait," said Niko, not asking but telling, gliding toward the corner of the room, one finger in the air. While his sculpted forearms groped around in the depths of his bag—since when had he carried around a bag?—I replayed his injunction in my head—*wait*—that earlier power slipping through me, as he, in one swift motion, lifted them out—

The photographs.

He sidled back over, the envelope in his hands, my wallet too, and on his face, uncalled for: a self-congratulatory smile.

"You left them," he said.

"Right," I said, cautiously. "Thank you."

"In my car." His words sliced through what I believed to be our unspoken agreement of confidentiality. Alec stared at us but said nothing.

My body tightened. I was angry at Niko for allowing last night to bleed into the present—but angrier still at my own negligence. To have left the photographs in his car. To have been in his car at all.

"Right," I said again, this time sterner. "Thank you."

Niko handed me the wallet, and then the envelope, the latter of which he held a moment too long, his eyes lingering, as though amused. A miasma of developer emanated from the photographs, so thick I could almost see it—or was it the smell of raki, of rue—seeping from my skin, trying to rid itself of me? I flooded with nausea as he and I searched each other's faces for answers, or more questions—or both. I couldn't be sure what we wanted. But I knew it was something neither of us would get. And then, finally, he let go.

14

It was mild outside, though breezy, those sirocco winds not yet letting up. The evening sun poured over everything, and the streets were busy, the traffic a bit heavy, a cabal of elderly people congregated outside a church in black attire, clutching one another under the shelter of primordial junipers. Even they seemed shifty. I wondered if I could trust anyone. What if William had sent me here not as the Hellenistic specialist, but as the sacrificial lamb? When I was first offered the trip, the thought did cross my mind. Why me? It wasn't impossible to think it had been a front for something. Either I brought back the statue and he named me his successor and was lauded for shaping me into the ambitious curator I'd become, or if things went awry he'd place all our misconduct on my lap and offer me to the media for slaughter, then give the position to Madison, or someone new entirely. William had had enough dirt on me—all the things I'd done for him, all the times I'd looked the other way. Though I had dirt on him too. Enough to take him down with me. But that seemed ridiculous, too conspiratorial. It would never happen. Not to him.

I walked past a buzzing internet café, emanating a lactic smell, its door held open by some leather-bound tome, and decided it might be a good idea to stop for a moment and take a breath, look at the photographs. They would regulate me, remind me of the importance of the task at hand. Plus I still needed to send them to William. I couldn't believe he hadn't asked. Better he'd forgotten too. Two days and I'd be back, and all would be sorted. Behind me, a set of brakes ground to a halt, and I turned to see a cab parking a few yards away. I remembered that cab driver, the man I owed money. Was it possible he'd been looking for me? I went inside.

At the counter, I ordered a Nescafé and sat next to a straight-postured woman who stared at a computer screen with boredom. On the other side, a young girl diligently worked on homework, her concentration unbreakable, worrisome. Softly, I cleared my throat to let her know my presence, then scooted my chair closer to the monitor. It felt too busy in there, too chaotic. It wasn't the right place, the right time to open the envelope. I decided to check my email.

I saw, first, a message from Julian. His divorce lawyer wanted to know my exact return date. The tone was cold, professional. I envied him this, and replied without thinking: *Strange things are happening here.* I deleted it and wrote, instead: *I might never come back.* I stared at the proclamation for a while, charmed by its unabashed dramatics. I added *ha-ha*, then deleted it too.

I wondered what Julian was doing now. Waking up to the smog-filled LA air. How I didn't miss those dried-out hills veined with asbestos, the threat of an earthquake or a fire swallowing our house—a house I didn't want, ungrateful as that might be. I grew tired of pretending to appreciate its rustic charm: the tick-infested garden, the drafty windows, the broken AC. And every summer, the rattlesnakes, dead and tire stomped in our driveway, or worse, alive and rustling around the edges of our home. I tried not to remember how I'd once killed one because Julian couldn't. He found it in the garage after dinner when he'd gone out to grab something from his car. He paced around the kitchen, talking himself into the unavoidable deed, but I'd had a meeting the next morning and needed sleep, so I'd strolled into the garage with the shovel and guillotined its head. I didn't internalize what I'd done, the death I'd caused. Instead, I turned around and calmly walked into the kitchen, handing Julian the shovel, then quietly slipping back into bed. The next morning, he regarded me timidly.

By the time I left for Greece, Julian and I had listed the house, and he was nearly packed and gone. It had taken him weeks; he kept dragging it out, I think, because he was worried about what I might do when left alone, because he often treated me like I was one disappointment away from catastrophe. *If it doesn't work out for you, this work thing,* he'd said, before I left, *I'm concerned for what you'll do.* What I really think he meant: *I'm concerned for who you'll hurt.*

Madison had emailed me from his personal account, which turned out to be a spam advertisement for Viagra. I responded to him, not phrasing anything kindly, as I usually would have.

Madi, I wrote—he hated to be called Madi—*you've been hacked.*

For a moment, I felt close to laughing, but the sensation was quickly replaced by worry. Did his wife check his email? I thought about her, but not chronically. I assumed she was spectacular. From a distance, it was easy to assume other women were spectacular. And what did Madison think of me now, so close to the statue, while he had to stay back, shackled to newfound fatherhood? A part of me worried that he'd given up too easily. That he didn't think I could handle real competition. Once, after a meeting, he'd confessed that he'd found my desire to outshine him attractive. I winced at his choice of words—my *desire* to outshine him. Not my ability. He'd led me on, made me believe I could be an adequate match, a worthy adversary, but all along it had been only fetish, only fantasy. So easily breakable. I glanced at the envelope of pictures—their budding heat.

As the café filled with more and more people, I opened a search engine and input information about the statue, finding several journal articles of similar acquisitions. An Italian man had written a dense blog post about the difference between the peplos and chiton. He discussed a statue from Rome, a clothed female, including several photographs, each of which took minutes to load. While I waited, I researched information about art vandalization. A few years back in Berlin, a group of vandals sawed off the toes of several Italian statues. In the eighties a man threw sulfuric acid over the *Mona Lisa*, then sliced her face with a knife. This one I remembered: the suffragette who took a meat cleaver to the *Rokeby Venus'* nude backside at the National Gallery. But my statue wasn't technically harmed. At least not permanently. Not yet.

I clicked back to the blog, which was still fuzzy, so I opened another search engine. I typed: *Theo*—then stopped. I didn't know her last name. I tried a second time—*Theo, photographer, California*. This yielded more results than anticipated. Deep in my body, I started to feel a strange sensation, almost like a menstrual cramp, but not quite as intense. I clicked back to the blog again. Nothing. An advertisement popped up. Something about horoscopes. I turned the computer a bit toward me. The movement made a loud noise, but no one paid me any mind. In English, the message said the moon was in the wrong place and that an astrologist could let me know the date of my death. Then, it said, what I did, and who I was, had cosmic value. I blinked at that sentence, dread rising inside me, the dizziness of an oncoming migraine.

I tried once more. I typed: *Theo, Greek photographer, Los Angeles*. On the second page of the search results, I came across a bland website. On it was Theo's artist bio. I scrolled through the text. *Theo Siarras was born in Athens, Greece. She utilizes found materials to expose the materiality of the self, offering the personal (the body) as a way to understand the universal (the body politic). Currently, she's working on a project that hopes to question the institutionalization and commodification of art and fem*—and there, it stopped. I was disappointed. The description of her work felt hazy, insincere. I doubted she even wrote it.

A voice, surprisingly deep, jolted me out of the thought.

"My seat," it said.

I turned around. A boy of fourteen or fifteen with the whisperings of a peach mustache, freshly washed hands, stood over me. Had he spoken to me in Greek or English? I hadn't been able to register. I watched his inchoate eyes scan my face, my chest. His wet fingers slipped inside the pocket of his baggy cargo pants as he asked for my name. I smiled and pretended I didn't understand, and then, for a moment, I stalled. There was nowhere else in the café to sit, but I didn't want to leave. I couldn't return to the museum or go back to the rental and rot in the quiet blankness of that transient space, a place that belonged to no one, especially not me. The nettling silence between us grew and grew until in exasperation, the boy crossed his arms and demanded I move. So audacious was his tone, it stunned me into action.

Outside, I tried to shake off the tenor of his voice, but couldn't. I felt displaced. Violently uninvited. Maybe it would be nice to vacate the island for a day or two, see Athens again. Even if it was risky to leave the statue alone. I hoped William hadn't been able to sense my unease during our call. I could never be sure how I came across to him but was certain he'd known more than he let on. He might have even known about Madison and me; he might have even liked it, gotten off on the idea of personal and professional boundary crossing, hoped it would heighten the competition between us, make us work harder. William was the kind of man who thrived on seeing his subordinates for who they really were, and when the time was right, using it to his advantage.

About a year after I'd been hired, the antiquities team went out for mid-day drinks to celebrate the acquisition of a vase from Zurich, in near-perfect shape. After we wrapped up, Madison went home to his wife, the others returned to wherever they needed to go, and William and I were left alone. We stood outside on the edge of the curb, waiting for cabs, making small talk. He had a celebratory cigar in his mouth, unlit, and he was laughing at something I said when he tripped on himself and fell off the curb, causing his cigar to fall into a gutter full of trash. With him now inches below me, he and I were eye to eye; he wasn't a tall man, but you couldn't act like he wasn't. I offered him my hand and he sprang back up to my level of the street. People walked around us, not paying attention. The sky was clear, the air, warm. When he said goodbye, his sloppy mouth hit the side of my lips, and for some reason—perhaps not to disappoint him, perhaps because I knew, deep down that at the end of the day, if I embarrassed him, I would be the one to pay—I turned and made contact. His lips, a shock of wet, and then, a heavy, gristle tongue, gliding inside. It didn't last long. He pulled back and we both went quiet. He might have cleared his throat, turned his head away, a shadow of him might have cast onto the street, and I might have laughed, acted drunker than I felt. It was nothing. An accident, a slip. His actions did not feel predatory so much as they felt pathetic. I said goodbye and hailed the next cab, hoping I would slink away unnoticed, but he hopped in beside me and buckled up, his loose chin pointed downward, liver-spotted hands spread across his lap. The sun fanned over my legs and arms and the driver sped through back-streets, taking every sharp turn he could, the cab's chassis rattling, as he and I kept silent. It was the act of speaking that would kill me, and I wouldn't give William that pleasure. I'd show him how quiet I could be, how little of his lips I'd remember. I squinted at the brightness of the sky, closed my eyes. The golden Los Angeles hills rolled on behind us, unmoved.

15

It began to drizzle as I walked around, a little shaken, a little hungry. A lot hungry. Ever since that dinner with Theo and Niko, I'd been insatiable. Back home, I rarely indulged, certainly no butter, oils, not much salt, or sugar, and if I'd had a particularly rough workday—said something idiotic, messed up paperwork, etc.—I'd fast. Water for twenty-four hours. Some tomato juice. Devoid of religion, restriction offered me a set of rules I couldn't find elsewhere, and I sensed a commonality to many women on this level, passing them by on the street, recognizing grotesque hunger in their waning gazes, the glory of self-punishment. Restraint as a net positive, a moral right.

In my younger years, I tried to keep these ruthless sentiments from Margaret, shield her from the banality of vanity. I would have given anything to keep her pure, because she was better than me, she was going to be better—stronger, self-actualized, less liable to fold under the eyes of others—but I could do only so much, and before long, the systems took hold, and I began to see glimpses of her self-consciousness: how she'd take her time in the bathroom, emerge with dark kohl smudged above her lash line, hair straightened with heat and cans of cola; how her big, deep-set eyes cruelly caught herself in unexpected places. During meals, I'd see her admiring—or else hating—her likeness in the reflection of a water glass. I'd watch her push food around on her plate, but only because I—or my mother, who often ate nothing but grapefruit for weeks—had done so first.

All of this, no doubt, had buried my hunger over the years, so that I wasn't sure what real satiation felt like. I'd either eat not enough and feel sick, light-headed, or eat too much and feel horrified at how much my body could willfully consume. Maybe today I could succumb to my innermost appetencies, eat to the point of pain, to the point of erasure, eat so much I'd forget my mistakes, forget my name, my skin, and then disgorge, revel in that release. Or better. Keep it inside, feel it expand and contract and crawl through me. As I pictured this—a plate of food like an implantable fetus—the cramping near my pelvic floor grew more acute. I ignored it, found a fork in the road, and went left.

I came across a café with ivy coiling up the stucco building, a view of the water, whitecaps glittering like mosaic glass. I wasn't sure what time it was, so I decided to have an early dinner or maybe dessert. The tables and chairs were located across from a wide and relatively busy road, which the waiter had to cross every time he brought something, and though he didn't seem to care, I felt guilty putting him in danger. Once, a knife fell onto the street and he, lackadaisically, bent down to retrieve it. The draft caused his white apron to billow.

He was friendly, if a little louche, his skin pocky like a citrus peel, the pads of his fingers stained with tobacco. I ordered a coffee and two slices of galaktoboureko, a custard pie gilded with fresh oranges and honeyed simple syrup. "You have a hungry?" he asked. I said yes. When he came back, I ate everything with my hands because the waiter had given me a dull spoon and it seemed silly to risk this man's life for a fork. When I picked the pie up, the syrup dripped onto the porcelain plate, which had a crack that ran down the center. I licked the sweetness off my palm with a desperation, sucked each finger, then remembered I was in public. Two tables over, a family of four played cards. Behind them sat a quiet couple, the man's arms folded over his wide chest. Across the street, a determined woman in a gray sweat suit ran back and forth alongside the traffic. Witnessing the weight of her unsupported breasts, I felt a secondhand pain. When she moved, an ambulance rushed through the streets, followed by a cavalcade of teenagers on mopeds and a slow-moving cab, about which I tried not to be suspicious. It was nice to know that regardless of what happened inside the museum, life went on. I sat still as I could for a while, wondering if the waiter would return, as clouds split the crisp blue of the sky, and wind rippled through a white umbrella, the swish of it a soothing melody. Low in my stomach, the pie settled like sediment. I put my elbows on the table, my forearms, thought I'd rest for just a moment, thick-trunked trees murmuring somewhere in the distance, a donkey brayed, and I fell into a hypnagogic state, not quite awake, not quite asleep.

I dreamed of Madison fucking me, his entitled, thrusting hips bucking as he sipped a glass of goat's milk and grinned. At least, at first it was Madison, but when I blinked, it became a headless man, a pair of aviator sunglasses tied around his neck and missing their lenses, though still, somehow, reflective, the frames bouncing up and down with each plunge. The decapitation cut was clean, unbloody, and from it, bees sprang, their wings glass-like and slick. In front of us, I could see the Mediterranean, so pale it was nearly a specter of itself.

A moment later, I felt a tap on my shoulder and lifted my head, mouth open, forearm wet with drool. No one was there. I looked around, then paid the check and tipped the waiter with whatever coins I had in my wallet, unsure of their worth. I considered giving him my number, even though I didn't find him attractive. On the way out, I stopped in the restroom to wash the honey-syrup off my hands. An indent from lying on my arm ran across my cheek and I tried rubbing it off, but it wouldn't budge. The scratch on my neck, too, had, somehow, darkened. I splashed my face. I couldn't get the smell of the museum—or the adhesive—off my skin. When I walked out, a teenage girl wearing a balaclava mask wandered inside. She put a finger to her lips. "*Shh,*" she said. Without thinking, I nodded. I watched her enter the stall, and then hurried away, wondering to what I had consented.

On my way back, I decided to run into a corner store. Bells rattled above when I opened the door. Some of the walls were papered with old magazine covers, European *Vogues* from the seventies. Three women achingly thin, wearing baggy dresses and beige swim caps, populated one such cover. They had an ethereal, epicene beauty like the statue's—like

Theo's—though one of them came across sadder than the other two. She stood facing the camera, sucking in her concave stomach, her waist the size of a soda bottle. Another stood in a contrapposto stance, all her weight resting on that rawboned, rear leg. The third was on the ground, her head propped up by a column-like hand.

I shopped around for a while, marveling at the cheap curios: a string of worry beads, handmade leather sandals, olive oil soap, then made my way toward the foodstuff. Canned tomatoes, creamy cheeses, burgundy olives, jars of fresh honey. I picked up a dented tin of dolmas, a sleeve of water crackers in a shiny black box—which reminded me, for a moment, of the tape, so I replaced it with a lesser-looking cracker in a red box, before I grabbed a fat square of goat cheese, wrapped in white paper and sealed with twine. In the corner, I opened a small refrigerator and touched the tops of several sodas, indecisive. Behind the register, a tiny woman with white hair and large ears watched a miniature television. The Greek was indecipherable, but the tone seemed one of concern. I chose a cola. Diet. No. Regular. The bells chimed again as two men shuffled inside. One carried a cat, which he brought to the counter and plopped next to a jumbo jar of marble-foiled chocolates. Another passed behind me, pressed his hand on my back.

"Excuse me," I said, "sorry." Both men disappeared through the shop's rear, leaving behind a miasma of smoked lamb and raki.

I wended my way to the register and placed my items next to the cat, who greeted me with disregard. The clerk kept glancing back at the television. Words flashed on the screen, but I found them impossible to read. Then the picture changed: a graphic airplane accident, black smoke, and the remains of white titanium. Three dead. It was a hopper plane to Athens.

"Does this happen," I choked, staring at the screen, mesmerized, "often?" She misunderstood, and changed the channel, showing a different news story. A group of young people—high-school-aged, they seemed, perhaps college—held posters above their heads, a unifying countenance of anger, determination. What vigor it took, I thought, to care about something so deeply. I recalled then Niko's comment at dinner, his mention of protestors. When I tried to interpret the words on their signs—painted in thick, black brushstrokes—the story changed again. Coverage of a carjacking. A woman alone. Her skull beaten by a tire iron, though, apparently, she'd survived.

A motorcycle blew past the storefront, the guttural sound of its engine filled the store, and I felt the cramping again, far down in my stomach, but this time, sharper.

The clerk began speaking to me in Greek.

I couldn't understand. She tried again. I got every other word: *yesterday, figs, early*. I glanced back at the television's harrowing images. Losing, then catching, my breath.

"What?" I said.

"You."

"No," I said.

"No?" she said. "Yes."

"No," I said again. "Not me."

The clerk left the register and ambled toward the back of the store, as a woman came inside with a baby affixed to her chest, wrapped in a soft beige fabric, its bald head bobbing, cloddish feet akimbo. The woman bounced her hips, side to side, and hummed as she roamed the store, seemingly on a mission for something specific. The baby was so quiet I had the passing thought it might be dead.

The clerk returned with a paper bag, opened it, and nodded. I leaned over the counter. Inside was a green basket of plump, rotund figs—a nearly black, necrosis purple. My mouth watered. They would go beautifully with the goat cheese, the crackers. I pictured it all on a platter, laid out before me, my appetite impossible, eternal.

"Yes?" the clerk said.

"I don't know," I said.

The woman with the baby left the shop, and in her place, a warm gust of wind came through, suffusing the store with air, with metal, the smell of street urine and seawater.

"Yes," she said.

It was clear language would not resolve this for us. The clerk was obviously confusing me with someone else, and because it would be too hard to navigate her mistake, I took the figs and said thank you. When we exchanged money, she grabbed hold of my hand. Hers were much older looking than her face, wizened and sliced with deep lines, raised blue veins, knuckles like knots. What kind of life had those hands endured? Behind her and next to the small television, I noticed a security monitor. It bore my image in black and white; the visual information of my likeness carried by radio waves, a brutal facsimile, grainy and distant. The clerk let go and I stepped back, disappearing from the screen.

16

Back at the rental, I set the envelope of photos down, resolving to take them out after eating, when I could concentrate on something other than the gnarled, nagging promise of filling myself to oblivion. I pummeled through everything, delighting in the tang of the goat cheese, the unctuous slip of the dolmas. I opened the bag of figs—they were smooth and bulbous, moldable to the pressure of my fingers. Piercing through the skin with my nail, I watched their tannic juices run down my thumb. Witnessing this exsanguination, my mouth flooded, and I could take it no longer. I lobbed a whole one in my mouth, the sweetness, more subdued than honey, the aftertaste, floral, like a wild berry. I'd only ever had figs dried, or else jammed inside the depressing confines of a low-calorie snack. I ate one after the other, licking the green basket in which they were held. When I finally caught my breath, I checked the bag again. One final fig jeweled at the bottom. Glutted, I picked it up, cleaved it with my teeth.

My mouth registered the intruder before my brain. A little bit of life— the size of a seed—writhed over my tongue. I spit the fruit's guts onto my palm.

Early in my time at the museum, a broker had wrongfully sent our department a sixteenth-century oil painting from Italy. When we opened the package, I saw movement behind the canvas, but didn't speak up. After

Margaret died, I used to see her, bits of her, here and there: the back of her head reflected in the oven, a tendril of hair swiping across my arm, her tanned foot peeking out of a blanket. That day at the museum, I could hear Henry's voice telling me I was imagining it all. *No*, he would have said, sitting back in his wooden chair, glasses cocked, chin tucked and doubled. *You didn't see. You* thought *you saw.*

But at the museum the next morning, the front of the painting had torn, and a swarm of wet, shiny maggots crawled out, fell onto the floor, slowly, one by one, and then faster, the sound like soft hail hitting a roof.

And there was one now, squirming in my hand: cream body, tan head glistening from the fig's juices. I dropped it on the floor, ran to the sink, and washed out my mouth, scrubbed my tongue, put a finger down my throat, and tried to throw everything back up, to no avail. I returned to where I'd let the insect fall, but couldn't find it.

I slept with the lights on, and all night, kept waking to the phantom feeling of a legless little being, opalescent and determined, prying my lips open, burrowing between my molars, thrashing against my soft palate.

17

On Monday, the takeoff to Athens lasted longer than expected. We were caught in a queue on the tarmac for an hour, right before sunset, the sky a scathing yellow against the city's shadowed landscape. The airport was the smallest one I'd ever been to, devoid of real security; a one-eyed cat in the middle of the check-in area had begged me for food the whole time we waited. I'd felt horrible that I'd nothing to share.

Inside the plane, I leaned against the window, trying to dodge the aggressive air-conditioning, but it found me anyway, blasting cool air onto the top of my head. Theo and Niko sat three rows behind.

Niko had come in case I'd needed a translator, and Theo had come because Niko had. In the moment she'd shown up beside him, no luggage in hand, I realized they might not have been as easygoing, as bohemian, as I'd previously thought. Underneath the careful varnish of their tousled hair, their sun-blown skin, there it was, glinting through: a grain of frailty.

I wasn't comfortable with Niko abandoning the statue, but I was so thrown by Theo's arrival, I could not find the will to tell him what I'd wanted to, which was, *Please. Don't come. I don't need you.* Because maybe I did need him—or them. Maybe I felt some relief at not having to do this alone.

When Theo left for a smoke, Niko promised the statue would be safe. Alec would keep watch. "He will not leave it out of sight," said Niko. I asked him about the locks, the cameras. Had he done as he promised? He said he'd make some calls, but he didn't want to get my hopes up. Things never happened that quickly on the island. I tried to reiterate how important the statue's safety was to me. I told him my future was on the line, and he said, with a serious tone, something he didn't take often, "It is understood."

"Wait," I said. "Does Theo know?" I wasn't sure if I'd wanted her to, if it mattered.

"No," he said, his face stiff, careful. "No, I do not think so."

After we boarded, there was a delay. Passengers stirred in their seats, expressing their dismay, first privately, then to one another. A collective anxiety grew like a film over every window. Eventually, the stewardess announced that the pilot on the plane in front of us had endured a medical emergency, but we would be taking off soon. I'd flown enough to know that *soon* meant "within a few hours." I settled in, reached for my bag, my hands fumbling around the unopened envelope of photographs, and found a pill, then swallowed it without water. I felt foolish that I'd waited this long to return to the pictures of the statue—but also, a bit fearful. The thought of seeing her through a new set of eyes held an absurd amount of power over me. I was afraid that she might have looked different—objectively more important, or objectively less. Either way, I needed clarity in my surroundings. I was hopeful that Athens would feel like a fresh start, a respite from the claustrophobia of the island.

When the woman next to me got up to use the bathroom, Theo took her spot.

"I swear this plane is cursed," she said, her voice cracked and sleep-deprived. She was wearing a blue cardigan and a pair of light-washed jeans with faint grass stains on her left knee, which kept moving, perilously, toward mine.

"Last time, I was mid-air when the pilot had a heart attack," she went on. "Or was it a seizure?" She paused, waiting for the answer. "I can't remember. But the point is—what if I told you all that happened on this plane?" she asked. "This *exact* plane."

"Even if it was the same airline, they all look identical. Don't they?"

She shook her head and pointed out the window, where we had a view of the wing. I craned my neck, pushed my face closer to the glass. The window rattled.

"What am I looking at?"

"On the left wing," she said. "There's an extra stripe of orange paint. None of the other planes have that."

I moved back.

"I see."

"You're not scared of flying?" She seemed, almost, shocked.

I thought of the crash I saw on the news yesterday, on that small television in the shop; the plane bowed and broken in the middle, the melted seats, the mouth of flames, the stone-colored fumes. Had she seen it too?

"No," I said. "I mean, not usually." I looked down. "Which part of it do you fear?"

She laughed. "What do you mean?" she said. "The dying part. The ultimate vacancy. The infinite confinement. The worst part about dying in a plane crash is the two minutes it takes to fall to the ground, when you know you can't do anything but wait for totalizing emptiness, endless static, or whatever it is."

Her hands moved as she spoke, the right one shooting up first, and then both together, her fingers loosely extended. The seats were so close. I could feel the heat of her worry. At one point, her hand accidentally brushed my elbow. Overwhelmed by her touch, I kept glancing at the point of contact.

"I've asked a pilot that before," she said, "and that's the right time, by the way. Two minutes for a plane to drop straight down. Boom. Doesn't seem like a long while, does it? Well, it would be."

She glanced out the window, then glanced again, and stopped to stare. The white noise from the engine whirred.

"The rational part of me knows that it's unlikely to happen, that I'd sooner die in a car accident or from some disease, but everybody thinks that, don't they? So every time I buckle in and feel the wheels under the plane start to rattle, I think, *Today, it could be me,* I think, *two minutes.* Two whole fucking minutes."

I twisted my neck and tried to spot the woman who'd been sitting beside me, but I realized I hadn't seen her face and so I didn't know who to look for. "Are you listening?" said Theo. I nodded, but my head felt funny, encased in mud, overcome with a thick, stoic dread.

A raspy voice on the intercom spoke and the plane lurched forward. As Theo got up and returned to Niko, the cramp from yesterday dug deeper into my lower abdomen, almost near my spine, and a baby began to wail. The plane sped forward, the noise of the engine uncompromising. Outside the window, tufts of feather grass cracked through the tarmac's asphalt and flailed in the wind, while men and women in reflective vests directed air traffic, arms outstretched, their faces deadened by night.

18

After a thankfully unclimactic landing, Niko, Theo, and I took a silent cab ride to our hotel. The streets felt different in Athens, wider, more crowded, the buildings jagged and half-finished. The sky a dull, hazy ink. When we arrived, a rush of relief overcame me: all I wanted was sleep. The quicker this day was done, the quicker I could return to the statue.

Our hotel was filled with expats and plain from the outside, facing Mount Lycabettus, but better than my place back on the island—sturdy architecture, a long, glimmering pool and lush courtyard. On the side of the building, someone had spray-painted the words *AMERICA IS A FASCIST* in red.

It was late enough for Niko, Theo, and me to part ways, so we said goodbye in the lobby, and I went up to my room. Once I settled in, I began preparing notes for my lecture. I'd planned on repurposing a talk I'd given at a conference many months ago, but when I recalled it, the subject felt uninspired. I wanted to discuss the statue. To focus on an item we were in the midst of purchasing—especially when its provenance was not exactly ironclad and its sale not exactly public knowledge—went against my better judgment, but I felt a momentum, an allegiance to the figure. She'd needed to be seen. And I wanted to be the one to show her. Plus, I had notes, and Niko's photographs, which I could project for the class. For a moment, I fantasized about the lecture going well; about students approaching me after, trembled excitement in their eyes—such theatrics seemed unlikely, but, I supposed, possible. I paced around the room, took a cold Mythos beer from the mini fridge, opened it, and sat on the bed. When I caught a glimpse of myself in the television's reflection, the reality of my aloneness shone back at me.

But this was ideal; it was what I needed. Space to think. I got up, opened my luggage, and slipped out the envelope of Niko's photos. After a few breaths, I unsheathed the one on top.

At first, witnessing the statue through Niko's perspective disoriented me. The images were taken at odd, unflattering angles. Some of them appeared almost fish eyed. In one, Niko had taken a full shot of the statue's body down by her feet, so that her curled toes appeared gargantuan, larger than her head. I didn't like how his lens abutted her most vulnerable parts—the most broken, the most eroded. An extreme close-up of her nose that I, at first, thought was part of her knee. In real life, she had been total and mesmerizing, but in these photos, she was warped and siloed into pieces: a hand, an ear, a lower back. I recalled the conversation Niko and I'd had about that man who sold photographs of paintings, passing them off as originals, and I wondered if these reproductions were causing my normal viewing processes to glitch—it was as though I was merely going through the *motions* of looking at her, rather than *experiencing* the sensation of seeing her. But I'd surveyed thousands of pictures of art objects and never felt so personally affected. Was it Niko's fault? His undistinguished eye? Or was I, myself, too close? I put the photos down and walked away. Steeling myself, biding my time, I sat on the bed. My desire to return to the images—to not return to them—equal in strength.

After marrying Julian, I temporarily lost my vision due to a particularly debilitating migraine. I told him this had happened once before and to please not freak out. "You can't see? What do you mean you can't see? Your eyes are open." I turned to him. "I mean exactly what I'm saying. I. Can't. See." When the blindness lasted more than a few hours, he drove me to the emergency room, where they gave me a CT scan, an ECG, tested my blood pressure, reflexes. The doctor called it hysterical blindness. I told him he was wrong. It was due to migraines, and it had happened when I was younger. "And how long did the episode last?" he asked.

I told him not long—an hour maybe—but I couldn't really recall. He said, "Well, that might be, but this is something else. You have normal fundi; your pupillary reactions are normal. It is hysterical."

Right, I repeated, a formless rage taking hold, *hysterical*. Who did this man think he was, pathologizing me with such conviction? I was certain he was wrong, but then, when I felt Julian squeeze my shoulder, my anger wilted under the heat of his palm. I was outnumbered. The doctor told me to "take care" and "perhaps draw a nice bath," and wrote me a prescription for a few different antianxiety medications, and then, on our way out, handed Julian a pamphlet for some psych ward: a smiling, dead-eyed woman on the cover, I saw later, and laughed about, before tossing it in the trash. The entire car ride home, my face felt cold and vacant, like it belonged to someone else. I reached to pull down the visor mirror—and then, I remembered. Once we got back, Julian escorted me inside, his warm palm gripping my elbow with what I could only assume to be glee. He fed me, helped me take baths. He washed my hair, shaved my legs—for whose benefit, I didn't know, but that I allowed him to run a razor up and down each thigh, each calf, says more about me than it does Julian. Each act left me feeling more naked than the last. More helpless, dependent. Of course, I couldn't work. I took a few days off, capsized under the covers of our bed as I thought about the blind figures of antiquity: Tiresias, the seer, for example—who went blind after he watched a nude Athena taking a bath—and Orion, who was blinded as a punishment for attempted rape. In every one of these stories, blindness had been the ultimate damnation for these men—a kind of castration. Without my ability to see, I realized how little of my senses I'd noticed—salty foods tasted saltier; fabrics felt softer; I could hear mosquitos buzzing outside the screen of our bedroom window. It became too much. I plugged my ears with cotton. I scratched at my skin, at the walls, like some kept animal. I wanted to be nothing but a pure, single pupil; sentient, yet unfeeling. And then—finally, a day and a half later, my vision returned. For the first few hours, I could see only static outlines. The flatness terrified me. I would have rather died than have gone through the world like that. But then, slowly, came the details, the dimensions of my space—an empty, finger-printed glass on the dresser, an accumulation of dust, icing the idle blades of the ceiling fan—and I felt, for the first time in a long time, genuine gratitude, like I could finally open my mouth, take in a gulp of resuscitating air. "You should wait it out," Julian said the next morning, while I buttoned up my white shirt, six-forty-five am. "A few more days won't kill you." But hadn't he been there? Hadn't he seen what it'd done to me?

An image of the statue's eyes entered my mind: her expectant, thalassic gaze. Her bloodless self-possession. Sick of myself, I got up and went back to the photos, my face hot, my hands unsteady. I turned to the next one. It was developed incorrectly, the exposure too dark. And in the next, the exposure was too light. Both would be unusable. I kept flipping, tossing all the pointless photos on the floor, growing more agitated until finally, I reached a clear image. I pulled it closer to my face. It was of the statue's torso, but something was printed on top of the marble, something that didn't belong, a small hand. I didn't recognize it as my own, or Niko's or Alec's. It was too petite, hairless and smooth. I traced the outline, following the curves as they led into a human arm, a chest. Over the top of the torso, an entire second figure came into focus. It was Theo.

This could easily be explained. Niko had given me a double exposure, two negatives stuck together in the darkroom. Or had this been purposeful? I turned to the next photo, holding my breath, careful not to smudge the edges.

It was Theo again, and not overlaid onto a different photograph, but alone, prostrate on a stripped mattress, limbs splayed like the Vitruvian man, two eyes screwed shut and a closed mouth. Her facial expression appeared either blissful or pained—or both—and she would have been nude, if it weren't for the coins covering her breasts and pubic area. They were emblazoned with some Grecian inscription, so focused I could smell them—ferric and ancient—and sense them on my skin too, heavy and cold enough to feel wet. They were adhered to her skin by either paint or blood or a mix of the two or something else entirely. An old but familiar emotion resurfaced. Something akin to annoyance.

The photo called to mind this project I'd seen in San Francisco, in the late eighties, right after college. The artist had gathered hundreds of thousands of pennies, laid them on a gallery floor, then painted over them with a thin film of honey. In a small, barred room at the back—like a jail cell—

three sheep brayed and grazed on grass. In front of them, the artist dipped her hands in a felt hat filled with honey, over and over again, warming it, wringing it out, staring off into nothing, completely silent, while beside her, two motorized mortar pestles droned on. One ground pennies, and the other, human teeth. I'd been sick with nerves that night and all the conflicting senses intensified my queasy state of being: the smell of copper, musk from the sheep, the squishing sound of the sugary secretions, the braying, the pestles grinding. I didn't know what it all meant, or how it made me feel. But I knew that it threatened what I'd come to value about ancient art: those clean, classical certainties of technical prowess; beauty for beauty's sake.

I'd gone to see the show with a man I was dating in Berkeley. I wasn't sure about him, but he seemed sure about me. He talked about how the installation was a representation of commodification, death, the filthiness of greed, and as I nodded along, I knew he understood what I couldn't then, and therefore, I'd have to sleep with him. If I didn't, this feeling of idiocy, of smallness, would never leave. That night, I performed my own show, everything I thought he'd want—I left the lights on, exposed my stomach in subservience, let him come on the cool skin of my chest. If I was going to be put on display, I might as well dictate how. As I lay below him, I wondered what kind of woman he wanted. What parts of myself should I hide? In a world built on hierarchies, it was impossible not to compare yourself, not to feel like you should be a little less or a little more of something. If you didn't size yourself up, someone else would do it for you. Once, at an event for work, a famous investor—a man who was nearly royal—made a joke in front of my colleagues. *Does Elizabeth have a bad back?* he'd asked the group, as they regarded him, confused. *She seems to be carrying a lot of weight.* At the tenebrous memory of his hands pantomiming large breasts in front of his chest, and the group's subsequent laugh, humiliation rippled through me.

But to say I was merely demeaned in that moment would be misleading. It would bypass something uglier, truer, more complex. Who was I to complain? Doors open for all types of unfair reasons, and I thought then: Look at me now; a powerful man knows my name. I hadn't heard him say a thing about Madison.

The picture of Theo continued to capture me, cannibalizing time, as city life went on outside the hotel, the darkling mountains lit up with life.

In every minute that passed, I noticed another detail: a wimpling on her thigh, a prominent vein on her hands, a faint scar running across her belly button, a peek of delicate body hair. The perspective did not force the eye toward areas of imperfection; rather, it dared the eye *not* to notice them. The lens dispassionate, the camera angle neutral—and therefore, free, stripping all nakedness, all shame, from her nudity. My vision blurred with tears. I thought of the statue and the tape—the control of the adhesive, how tightly it had mended to the stone, had made it seem as though the head had been replaced by a new one, or else never existed at all. What was the line, really, between destruction and invention? I examined the photograph in every way possible. I let it bury me. By the time I fell asleep, it was almost daylight.

19

That morning, Niko and I left for the lecture a little after nine a.m. He appeared oddly professional in his black blazer and linen slacks, as we threaded through the streets of Athens, pausing for long periods of time and waiting to cross the road because of heavy traffic. Inwardly, I asked him about Theo's photograph: *Which one of you put it in there? What are you trying to tell me?*

In certain areas of the city, protest slogans littered the ground, and the air was layered with exhaust fumes, the acidic smell of residual tear gas. We trekked past a cluttered chain of establishments: a bank, a café, a bookstore, many of them boarded up, until we came upon an open souvenir shop with a headless mannequin out front wearing a *somebody in Athens loves me* T-shirt. Niko stopped inside to get a cold bottle of water. Pamphlets for international travelers lined the wall. I picked one up about the Acropolis, a food guide, and then another that read: *Women Traveling Alone*, prepared by the U.S. Embassy. "The social cues abroad," one page said, "can be quite different than those at home. You cannot be sure which signals you are sending, so you must be extra cautious when engaging with strangers."

I folded the pamphlet and tucked it inside my pocket, then felt bad for Niko's measly purchase, so I bought the *somebody loves me* shirt—or, tried to buy it, but I didn't have enough money on me. He ended up paying, and for the rest of the way, as the small, clear bag bumped against my thigh and we both disappeared back into the crowd, I had to pretend like I was grateful.

When we finally arrived on campus, students sat outside, basking in golden light and chatting with one another, book bags slung over their shoulders, zippers flashing in the sun. We walked into a building where fans the size of cars whirred above us; along the walls, advertisements for roommates, nannying jobs, lost cats, and antiwar sentiments decorated the bulletin boards.

"Wait," I said to Niko, before we went in. "Have you heard anything about—?" I didn't want to state it explicitly, to risk shattering the glass of silence—of secrecy—we'd spent the morning building.

He said he'd talked to Alec an hour ago. The statue was fine.

"Good," I said, smiling meekly. "Thanks."

I felt his eyes flicker to my bag, the stupid shirt.

"I'm discussing her today," I said, under my breath.

"Is that so?" he asked, his tone taking on an air of gleefulness. "And will you utilize my photographs?"

"A few of them," I said, glancing at the room's open door, not wanting to confess how many of his pictures were unusable.

He leaned against the wall. "I wish I had what you had. Or Theo. A central muse. Creativity."

"I don't have much creativity," I said.

"Always so humble." He laughed, ushering me in.

"What you do," he said, "it requires a specific idealism. No?" As I walked in, he went on, his voice trailing behind me. "I gave up, too early. Perhaps. Perhaps I could have made of myself something."

It hadn't occurred to me that Niko would be unsatisfied with any part of his life. Then again, I'd never asked.

The lecture hall itself was sparse, dank, with a sweet, rotten smell, wood-paneled walls, and a whiteboard penned with the ghost marks of someone else's thoughts. An oak-colored lectern sat in the dead middle, too tall for me. The microphone would hit my forehead. I wondered if a woman had ever stood up there.

A tall man approached me and Niko and said the air con wasn't working. He was perspiring and apologizing profusely, and in nervous anticipation of disappointing him, I apologized back, like my presence had caused the malfunction.

"How many students will be here?" I asked. He said he didn't know. Niko shook his hand and thanked him, but when I went to do the same, the tall man did not reciprocate.

A few minutes later, the students filtered in, backlit by the hallway. Warm bodies thronged the entrance. The sheer number overwhelmed me as they sauntered in, textbooks in hand, disheveled hair, clothes I didn't understand. An undercurrent of confused, unrequited desire hummed between them. I couldn't recall being that young; did I ever possess such palpable callowness? Niko tapped me on the shoulder and said, into my ear, "Wow, so many, no?" The tall man whispered to us both, "Five minutes." I felt the time tick in my throat.

I walked to the podium with the cards I had scribbled together the night before and shuffled through them, hunched over with my chin propped up by my fist. Niko approached me. There was a silent tension between us, and I could sense he wanted to fill it, whether I obliged or not. "Is your hotel room pleasant?" he said. I told him it was, and was his? "Yes," he said. "Yes."

He turned his head away from the crowd and lowered his voice. "Did you have fun with us? The other night. Leon said he enjoyed his time."

I stared at him, confused—and then, it clicked.

"Oh, I am apologetic. Did I say something wrong?"

I told him no, it was fine. And yes, I'd enjoyed it, too.

He began to saunter away, but stopped himself, and then turned back to me once more.

"May I ask of you something else?"

I didn't look up. "Can it wait?"

"What did Theo say to you on the plane?"

My eyes shot up to his.

"Nothing important," I told him. "Why?"

"Never mind," he said. "Of course. Never mind. Forget I said it. Would you? We have been, well, having disagreements."

"Oh." I glanced at the clock, then at the students, my forehead hot.

The cramping from earlier intensified, pulsated in an almost incomprehensible area of my pelvis. I breathed slowly and massaged it, hoping the discomfort would subside.

More male students entered the auditorium than female. Or did it only seem that way because of the gap in each group's loudness? I set my note cards down and walked off, past the tall man and Niko, who touched my arm on the way out and said, "Where are you going?"

I told him I'd be right back.

"Everything is OK?"

I nodded and slipped out. When I got to the restroom, I wiped my face with a scratchy brown paper towel. I went to wash my hands, but the water came out too quickly, splattering all over my white blouse; transparent cloth clung to the outline of my left breast, my stomach. Visible now was the shadow of my navel, the texture of my skin. I touched the scratch on my neck and tried to picture someone kissing or grabbing me, willing myself to recall what I'd asked for the other night, if anything. But I couldn't conjure a single image. At least no believable one. Had Niko seen something with me and Leon? Had we left together?

When I was younger, Henry had this friend. He had broad shoulders and silk for hair, and he used to come over and swim with us. This was a year after Margaret died. We'd just installed a pool in the backyard because Henry had received a research grant, and because according to my mother, he'd needed to get out of his office and stop moping; he'd needed a project. I was fifteen, and my breasts were the size of grapefruits. I wore my mother's bikini, filled the top out to the brim, skin pinched over the fabric's edges. The friend wore black swim trunks and a monogrammed bathrobe that trailed behind him when he walked. He was a wealthy and important man. I knew this because of the perfume my mother wore around him, because of the kind of scotch Henry brought down from the bookshelf once the man rang our doorbell—and because I'd seen him on the backs of some of my mother's favorite books. I hadn't liked being in the pool, or water, at all, but my mother had insisted on my participation. One evening, the man asked my mother to take a picture of us. "Just us two?" I asked. He motioned for me to sit on his lap, and so I did, the wetness of his trunks seeping onto my thighs. In a split second, as my mother looked away to slap a mosquito off her arm, the man's cold thumb slipped inside my bikini and touched my nipple, then just as quickly retreated. The pool water stilled. We grinned on cue. I felt what I would later come to recognize as shame, but something else too, something more lurid: a secret pride, his attention as confirmation of my worth. Nobody had touched me since the night Margaret died. Years later, I came across that photograph in an album and was shocked to see some unrecognizable chimera—the head of a child with crooked teeth and a snub nose and the body of a developed woman. In retrospect, it was easy to see why the man had been so bold, so careless, in his approach—he understood which parts of me did not belong to me, long before I ever did.

I slipped into one of the stalls, but it was broken so I held it shut, the floor puddled with liquid. It was disgusting, but I felt disgusting already, my clothes stuck to my skin with sweat and faucet water. I smelled a hint of chlorine as I remembered my mother's cautions. "Don't get in the pool with George," she'd say, a secret caught on her face, as if to pronounce, *We're in this together.* One time, she came inside the kitchen dripping wet with a towel around her chest, the tie of her bikini undone. "He's grabby, isn't he?" Was I supposed to answer? It seemed like a test I would fail either way. Soon, she began dictating what I wore. The bikinis were no longer an option; neither were halter tops, or my most prized pair of frayed denim shorts. She told me if you catch a man staring at you for too long that means he's undressed you with his eyes. "And what are you to do then?" I'd asked. "Nothing," she'd said. "I only wanted you to be aware. Knowledge is power." Though it didn't feel that way; it felt burdensome. It felt like I'd been standing on the mirrored side of a two-way glass. Not only did I have to care for how I looked; I had to care for the ways in which I was looked at. This was a violence I never came to terms with. I think I've held it over the head of every man I'd ever met. I'm not saying that's fair.

I heard someone come inside. They went to the stall to the right of me, and then unhappy with that, walked back out. I heard banging on the door—violent banging—and stepped back, keeping the door closed with my foot, balancing on one leg. "Someone is in here," I yelled, in English, then tried to yell again in Greek. It did not stop. The stall shook. The handle clattered. Words written everywhere, a tiny, detailed drawing of a dog with a lizard immured in its maw. "What the fuck is your problem?" I said, opening the door.

A man stood there.

The sound of liquid splashed; the air inside was stiff. Ripe. I saw another young man standing at the urinals—had he been there the whole time? "I'm sorry," I said, and they both said nothing. Just watched me leave.

Niko was waiting for me in the lecture hall doorframe, hands behind his back, head bent down. I stopped and asked for his blazer. He took it off and handed it to me, but not before glancing at my wet shirt. I covered myself, then thanked him quietly, the cramping still present.

"Good luck," he said.

He went to the side of the room and sat down in a small, blue chair, and in the weakened fluorescent light of the hall, I noticed a streak of gray hiding near his temple.

The tall man introduced me, said a few words, and then the room hushed, and the lights dimmed. My hands trembled and I could barely see the words I'd written on the note cards; the lectern seemed to grow, threatened to swallow me. Then, as if out of my control, and despite the gaping silence, the students' bored yawns, I set the cards down and began. The crowd seemed engaged with the few photographs I was able to project. I discussed the sequence of concavities that made up the statue's form: the slight hollow of her stomach; her cupped hand, the depressed space under both collarbones, and lastly, the forward push of her hips, which caused the pubic region to appear especially sunken. In many ways, the figure exemplifies an opening, the physicality of female genitalia. And yet the turn of her head suggests an aloofness, an ignoring of her spectator. A warning to not come close. Her body is a paradox.

Part of me delivered this lecture, while the other half watched, awed at how the words flowed, how I was able to maintain eye contact, a near-perfect posture. Even the cramping had subsided.

At the end, I reserved ten minutes for questions. Mostly, the inquiries were dull and obvious, or else half-formed opinions, statements disguised as queries. I took my last one from a student in the back right corner, who had been watching me thoughtfully, almost *too* thoughtfully. I squinted to try to make out her face, which was oddly familiar, but soft and round and defiantly open. Onto it I could have projected anyone. "Your name," I said, though I hadn't asked that information from anyone else. I tried to remember to smile.

She stood up and came into the light.

"If the aim of your museum," she began, "is to spread cultural knowledge about antiquities, then why do you consistently turn a blind eye toward the kinds of illegal activities that bring irreparable cultural loss?"

Her English was crisp. The crowd murmured and turned to look at her. For a moment, her skin appeared gray, inhuman.

"And what kinds of illegal activities are those?"

"Purchasing items from known looters," she said. "For one."

My lips went cold. "Huh," I said, "thank you for your question." Quickly, I ran through the codified messages I knew by heart, the ones I'd heard William say time and time again. "It's true that not every antiquity has a verifiable provenance. In fact, many do not. But that doesn't necessarily mean that they are thieved."

"If you find something on our land," the student said, "then it belongs to us. Not some looter."

I took a deep breath in. Adrenaline ran through me. "But if it *was* sold to a private collector," I said, "then at one point, however far back, however much a looter he was, however unethical, then it belonged to him, and then it belonged to whomever he sold it to, and so on. As long as these objects hold value, they will be bought, and they will be sold. The land, technically, doesn't own anything."

"But don't you think it should?"

"Well, whether we like it or not," I said, "these pieces of art have been deemed valuable, and because of this, they've been given a price, and once something has been given a price—" I lost my train of thought. Suddenly, it seemed criminal that I should be allowed up here, behind this lectern, trying to explain something that I could not fully understand myself. Sweat accumulated on my palms. I saw William's nagging eyes, warning me to stop, alongside all the authoritative men on the board, their mouths slumped down in spurn.

But I didn't want to stop. I wanted to say something honest.

"I do think these incredibly significant antiquities should be seen, widely, as widely as possible, and when you want art to be seen widely, it becomes a product, a commodity, something to be owned." My mind spun. "People are drawn to the power that comes with that ownership."

"People or institutions?" she asked.

"Institutions are people."

"You're not getting to the heart of the matter," she said.

"Which is?"

"Why can't objects be kept in the countries they were originally found?"

I wiped my palms on my slacks and considered this. Silence rumbled through the room. A pen clicked.

"The truth is that many large-scale museums are better equipped to handle, restore, *preserve* these objects, better equipped to make them available to both the public and academics."

She scoffed. "By *large-scale museums*, you mean *your American* museum."

"As it stands now," I said, "yes. And I can assure you that our aim is always to put the art first. We do the best we can with what we have."

This time, she spoke louder. "You can't really believe that."

"I have to," I said, too quietly, unsure if I'd meant it.

In unison, the crowd murmured and began to stir. I looked at the clock. I'd gone a few minutes over. The tall man regarded me with curious, yet unmistakable, insouciance. He wouldn't release me. I'd have to release myself.

I stood straighter, and over the chatter, I called out, "That's all I have for now. Thank you for coming."

The students, seemingly ambivalent at the unresolvedness of our ending, gathered their things, then forged toward the exit, moving on and out into daylight. I stood at the lectern for a moment, collecting my thoughts. I was glad time had run out. If she'd kept pressing, I might have folded. Maybe even told her the truth. Which was that I didn't worry—as often as I could have—about who owned what. I worried about how it benefited me—and yet, every morning, I woke with equal parts fear and desire for it all to be over: the pressure to perform, the useless ladder climbing, the charade of teething my tongue, and though I stood before her and her classmates, physically, amongst them and their fresh-faced, blood-pumping bodies, I was both present and not present, both dead and alive, and frankly, her questions didn't matter and conversations like ours would always prove to be futile because as much as I'd wanted to *believe* in ethics, ethics were not reality and, in reality, curation was a business. And in business, money won.

20

The cramping had not abated, but the faster I walked out of the university, the less I noticed. I hadn't stopped to say more than a quick goodbye to Niko, who had stood there in silence, dumbly watching me leave. As I blew through blurry crowds of people, the young woman's questions caromed in my head. I envied her clarity of anger—her clarity, in general.

Once I got to the hotel, I could barely remember the trek back. The top of my head and shoulders were slightly damp. Had it been raining? I took four ibuprofen and ordered the most depressing room service I could manage: an underdone hamburger, bleedy and tepid, and a basket of wimpy fries. With each bite, I felt the tickle of the maggot from the other night, squirming up and down my esophagus, which, every few moments, caused my throat to contract. I panicked and spit the food back out onto the plate, before trying again, washing everything down with a lukewarm beer from the mini fridge, my greasy fingerprints slipping on the bottle as I moved on to dessert: a stodgy cheesecake with the faint aftertaste of refrigeration, the sweetness of which only increased my hunger, before giving way to all-encompassing shame, and then, finally exhaustion.

The hotel sheets were coarse and smelled of cigarette ash and bleach. I curled up under them and closed my eyes. Noises of the outside world infiltrated my room: the red roar of sirens, blaring car horns, groups of intoxicated caterwaulers. In the room beside me, a television murmured. I thought of Theo and wondered if this was the kind of death she'd meant, the ultimate vacancy: alone in a dark hotel, the imperceivable white noise of your neighbor's television. I crawled closer to the mumbled voices and pressed my ear to the wall. It was the news. They were discussing some recent NATO protests. Dozens of shops had been damaged, a few set on fire. A man called the US president a murderer, and regarding his potential visit to Greece, said, "Keep that pervert out of our country." The television turned off.

I entwined myself back in the covers, irritated by the discomfort inside me. Was the pain real? All my ruminating had surely made it worse. I got up and ran a bath, hopeful that the warmth of it would help. The water came out in pins, like rain. Swollen from the alcohol and salt, I didn't want to get undressed and be forced to engage with my body, but I disrobed and got in anyway, the edges of the tub slippery. Steam fogged the mirror, the brass knob of the sink, the edges of the cracked door. An engorged mosquito flew into the bathroom, landed on the wall, and stayed.

I breathed deeply and closed my eyes, my mind flittered to Theo and Niko's bed, sprawling and messy and feather soft, an adjustment of pillows. A soft kiss behind the ear, goose-pimpled skin, Niko's hand wrapping around Theo's bucking hips—and then, another hand made of marble, ice white, reaching for me, pulling underwear to ankles.

My eyes shot open, and I recalibrated and glanced around the room, repeating to myself the various objects I saw: light fixture, sink, door. I looked down. Dark hair spilled between my legs and floated in the limpid water. It had been weeks since I'd trimmed or groomed. *I like it*, Madison told me once, when it had been like this before. *The rest of you is so neat, so controlled, and yet here*, here *you are wild*. I thought of my statue. I thought of how depilated pubic mounds proliferated the female sculptures of Ancient Greece, each one smooth as glass. It was believed that the inclusion of hair—or frankly, any detail of anatomy—would make the female body appear lewd. There was a certain kind of museumgoer who would circle the nude figures like they were prey—if you looked close enough, you could draw a line from their eyes to the spaces between the statues' hips. I was giving a donor a tour when one such patron approached me with a grin and nodded toward a crouching *Aphrodite*. *I've heard some were modeled after real women*, he said. *Their lovers must have been very pleased.*

I cleaved the water with my fingers, then ran them through the curls and pushed one inside myself. It felt good at first, and then, tender, like thumbing a bruise. Something strange, foreign, was stuck inside, but I couldn't reach it, even when I relaxed my muscles. My legs now splayed, one ankle on either side of the tub, the edges like stirrups, I tried again, dug my fingers deeper, as though I was reaching for a ring at the bottom of a drain—just a little more now, almost there. Pressure built; everything began to throb—my wrist, my tailbone, the latter of which ground into the porcelain of the tub. The cramp almost unbearable now, I tried again and again until finally, I got a hold and slipped it out with one silky movement, then let go. I watched it bob to the surface of the unclouded water, flaccid and coiled. In some ways, I was relieved. In other ways, I felt, rising in my throat, the physical manifestation of repulsion. I couldn't bring myself to touch the object, or else risk confirmation of its existence. I gathered my legs up to my chest, and squeezed shut my eyes. I thought I should clear out the water, but then I pictured the condom, bare against the tub's porcelain, curled up like a small fetus—slick and stuck to the ceramic—and the image nauseated me further. If I didn't leave the tub immediately, I would vomit. I grabbed the edges and hoisted myself out of the water, the warmth rushing away from me, my blood pressure dropping as my foot slipped on the warm tile and my hand slammed the door behind me—all in a single motion. The room spun—or I spun. Maybe my organs spun, out of fury. I pulled myself to the bed and lifted the covers, breathing—in for six, out for six.

Eventually, everything quieted, and I sank deeper into the mattress, trying to forget what I'd never know, as I searched my body. It all seemed fine—the same as it always had. I closed my eyes, took another deep breath, and plunged my pointer finger inside myself, then my middle, pressing against the wet, ribbed walls, comforted at this erasure. How one part of me could so easily swallow another.

21

Sun fell through the windows and flooded the clinic with migraine-inducing light. In between the freshly painted walls, the waiting room teemed with children, their mothers tracking them as the floor creaked under my restless feet, and the ceiling fan lazed, then sped up again. I locked eyes with one such mother, beleaguered in expression, a baby's hand groping through the knots of her hair. Did she ever tire of everything it took from her? My mother used to call me her greatest thief.

I waited forty-five minutes to see the doctor, an older man with brittle hair and chapped lips who squinted at me with austerity. When I was done talking, the man grimaced and said it was too early to run any tests for transmitted diseases, and though he advised an antibiotic for the infection I'd likely received from what he called the "exited contraceptive," this office didn't have the medicine on hand, and I'd have to visit a pharmacist. I wondered if he saw me as an uncultured American woman traipsing around Europe without care, or if he pitied me, or worried for me. Maybe he had a daughter himself. I asked if he could write me a prescription for migraines. I said I'd taken Sansert—methysergide—before. He said he didn't know what that was, and if I'd had a headache, ibuprofen should work just fine. He escorted me out of the room with his hand on my shoulder and told me to be well.

I left, intending to find a pharmacy, but looped instead through unseen pockets of the city, nothing I would have recognized as the Greece I'd come to know. Though what did that mean, really? That morning, a fire had erupted hillside and ashed the city. Under the mauve sky, shops were beginning to open, but nobody was out. I stopped in various restrooms to cool my neck with water and challenge my reflection in different iterations of the same, hazy mirrors, every time hoping to notice a marked difference between the person who arrived on the island and the person I was now. But I could detect no visual change. If anything, I was prone to mistaking myself for no one. A ghost of a ghost. A copy of a copy.

Sometime after—between the clinic and the hotel—I stopped for a coffee, a place I'd heard Theo mention on the cab ride here. When I was on my way out, I was shocked, but shouldn't have been, to find her, sitting at a corner table, half faced away from me, reading an Athenian paper. I considered leaving, acting as though I hadn't seen her, but there was a possibility she'd already seen me too. When I sat across from her, she barely looked up. I felt too aware of my surroundings, too alert. The smell of fresh ink on Theo's paper, the steam rising from her coffee, the lemon dregs of light inside the shop.

"Have you ever been to the Acropolis?" said Theo, then laughed a bloodless little laugh, eyes still away from me. "Right. Stupid question." She conceded that she hadn't. "I'm not one for sightseeing, but I've decided to try it." She looked off and into the street, her hands still clutching the paper. She waited a beat. "Today. Now actually."

"Now?" I said, to say something.

She shrugged, put the paper down, and finally eyed me. "Come with me? Unless you have something better to do." I considered the pharmacy.

"No," I said. "Not at all."

Minutes later, we hopped on a crowded bus with carpeted walls and internally exposed wiring. Theo suggested we sit in the front. The driver had a crew cut and a bouquet of bougainvillea on his lap and the smell reminded me of the island, but only vaguely. From all the way out here, how unreachable its particulars felt.

I looked out the milky window. The light shifted over my face, there and gone. Orange trees sprang from the sidewalks, rows of them lining both sides of the streets. Theo leaned over and told me that once, as a little girl, she'd picked off a piece of fruit. "I couldn't believe it," she said. "The juice tasted like gasoline." Ten minutes later, we disembarked, stepping over an orange splattered and frothing in the middle of our path. "I read once," Theo said, "that the navel of the orange is a mutation." "A mutation how?" I asked. "It's a second orange. A nascent orange that didn't make it."

We walked by kiosks of postcards, water bottles swimming in the melted ice of squalid coolers, a joyful man with browned teeth selling newspapers, as piebald pigeons crossed back and forth over the cobblestone road. Up ahead, the citadel loomed: stark columns gilded by sunlight; escarpments bathed in shade. We proceeded onto a busier street, marked by the furor of some small but loud protest: men and women of all ages handing out flyers and lifting signs. One said: *All we want is ours.* I wondered if any of them was the student from yesterday. I liked to think I could have recognized her—or at least recognized the stare she gave me, that deprecating, paranormal glower. And would she have identified me? I put my head down, hoping to appear like anyone else. A young man shoved a small piece of paper into my hand, which I pretended to consider, but which I then folded and slipped inside my pocket.

I'd re-worn my clothes from yesterday's lecture, the hems of my slacks caked with dirt from the street. Theo wore a sleeveless white top and a pair of flattering jeans. Her hair tousled into a low bun. She had mastered effortlessness in a way I never could, and as we moved through the cluster of protestors, I watched the men and women look at her, taking a secondhand pleasure in their gaze.

We paid for our tickets and started to climb. The vertiginous steps took away my breath; my throat ached with thirst, and my thighs shook, my calves immediately sore. But Theo didn't seem winded at all.

Once we made it to the top, the city's neighborhoods surrounded us; a sea of white and beige buildings; places emptied of particularity. Clouds dispersed and the sunlight sharpened, the air heavy with the scent of thyme and mud. A gray dog with black ears lay under the shade of a hillock of stones, its back pushed against rock, its nose rough as bark. It reminded me of the dog I'd seen on the island my first night, but mangier, more wrung out, with trepidation in its eyes. I knew its presence was merely coincidental—there must have been thousands of strays just like it—and still, I felt unexplainably pulled to the dog, as though it were an old friend from some Delphic past.

"What are you looking at?" asked Theo.

"That dog," I said, "Do you think it's OK?" She said all the strays around here were well-fed. But that wasn't what I meant.

Elsewhere, people viewed the site through the lenses of their cameras, ran into one another, talked loudly, pointing everywhere with abandon. A group of construction men worked on the east-end metopes; their orange-yellow hats and loaders sored the gray, monochrome palette of beige marble and limestone. A pair of nuns in white habits wandered hand in hand wearing flip-flops patterned with daisies. I recalled Theo's story, the one she told me at dinner. Ever since that night, I'd wondered about the nun's near self-immolation—the missed-ness of it, the onanistic almost. Why hadn't she gone through with the abasement? When Theo had first relayed the anecdote, I'd thought she was relaying something about artifice, about exhibition, about how the performance of pain can be its own kind of relief, but up at the citadel, overlooking the whole of the city, I wondered if the story wasn't more about the audience than the act. That Theo had not only perceived this woman's pain, but had promised to create something from it, something that had the power to outlast. A photograph.

Theo and I made our way over to the Erechtheion, the south porch, the roof supported by five statues of maidens, the Caryatids. We passed the protestors, who had now formed a line near the center of the temple. They were standing still, and silent. Holding up their signs, eyeing all the passersby with what I assumed was contempt, but on a second look, appeared closer to grief.

"I heard you took a bit of a beating," Theo said. "At the lecture."

I peered at her with suspicion. If she knew about what happened at the lecture—what else did she know? "No," I said. "I mean, I wouldn't put it like that. It was one student."

"Niko said you were brave," she said.

"All I did was answer a question."

"It sounded like she went up against everything you believe in," she said, pausing for a moment, her tone impassive. Pleasant, even. "Right?"

"Yes and no," I said. "You could say my thoughts are—well, tangled." I told her I stood with museums on principle. They believed their acquisitions to be fair, the statues and paintings put to culturally important use, their acquisitions not only just, but necessary—acts of preservation. Could I see the other side's points? About objects belonging to their own heritage? Intellectually, of course. But pragmatically, no.

We stopped at the maidens, each one's fishtail braid the width of her neck. I jutted my chin toward them. "What do you think of the detail on the hair?" I said.

She ignored me. "But it isn't about pragmatics," she said.

I nodded. "I'm sure you're right. But I have to be realistic, don't I?"

"Do you think you scared her?" she said.

"Why would I have scared her? If anything, she scared me."

"But you're the one in charge."

I shook my head. "Not as much as you'd think."

"Then you're very invested, for someone who isn't running the show."

"She had her own investments too."

"Of course," said Theo. "We all do."

We began to move again. I tried to distract myself from Theo's questions. I wanted to believe that her intentions were good, but that, like the student, she had no idea how these things actually worked. The bureaucracies. How impossible it was to make change—even from the inside. But perhaps I wasn't giving Theo enough credit—or else, was giving her too much. Perhaps I was blinded by her mystique, the mystery of her perceptions. Everything about her I could never know.

As we came to the Parthenon and then the east pediment, I was reminded of one of the last statues I'd studied in graduate school: the figures of three goddesses. Now housed in the British Museum, a group of headless, ornately draped marble figurines, representing Hestia, Dione, and Aphrodite. To me, it had always been unclear if the figure on the far left, Hestia, is trying to stand or sit, her right foot stowed under the cloth, her other knee popping outward. To the right of her, Dione perches lower, and in her lap rests Aphrodite. I always found the intimacy of Dione and Aphrodite compelling: the way one leans so heavily into the other. I remembered this classmate of mine who took me for a cup of coffee once to discuss our final projects. I told him all about the three goddesses, thoughts rushing out of me, roiling over and onto the table. Their drapery had enamored me: the wimpled folds, the movement, how the stone, somehow, appears mobile, liquescent, like if you blink, you'll miss the moment the chiton slips right off. Though the goddesses are clothed they might as well be nude, their drapery the equivalent of the hand in the *Venus Pudica* pose—drawing the eye toward the very spot being hidden. Hestia especially, sitting with her legs wide open, just daring the spectator to imagine. (Interesting, or predictable, that the word *pudica* is related to the Latin *pudendis*—which means both shame or genitalia—or sometimes both?) At the end of the date, he asked me to come home with him. He laid me on his bed, the air in his room freezing, all the lights on. His long fingers pulled off my underwear as he told me to relax. He went down on me for some time, my hips pinioned by his water polo hands, his tongue arrowed and misguided. My mind wandered; I ruminated over the three goddesses, tried to count all the folds of their drapes but gave up at twenty. When he was done, he told me which figures of antiquity he found fuckable—Helen of Troy, fuckable; Cassandra, not fuckable. I said nothing. After that, he phoned me every day, would wait for me after class. I tried to cut him off. I found out later that he'd told everyone I was terrible in bed—lifeless, he'd said, like fucking a corpse. But, worse, he'd taken my ideas about the goddesses' drapery and written a paper himself, passing the observations off as his own. I went to the professor and told her. But she only smirked at me, seemed agitated I'd snitched. She leaned forward in her office chair—sweat on her upper lip—and shared some platitude: something about working smarter, not harder, about beating the men at their own game, before ushering me out, falsely assuming she'd told me something I didn't already know. Either way, she'd been wrong. Or not, wrong, exactly, but ignorant of the whole picture. I saw the way the men in the department looked at her, passed over her. She hadn't beaten anyone at anything.

"What are you thinking about?" Theo asked. "You're not upset by my comments, are you?"

"No," I said, recalibrating myself. "No, sorry. I was just—I was just observing."

We made it to the Theatre of Dionysus, sat down on a ledge, and gazed over Athens. Sun rays fanned out from the clouds. How Godly the city looked from up there. Theo turned from the restless wind; her hair lifted and stippled her face, her posture rigid, yet her composure, soft.

"There was a story my father used to tell me," she said. "Of a woman who jumped off and into that theater. This was in the sixties, I think. She was an Italian actress. A painter too."

I surveyed the theater and imagined an elegant actress's neck cracked and broken, but I could barely look at any of the steps directly. Theo took a cigarette from her bag.

"Can you smoke up here?"

She lit the end. The smoke anointed me, coated my throat. I coughed, then apologized. I was dying for water.

"I fell in love with her. Or the lore that followed her. They said she was an MI5 agent. She modeled for Warhol. She had an affair with John Wayne—or JFK. Could be both. We had a summer place out here—well, on the island—and I used my father's portable TV to watch her films. Over and over again. I was searching. But you know what? She was completely, utterly—"

Here, Theo's voice cut off, her eyes narrowed, and she took in the city, flaking ash from her cigarette with a quick flick of her pointer finger. Garrigue rustled on the hillside.

"I would like to go like that," Theo said. "Unquietly."

I nodded, said nothing. Was she toying with me? Did she want this to elicit a response? It felt so different being with her, alone, without Niko. She was a dangerous person, but not in any of the ways she would have had you believe.

My thirst turned lethal. I coughed again, breathing through the dis-comfort. I asked about the summer place she'd just mentioned. Her father was Greek, she said. When Theo was four, they moved to America, and he became a textile tycoon, founded the company Siarras Fabrics. For a moment, it sounded familiar, like a name I'd seen embroidered on the tags of my sheets. "And then my mother," she said. "My mother. She tried to come on to Niko. When he was eighteen. Still, though. She showed up to his room in lingerie and a long cigarette and said, 'I won't tell Theo if you won't.'"

"You're kidding."

"I am," she said. "My mother would never be so bold."

I didn't know which version to believe, but I knew that neither was the actual truth.

"And your father?" I said.

"What about him?" she replied, and I did not know how to read her tone—as one of disdain or playfulness—and so I did not press.

The summer place was inherited. Niko's family had one too. Both families came every year. To think of Theo and Niko as children swim-ming in the warm Grecian sea, playing in the sand, rubbing aloe on their innocent, sunburned backs. Half-asleep with salty hair. Pale sun on their skin. Some prelapsarian paradise.

"How old were you when you two met?" I asked.

"Twelve," she said.

"And him?"

She did some math in her head. "He would've been, let's see, fifteen, sixteen."

"And you two?"

She nodded, a wildness in the gesture, her cigarette burnt close to the filter, the spark almost touching her fingers.

At that moment, the protestors began to chant. At first, quietly.

"It sounds bad, but it wasn't. I looked like a little girl, but I was self-possessed. I knew what I wanted. People always say that, but it's true."

"Do they sell water up here?" I asked, light-headed at the thought of a twelve-year-old Theo entering the dark, cold bedroom of a sixteen-year-old Niko. I'd reached my capacity—I didn't want to know more.

"Oh," she said, scanning the grounds. "I don't think so." I watched two people—one holding a large camera, the other a microphone—plod toward the battalion of protestors, whose general din steadily increased into a single, anxious mantra.

"It's good they're getting some coverage," Theo said, nodding their way, "but this will barely make a splash. Look around. No one even cares that this place has been robbed of all its most important objects."

"I didn't know you knew much about the matter."

"Maybe you inspired me."

I feared taking her words at face value, but just in case she was speaking the truth, I tried not to appear flattered. And about the protestors, she was right. We watched as they remained largely unnoticed, even with a camera's presence. A cabal of schoolchildren—kitted out in striped shirts and navy slacks—cut through the group as though they were part of the property. Every so often, an errant traveler gazed in their direction, squinting at their signage.

Theo turned toward me. "It's just not enough, is it?"

My temples began to ache, my eyes a little heavy, darting across the ever-moving target of her face, but I didn't want her to notice my fatigue, how easily she'd outpaced me.

"What do you expect them to do?" I asked.

She shrugged.

"Something with real consequences."

"Huh," I said.

A hunched man with a black trash bag approached us and picked up a few tiny pieces of litter by our feet. I asked him about getting some water. He pointed to a restroom on the other end. "I'll come with you," said Theo. "That's OK," I said. "I'll be right back." She regarded me with confusion, as though her company had never before been refused.

Inside, graffiti looped on the walls, words overlaid on one another, an interminable string of a language lost. The toilet was so low to the floor I didn't trust my ability to hover and not contaminate myself, so I decided not to go. We'd been up there for so long and I still needed to get down and to the other pharmacy before they closed. I turned on the faucet, which dribbled at first and then spurted out a sulfuric-smelling liquid. My hands were a distraction. When had I acquired age spots? When had my veins ever been so noticeable? They looked like my mother's hands. I thought of the statue's defacement—how carefully my hands had worked then, how useful they'd felt, purposeful, and then I thought of Theo's hands, the easy way they held on to things, like they were not afraid of losing them.

When I came back, she was where I'd left her, but this time, not alone. She was chatting with someone, an anemic college student, a young woman. I watched them for a little while. Theo seemed comfortable—though I'd never seen Theo uncomfortable—gesturing with her hands and leaning closer to the woman, as though listening with real intent, unselfconscious interest. The same way she listened to me. A few minutes later, they parted in an aggressively cordial matter. When the young woman passed me, she paused, and took me in, and I took her in too, paralyzed for a moment at what she might say. But I didn't recognize her, and she didn't seem to recognize me either.

"Who was that?" I asked, trying to appear open, slightly curious.

Theo told me it was one of Niko's many cousins. I did not feel it was my place to push. Or rather, I did not want to come across as paranoid as I felt, so we moved on, continued to walk, both our faces forward. The weather dropped in temperature, the sky remarkably clear. Our steps coincided with each other, heels gnawing on tiny stones.

"So, what about you?" I said. "Your work. Your art, I mean."

"My art," she said. "What do you want to know?"

"All of it," I said. "Start at the beginning."

She'd always had this fixation with capturing moments, she said. With remembering. At seventeen, her mother gifted her an old, heavy camera, the paint peeling off its sides. I wanted to tell her that my mother had done something similar for me—but in fact, it had been Henry. Henry who escorted me into the blank beauty of a cold museum before I understood what a haven it could be, what a lifeline.

"That camera was ancient," said Theo, "but I was obsessed." She took pictures of her friends, her sister. But soon, they got sick of her constant surveillance, and so, she turned the lens on herself. "I started to feel like I didn't exist unless I was documenting myself. I went sort of, I don't know; my work started asking more of me."

Eventually, she lugged her camera into her childhood bedroom, stripped, and indexed her body, capturing details in every exposure and position she could. In my mind's eye, I saw the shape of her backlit frame, blurred skin, a brow caught mid-furrow—the surprising bloom of a pale nipple.

She told me about this mentor, a prominent photographer whose work she greatly admired. He made promises of getting her into residencies and galleries, the most prestigious, the most covetable. He'd been impressed by a series of her self-portraits, wherein, in a blank studio, she stood naked, and began to wrap herself in cellophane. Twenty-nine images she took of the process, until she was fully entombed in the synthetic. At first thought, it sounded a little dull, a little overdone—betraying beauty for spectacle—but I knew the most provocative artwork resisted its own description, and when I pictured her body, her skin crushed against itself, all the shadows and folds this must have created, the feminine symbology it must have invoked, I felt that my initial reaction was probably wrong, and that I was being too austere, too stuck on outdated models of taste.

"I know what you're thinking," she said.

"I'm not."

"They did well."

The photographs received some acclaim. She'd been only twenty-two. She'd aimed to continue the project, make it a series, complicate her original idea by adding more objects to her body, more ways, she said, "to expose the commodification of the feminine self," to "indict the audience of their greed for the naked body." The image of Theo covered in coins returned to me—the metal catching light, winking. "Back then, I just wanted to elicit real emotion," she said, "disrupt the institution."

"And now?"

"Same thing," she said.

I wanted to tell her I understood. But did I?

"Does it ever bother you?" I asked.

"What?"

"To think of your image owned by someone else. Hung up in someone's home?"

"How do you know where my images are?"

I paused. "Well, I assume. I mean. They sold. Didn't they? Where else would they be?"

For the first time, her tone lacked confidence. "They sold," she said. "And to answer you, no. I don't feel that way. Because I created this version of me. Despite what anyone says, I was the one in control. I chose the lighting, the film, the angle. If anything, the process is incredibly empowering. Erotic, even."

I didn't know if I believed her—or if she believed her either. It seemed too simple a substitution to make. But then I thought of the photo with the coins—how her closed eyes shut the world out, would not allow the viewer to experience her, experiencing them.

As we followed the footpath that ringed the property, my breath quickened. Dirt befouled our shoes. Early crowds left and made room for a new set of tourists. We found a large rock on which to rest.

"Anyway," she said. "If I could go back in time and tell them all how I really felt, I would."

Apparently, after the series with the cellophane sold, her mentor told her it'd done well not because of its singularity, but because of how she'd looked. *How can you put the viewer on trial about its desire for the female form, if you possess the ideal female form?* he'd asked. I thought maybe he had a point. But I wouldn't have said so. About the matter, she spoke with an air of curiosity, rather than cynicism. There was no conflation of vanity with victimhood. She did not complain about being beautiful, or dismiss the virtues her looks had brought her, but instead, examined the value systems of beauty—how exclusionary and obsolete they were: how rooted in Western bias; how antithetical to art.

Theo told me her mentor was too obtuse to notice the particulars of her work. Her images placed pressure on the viewer's expectations, purposefully constructed, and fabricated to appear, at first, sexually gratifying, but upon second viewing, obviously incriminating. He told her she hadn't pushed it far enough. He told her she was in danger of stasis, of vapidity, of narcissism. That she risked falling into a certain category, one she'd never outrun. Meanwhile, most of her male counterparts were participating in what she called "a Larry Clark circle jerk of mediocrity," but they were never asked to change direction, their visions not questioned.

"The institution underestimated me," said Theo. "And I let them."

To this, I nodded again, perhaps too ardently.

"But what choice did you have, really?"

"I had a choice," she said. "There's always a choice." But when she relayed this, she appeared suddenly strained. Her eyes, sullen.

She snatched another cigarette from her bag, and I—not wanting to break how intimate I felt toward her—asked for one too. She placed it in my mouth; then against the wind, she tried to light it for me, my eyes on her the whole time, her concentration unbreakable, a quality I'd always admired, but in her, felt almost harrowing. When I inhaled, blood rushed to the roots of my hair, my mouth filled with so much heat I thought it might have been on fire itself, but I didn't care. When I exhaled, I felt like I'd been exorcised.

I coughed on some smoke, my knee anxiously bouncing. "There was something," I began, nervously, "something stuck to this—a photograph. In the envelope Niko gave me. It was of, well, you were on a bed, I think."

I was having a hard time explaining myself, piecing together the particulars of that image—I didn't want to say too much, risk giving away how long I'd studied it—when a museum attendee approached us and told us to put our cigarettes out. Of course, I should have known, and I apologized, profusely, but the interaction left Theo unbothered. Which for a moment, unnerved me.

"What were you saying?" she asked, finishing her cigarette as though nothing had transpired, powdery ash falling to the ground.

"One of your photos got stuck to another one of the statue."

"That's odd," she said, but there was something about her tone that left me unconvinced.

"Do you want it back?"

She cracked her neck. "Do you want to give it back?"

I didn't know what to say.

"What did you think of it?"

"I liked it," I said.

"You liked it," she repeated, her voice inscrutable. "Huh."

I wasn't actually sure. I was sure it bothered me. Ossified itself inside me. I was sure that it made my blood itch. That it made me feel as though I'd lost my head. But why? Because she'd seemed so liberated, so unrestrained—so entitled to self-expression—under her own lens? There was nothing radical about exploiting the aesthetics of a woman's nude body, but perhaps radicalism did not matter. What mattered was that the photograph had affected me. What mattered was that the photograph had a certain, undeniable freedom of power.

But I said none of that, and a distance grew between us, erasing the closeness we'd experienced just moments prior. I wanted to leave but couldn't. She might have felt the same. Either way, we sat in silence for a few moments, until whatever happened next happened.

The order of things was not clear. It felt, for a moment, like a staged production. A joke gone wrong. A misunderstanding. Which was not to say that it happened in abstraction, or that time halted, or events unfolded quickly. The pace was not abnormal.

It started with one man. Dressed in black, running toward us. Then another, and another. Sun bounced off their white helmets. Their guns held at eye level, the sound of their boots hitting the dirt, a succession of thuds. The sharp smell of metal. Of mineral. Polished stone. Yelling in Greek, fragments of English. "Get off the grounds." They looked so serious, I wanted to laugh. I might have laughed. They parted the crowds. Everyone shuffled, then sprinted toward entrances and exits. It was inchoate chaos. On the way down, every part of the Acropolis was full of steep, slippery stairs. People pushed one another. Tripped, and growled. You could smell the panic—the elemental fear. Theo got up and walked not away from the mayhem, but toward it, and I stood still, saying nothing. Beyond her, I could perceive only the broad strokes.

A kid—no more than twenty—with a sign.

A tackle.

Rising from the ground: bursts of dry, dusty clouds.

Something square, and black, falling out of his hands.

The kid on his stomach, chin smashing into the dirt, hands pushed behind his back.

A knee on his spine. A nosebleed.

A fight—and quick surrender—for control.

22

T heo, Niko, and I returned to the island the following morning. Theo sat next to me this time; Niko, a few rows behind us. It was a too-bright day already, and clear. The plane smelled of fresh paint, and vomit, of citric antiseptic. As we settled in, Theo nudged me with her elbow. "Did you sleep?" she said.

I shook my head. I didn't say that my sleep patterns had been erratic anyway, that what happened at the Acropolis had shaken me, but no more than I'd already been, and that in some ways, it felt almost bound to happen. Almost, expected.

"So," said Theo. "Do you want to know, or . . . ?"

Yes, I said. I did.

Apparently, the authorities were responding to an anonymous bomb tip. Two calls came through that day, said Theo. In one call, the bomb was inside the museum down the hill. In another, a protestor had smuggled the bomb onto the citadel and was carrying it around in the open. At first, the newspapers said the man was undercover, part of the Nihilist Faction, or Black Star. They said he was anti-capitalist, antiestablishment, mentally unhinged, or else Turkish, and seeking revenge for that F-16 shot down in '96. Whatever the media said, the police had gotten the wrong man because, in fact, there was no man at all. There was a nineteen-year-old boy, a student from the UK studying political science, and the bomb was not a bomb but a handheld television. The boy had taken a break from protesting with the others to watch Arsenal play Manchester United. It was the middle of the second half when the police attacked him and gave him a concussion and cracked two of his ribs. Upon waking—before he died later in the hospital, due to the stress of the injuries and a congenital heart condition—he only had one question for the nurse: *Who won?*

I wondered how she'd acquired these details. I thought about the young woman with whom she'd been talking.

"Did you know him or something?"

"No," she said. "Not at all."

And that was all we spoke, until, as the plane descended, the shadow of its wings lengthening onto the runway, she invited me to dinner.

Eight pm, her place. I told her I'd have to see, though I knew I'd go.

It was hotter on the island than it'd been when we left. The first thing I needed to do was check on the statue, but I didn't have the energy to carry my luggage around under the bleating sun, so I went to the rental first. As I walked up the stairs, the day Theo and I shared at the Acropolis had already taken on the hazy texture of events passed. I felt for the boy but only in a way that would not threaten my own livelihood—which is to say, I tried to keep the gloom at a distance, tried not to think of the boy's struggling body, or who would clean his blood, or if the newness of the blood would stain the old stones on which it puddled. Would his death make international news and therefore, help the protestor's cause? If it hadn't been for the heart condition, maybe. And where would the boy's corpse go? How did they fly the deceased back home? I had a maudlin vision of some sad nurse closing the boy's blue eyelids and sending him off in a padded crate, not unlike the ways in which we'd moved large pieces of art from country to country. Though probably not as careful. If a body broke postmortem, what would be the consequences? In the ancient world, steles, vases, figures—all were popular to mark the final rung of death, to let the spirit go. Depending on how much money a family had, the artwork would be bland and small, or large and heavily decorated. We kept a particularly stunning funerary vase in the east wing of the museum. The pattern geometric, almost prehistoric. In one area, a snake wraps around a woman's ankle; in another a cavalcade of horse-drawn chariots lead nowhere. On the neck, a succession of shadowed figurines dance with their arms up; below them are several unidentifiable animals—my favorite, some cross between a panther and a goat.

Once I got to my unit, I went straight to the bathroom and wet a cold towel for my forehead and thought I'd lie down for a second and wait for the exhaustion to turn into adrenaline, but I fell asleep without meaning to. I dreamed, somehow, in Greek. I dreamed of the statue: prostrate like she'd been the other day, but this time, her head tilted up, toward me, her neck strained. She told me that I'd been patient and that she had something to show me now, and I said OK, and then I felt an unimaginable pain tearing me apart. I peered between my legs, bloody and swollen and ripping—and out came a head made of stone, bald and slick. A weight pressed down on my stomach, and I couldn't move—and then, my mind woke, but my body did not.

The first time this happened, I was fifteen. I assumed it was a side effect of some medication—the combination of the antipsychotics for daytime, the tranquilizers for nighttime. It might have been the Sansert—which can cause hallucinations. It might have been the migraines themselves. My mother accused me of theatrics. I remember once falling asleep on the couch and opening my eyes to her head bent over and watching me, as hot tears fizzed down my cheeks. She shook me, but I stayed still as a board, completely paralyzed. I couldn't even blink. My prescriptions were tweaked after that, and I was put on Nardil, an antidepressant which not only numbed me, but disallowed certain pleasures, anything high in tyramine, anything salted, smoked, pickled, processed. If I had even a lick of something off-limits, I would get dizzy and sleepy and wake in the middle of the night to a sudden and severe headache.

But I hadn't experienced an episode in years, not since I'd moved out of my childhood home, and what if, after all this time, my body finally refused to unlock itself? I'd have to scream for someone to come find me. Even if they did—who knew how long it would take—they'd call a doctor, or take me to one, and then I'd have to deal with some stranger who wouldn't understand or believe me, and then what? I thought about the words on the US Embassy pamphlet: *you must be extra cautious when engaging with strangers.* Would I have considered Leon a stranger?

Or I could not scream. I could give in to this. Become immobile, immaterial, belong to nothing, not even time, or space. Enough thinking, looking, thinking more—and about what? Depth. Light. Texture. Detail. I tried, instead, to feel: the sheets puddling under my heel, the pilled texture of the comforter, weighing down my chest, the circulation, the insulation, of body heat—but nothing even close to relief beseeched me. I thought of the origin of the term *navel-gazing*. Omphaloskepsis, the contemplation of one's body—one's navel—as an aid in meditation, used in the fourteenth century by Greek monks. I liked to picture them—these sad, quiet men staring at their belly buttons as a way to induce spiritual reverie. I peered down at myself and tried to focus on what I was: a figure, a vessel, a navel. I thought of the statue's navel—how deep it had been, how perfectly round in comparison to mine, which was shallow and narrow, like a slit in fabric. A few moments later, I started to feel a removal of myself—a peeling. It was not as though I'd magically birthed some second version of me—a specter or a shadow—it was more like an exhalation, and the second me could see the first me, lying there on the bed with this look on her face, this feral, desperate look. Like an animal, caught. I wondered if this was death. Or at the very least, acceptance.

Movement returned to my toes, my calves, a searing of energy surging through my stomach and throat, reaching toward my mouth, which I opened quickly, swallowing a gulp of fresh air, like a backward laugh. I touched my face, my chest, my mouth. When it felt safe enough, I got up, took a sip of water, changed into something I could wear in public, and left. I stopped at the pharmacy and made it just before closing, lucky when the woman at the counter gave me the antibiotic the doctor in Athens had recommended. Out front of the store, without water, I took the pill, surprised when it slipped down without a choke, and then, dissatisfied. What did my health matter? I should have been prioritizing the statue, dealing with the rest later. It's what William would have done. Madison too. Had I not fallen asleep, gotten stuck, I could have made it to the museum, but it was too late now. No one would be there.

The bitter taste of the antibiotic hung like fur on the darkest parts of my tongue. I walked toward the water, passing an Orthodox church with iron grille windows, a flag rippling above its blue dome. I wondered if I should have gone inside and prayed. What would it have taken, to believe in a single, unifying force as power hungry as a God? I wanted to become someone who wasn't reliant on anyone or anything, who could fix herself through sheer will—and yet I feared that, perhaps, I didn't want to be fixed at all. What if the threat of personal abomination—the entropies of pain and subsequent dependence on the alleviation of it—was the only thing keeping me moving in the first place?

When I hit the seawall, I stopped. Knots of garbage whorled around in the water, clung to the undersides of the chained-up sailboats, which bobbed with the current. On one of the sailboats was a figurehead—a female, mid-eighteenth century, if I had to guess—dressed to an almost absurd, virginal degree, but phallic in form, with a billowing of fabric around her hips, the paint wizened from environmental exposure, cracked and dull and grimy where it should have been smooth and polished, alive with color. The lower half of her jaw completely eroded, giving her the countenance of some horrific ghost, stuck in purgatorial woe. But her eyes. Her eyes surprised me; they were open, wide awake.

Feeling chilled, I moved on, back toward the center of town, ambling down a side street, up another. After a few minutes, I had the feeling I was being followed by a taxi that kept turning every time I did. I thought of the cabdriver, my outstanding debt. I crossed the road and came upon a little café, where a woman sat alone—a languidness about her, an ease—spooning out bites of some delicate dessert, cigarette smoke pluming around her head. The café menu hid behind a cracked acrylic stand, its words illegible. I went in anyway. Feeling like I was intruding on the woman's lonely hour, I didn't want to make a fuss, so I ordered only coffee. Soon, the waiter returned with my drink and a glass of ouzo. I told him it wasn't mine. He said it was courtesy of another patron, then turned to point to the woman, who was—to our collective surprise—no longer present; her sudden absence, adding to the air, a disquietude.

Years ago, I was sitting at a coffee shop somewhere near Venice Boulevard studying for a large exam about Roman relief ware when a woman—not much older than I was then, twenty-eight or so—sat next to me. She was dressed professionally, a disguise intended to make her more palatable to the skeptic: a silk blazer with shoulder pads, a tasteful taupe shadow dusting her lids. She had a stunning aquiline nose, the kind of nose that has become rarer and rarer in Los Angeles.

She sat next to me and said, "I'll read you for free." She didn't ask if she could; she just began. She said I'd been a celibate nun in a previous life. She said she saw me traveling. She said I was often presenting myself as someone I was not; that I was obsessed with how I came across to others; that I was a shapeshifter, and I could use this to my advantage, but also must be aware that there is a cost to it, an emotional one. "It will take you a long time," she said, "to understand who you are." She asked if I wanted to know more, and if I did, it would cost. I had fifteen dollars in cash. That's all I had, I said, and though I did not believe in her pseudoscience, something overcame me, and I handed it over. Her fingers were soft, and she had the lightest touch I'd ever felt as she traced my lines. When the manager came by to say they were closing, he asked if I wanted anything else, and I said to the woman, "Well, shouldn't you know?" and we laughed. She put a cube of sugar in her mouth and sucked and then moved on from my palm to my auric field. At this point, I'd spent twenty minutes with this stranger, and I found her reticence to console me motherly, and so, I followed her tangents. She asked if I had a twin. I said no. She asked if I got headaches. I said sometimes. She scoffed and said, "Sometimes?" For a second, I believed that she could save me from myself. That she could observe my pain, my past, and, through such observation, offer me some long-awaited comfort—compassion without pity. But then she took my hands in hers. "You have one very deep line," she said, "on your palm." I asked what that meant. She closed her eyes. They moved speedily under her lids, like she was watching a film at double speed, and before I knew it, she let go, visibly shaken. "What is it?" I asked, still, stupidly hopeful. I watched her smile quiver, her eyes drop. "I'm sorry," she said, her face carved into a panic. "I'm experiencing a block." She was so apologetic that I became apologetic in return. In a frenzy, she returned my money and left, knocking a chair over and hobbling off like prey, trying to escape its fate. She did not look back. Not even once.

Since then, I've tried not to think of that woman, to invoke her at all—but I felt her presence then, all the way out here, the thickness of her fear leaching onto that café, an airborne sickness. I left the table, the gifted ouzo untouched.

On my way back, I stopped by a corner store to buy a bottle of something for dinner. A young girl ran the register. She couldn't have been over twelve, her hair a soft red, her lashes clumped together. A careless scar on her chin, a zit too ardently picked. As she rang me up, she answered the phone, and from the way her demeanor changed—from bored indifference to tortured elation—I knew the caller was a boy. I thought of Theo, of Niko. The blurry history of their youthful romance—if one could call it that. Behind the counter, a soccer match played quietly on the television.

"Is that Arsenal?"

The girl placed the phone on her chest. At me, she furrowed her brows.

"Arsenal?" I said, louder this time. But she paid the question no mind, shaking her head in dismissal, returning the phone to her ear, to the boy, her eyes far off now, a fingernail propped in her mouth. Where had she learned such a gesture? So bloated with the erotic.

"Never mind," I said. "Thank you."

Outside, it began to rain. Everything appeared closed and empty; every building, a little too close to all the other buildings. How could anyone breathe? I plodded through the slick street, through tangles of wet dross, a plastic water bottle crunching under my step. Two policemen riding on one motorcycle whizzed past me in white helmets, batons hanging by their sides.

A moment later, I saw that same cab, following closely behind me, then parking. I turned around and stared through the window, trying to make out the driver. The rain fell harder. It was dark out now. Emboldened by the sunlessness, and feeling like I had nothing to lose, I made my way toward him. What could he do to me now? Kill me? I straightened my back, cleared my throat, and tapped on his window. His hair was white and full of loose, thin curls. He squinted through the glass, seemingly perplexed.

"Who are you?" I said, loudly, in the clearest Greek I could muster. "What do you want?"

He rolled down the window, his hands shaking, not from fear, it seemed, but illness. He was older than I'd thought, his face brutalized by decades spent under the sun, but I could see the youth inside him, buried under years of fallen skin. My chest tightened.

"Nai?" he said.

A silence misted between us.

"Nai?"

Both English and Greek wouldn't come to mind. I searched the back of my brain for a different language. French. Spanish. Portuguese. I spoke nothing else.

"Never mind," I said. "I thought you were . . . Never mind."

I watched his hand move to the door handle and heard it pop open before I turned around and hurried off through the sheets of rain. A moment later, the man switched on his headlights, perhaps by accident, or perhaps so I could see the path in front of me.

23

An iron gate veiled Theo and Niko's property, ornamented with a knocker in the shape of a small hand. I pushed it open and walked into their yard, which was overgrown with pine trees and cluttered with fallen needles. Two laundry lines intersected. Wind blew between the fibers of slip dresses, mid-calf socks, and white androgynous T-shirts. I imagined they were the kind of couple who shared clothes; any shape of fabric would cater to the lines of Theo's body. Niko's too. I looked forward. On the bottom step of the front stairway, lurked a nymph made of stone, two feet tall. Its eyes were closed, a hand held up to its ear, as though listening for something. I wondered about its origins—based on the detailing and the shade of marble, I would have guessed Italian, late nineteenth century.

Opening the front door halfway, Niko welcomed me in a blue short-sleeved tee, unbuttoned to his hairless sternum. What must it have been like for him and Theo to touch? Frictionless? His gelled hair gave off the appearance of permanent dampness; an errant strand dangled over his forehead, skin gloomy with sweat.

He told me Alec was coming to dinner too, and he was bringing a guest—some mystery man Niko had never met before.

"He's not with the museum?"

Niko dropped his shoulders, hummed in exasperation. "And then," he said, hands on his hips. "My wife invites Leon. This is OK?"

"Of course," I said.

"It is a full house tonight," he concluded. "But please, Doctor, shall we?"

In the hallway alcove, I removed my mules and put them next to a pair of Theo's sneakers, which radiated an almost criminal youthfulness, belied only by their size. Niko watched and waited. I handed him the bottle of wine I'd brought.

Simmering garlic crackled on the stove; the smell of it overwhelmed the home, despite all the windows being open. The expansive floor plan surprised me. All was clean, almost barren, no signs of haphazard juvenescence. White walls, light tile, counters devoid of clutter. On the oversized terrace that overlooked the old town sat an iron table and seven chairs. Power lines crisscrossed above it all. But my eyes focused on the frosted glass door that opened into a dim bedroom, where I could see evidence of movement, a wimpled sheet—some beautiful, expensive linen on the edge of the bed, a silk brocade, and then, a reclining Venus, a twisting, tensing foot.

Theo got up when she heard me. The door closed. I flushed with embarrassment—excitement.

Niko told me to have a seat in the living room, where there was a long white couch, a stone coffee table, and an heirloom rug, handwoven and intricate—a subtle nod to some inherited wealth. The space was curiously shaped, with an extended, parabolic reading nook, which housed a three-legged lounge chair, and behind it, two tall windows dressed in gauzy, white curtains. I could sense that, during the day, the nook must have endured an incandescent light.

Moments later, in rolled Theo, on her skates. I wanted to laugh. Was she playacting? For whom? Her right hand carried a newspaper, and her left held the stem of a wineglass like a pen, the liquid sloshing and perilously close to a spill. Her collarbone shone with the oiliness of recently applied balm, and she wore a white gallant dress, ever so slightly crumpled, like it had just dried in the sun. She set the glass and paper down on a miniature side table and then moved a portable fan from one side of the room to the other and plugged it in.

Without looking at me, she said, "Do you hear all of that?"

Her skates rumbled over the floor. I said I didn't hear anything. She turned the fan on. "This place has spirits."

"Are you scaring our dear guest?" Niko called out from the kitchen.

"I'm only telling the truth," she replied, though not loud enough for Niko to hear.

The fan whirred as she made a gesture for me to sit. She joined me and started taking off the skates. She asked if I'd made it home safely after the flight and I said it'd been fine, though I worried that I'd been too eager during our trip to the citadel, captivated by her every word, and caught uncertain more times than I'd have liked. Had she thought, at all, about the boy?

"Good," she said. She studied me for a moment before offering a drink, at which point, I got up and followed her to the kitchen, where she poured raki into an outdated smoke brown glass. Copper pots and pans hung from the ceiling. Niko stood with his back toward us and chopped a red onion. My eyes watered. Next to him, a cluster of fish frowned as their blood leaked out and onto the counter.

Niko asked if I might step out and pick some lemons from the tree.

Raki in hand, I walked out the front door and back into the night. Moonlight shone on the glossed leaves of the lemon tree, its fruit bloated and overripe. Around me, the shrubbery shook. I didn't think it was possible, but the air whistled. I set my glass down and reached for a too-high lemon. Something shuffled behind me.

A deep voice said, "Need a boost?"

I looked around.

"Doctor Elizabeth Clarke," said Leon, as he came closer, wearing once again that orange batik shirt, mirrored glasses folded and hanging between the collar. A swarm of mosquitos formed a halo around his head. "You are still here?"

Next to him stood a woman. A simple red dress cinched her waist and her earlobes sagged with the heaviness of gold jewelry. Leon began telling her about me, that I was an art historian, that I was here on business. The woman smiled with large, exposed teeth, her gums preternaturally red. Behind us, Theo trounced down the steps.

"You're late," she said, then kissed Leon on the cheek and embraced the woman in a hug. The woman introduced herself as Amara.

I said it was great to meet her.

"I've seen you before," she said.

I told her no, she hadn't.

She said, "Then you must look like someone else?" She had a faint Eastern European accent. She turned back to Theo and said, "I'm going blond. What do you think? Vara went blond the other day." Her hair was gray and thick, halfway down her back. "She looks like a wraith now," said Amara, and I remembered her then, one of the women from the bar, the one who discussed the nocturnal orgasms.

Elsewhere, church bells broke into a booming ring, and I reached for lower-hanging fruit and plucked three lemons off the tree, before I shadowed Theo and the new guests inside. "I didn't realize this was a party," I whispered to Theo.

She shrugged. "I wouldn't call it that."

I returned to the kitchen and set the lemons down into an empty, faience bowl. Niko handed me a knife and a cutting board, and I started to slice. When I was done, he led me to the stovetop where butter seethed in a saucepan.

"Please," Niko said, wiping his forehead with the back of his hand. "Remove the foam on top. To make it, what is the word? Clarified."

I tried listening to the conversation between Leon, Theo, and Amara in the other room, but the purring refrigerator and the shaky oven fan drowned them out.

"Wait," Niko said. "It stains." He plucked an apron from under the sink and told me to turn about, and then he wrapped it around my waist, knotted the ties at the curve of my lower back. I wondered if I had ever owned an apron. When Niko finished, he patted the sides of my hips. Had Theo caught sight of us? If so, would I have been pleased? Niko turned from me and plopped langoustines into boiling water. I gave in to the cooking, the rhythm of it, removing the foam from the butter as carefully as I could, as the sound of a motor pulling up to the property fanned through the open windows. I peered out and beyond the gate, where two passengers got out of a small car. I couldn't get a view of their faces.

"The mysterious guest?"

Niko sighed. "I suppose."

I rubbed my hands on the apron and walked out and toward the front door, which had been left open. The wind picked up again. Needles on the steps accumulated, then dispersed.

"Elizabeth," said a familiar voice. "Do my eyes deceive me, or are you cooking?"

24

When word of William's imminent departure hit the museum, he called me and Madison into his bright office. It was a flat, blue day in Los Angeles; the sun beating onto William's oak desk. He was wearing one of his brighter ties—a pink and orange paisley—and his pores reeked of a lunch martini. Papers messed his desk—letters from dealers, contracts, photographs of a vase painted in the black figure technique. He sat down in his worn leather chair, his legs crossed, a navy-socked ankle resting on his knee, and began.

"No need for fluff," he said. "It's between the two of you."

Madison leaned back in his chair and cleared his throat. "I can see why Elizabeth would be a good choice," he said. Madison with his unremarkable face and insipid but expensive suit, the faintest tan line rimming his eyes, specter sunglass markings from a weekend boat trip. "She is, how should I put this? Scrappy. And it's bad timing for me. With the baby coming and all."

"Well, you have a wife, don't you? What's she for, then?" said William.

"I understand why you would go with someone like Madison," I said, fighting his fire with mine. "Ivy League boy, the right internships, the right family. He fits the bill. I mean, he might as well be you, William. But isn't the department—the museum—ready for, I don't know, a direction less obvious?"

I uncrossed my legs, then recrossed them and smoothed over my pencil skirt. William's eyes flickered to me, then Madison. I surveyed William's ceiling-high bookshelf. I was so close to the possession of everything in there, I could feel the dust on my hands, the weight of my body in his chair.

"You can't hold respectable credentials over someone's head," said Madison.

"Oh no, I would never. I'm just saying."

William chimed in, "What are you saying, Elizabeth?" He came around the table and sat on its edge, his knees pointed toward me. He peered at his watch and folded his arms.

"I'm saying the old pond is stagnant. We're entering a new millennium. We need a new perspective. A distinct—I don't know. *Vision.*"

"So. Go on then. What's yours?"

Madison chimed in—"*sir, if I may*"—but William waved a hand in dismissal.

The secretary stuck her head into the room and called Madison out for a phone call. William and I glanced at each other. When Madison left, William sat in his chair, then pulled it closer to me, his heedless feet almost touching mine.

Now that it was just us two, he said that, truthfully, he'd wanted to go with me, but he worried that the board wouldn't be willing. That even if he backed the idea, they would see it as risky. I mentioned several other female head curators in the history of our industry, but he stopped me. "It's not always about that, Elizabeth," he said. So then, what was it? But he wouldn't answer. He wouldn't even meet my eye.

Elbows pressed into my chair, I stilled. He leaned forward and scanned my face, placing a hand on my knee. A bone-chilling self-hatred quickly morphed into deflection, and I pushed my leg toward him, called his bluff. He backed off.

"How is your Greek these days?"

"Excellent," I lied.

He raised a smile, saliva gathered at the edges of his lips. "Then I've got something for you."

25

I didn't recognize Madison at first. Uneven patches of scruff bristled his upper lip, his chin. His eyes wiped of sleep. He reached the top of the steps and said, "So you are? You're cooking."

I said nothing.

"You don't look surprised," he said.

"I guess I'm not."

He put his hands up in surrender. "The acquisitions committee wanted a second opinion before the deal is sealed," he said. "That is all." He stepped closer, lowered his palms. He smelled like musk—like emptiness. The echoing halls of the museum.

"And he sent you all the way here for that?" I said. "An opinion?"

"He's a dramatic man."

I put my hands on my hips, but something about the posture felt strange—motherly—so I slid them back down. "Do you know something?"

"I know what you know."

"I don't know anything," I said. "How's the baby?"

"She's perfect. Nine pounds, three ounces."

"That's a little big, no?"

He grimaced. "I guess it's above average."

"So have you seen her yet?"

"My baby?"

"The statue."

He stepped closer. "I just got in. Alec was kind enough to pick me up. Bit of a strange man." He took note of his surroundings. I couldn't help but notice a hint of condescension in the way he looked around. I wished that it bothered me less. "We do need to talk, though," he said, "you and I."

"Here?"

"I never turn down a meal."

Niko stepped into the hallway and introduced himself to Madison.

"Welcome, welcome," he said, extending his hand. "Niko Yorgos."

Madison extended his hand back. "Thank you for having us."

Niko clutched both our shoulders. "Let us go back inside, yes? I will open a bottle of red. Madison, I have a very expressive Limniona from Thessaly. What do you say?"

As we stepped inside, Leon's garish laugh robbed the home of its air. The equanimity of all these men made me want to bash my head into the cold, hard tiles of this too-clean home.

I distracted myself by helping Amara and Theo set the outside table, where Theo was spreading a gingham cloth over its top. A napkin dropped and I picked it up and dusted off some dirt, then folded it inconspicuously under one of the mismatched plates. Amara whistled for the men, and then one by one, under a cloudless sky, we sat down to eat.

I was directly across from Niko and Madison. A row of candles flickered between us, and beyond the chain of flat-topped homes, a slice of ocean glinted.

Theo was to my right, Leon to my left. At the other end sat Alec—whom I hadn't spoken to at all—and next to him, Amara. The table was too small. As I reached for a drink, my elbows bumped into either Leon or Theo or both; I didn't have room to breathe.

Niko stood and tapped his glass with a dull knife.

"Everyone," Niko said. "My wife and I thank you for coming." He paused, peered at his feet, then to Theo. "May God be with us all?" he added, like a question.

I looked to Theo, who was looking at Leon, who was looking at Amara, who was baring her teeth in what I assumed to be a smile.

We passed the wine around, then the food: the salt-encrusted fish, the boiled langoustine, the warmed boule of black bread, dusty and served alongside a golden olive oil. I watched a fruit fly land in the oil and drown. No one noticed. At the top of the langoustine's neck, I slipped my finger under its shell and pulled. Its pinprick eyes stared back at me; I snapped off its head and sucked. One moment my plate was full; the next, only fingernail-thin remnants of the prawn remained. I had almost no memory of how they'd tasted, only faint impressions of sea, and salt and fat withering on my palate. It was unusual for me to eat this much in the company of men who had—at one point or another—been inside me. In my mind—by either memory or imagination—I saw the outline of Leon's frame in my rental, the outline of me, in my blacked-out state, on the bed. I wondered about all the things from that night I'd never know. Even if it hadn't been Leon, I thought about fucking him as a way to restore the balance I'd lost. I'd stay sober; he'd get obliterated. I would degrade him with spit or request he lie still in some uncomfortable position while I tied him up with scratchy rope. He would beg me to stop. But would I allow him the satisfaction of seeing himself as the quarry? I could try for a commitment more serious, nefarious. A real relationship. Something long-term.

"So, tell me," Leon said, glancing at Niko, Alec, and then Madison. "Two visitors in one week. What *is* it with this, this particular piece of art?"

My knee shook.

Madison eyed the outside of the house in mock admiration and turned to Niko. "When was this place built, do you know? It's got lovely, interesting bones," he said.

"The statue is unusual," I said. "It's got this—this *power*. I've never seen, I mean, you don't come across one of these every day."

"Well," said Amara, "I see why Leon wants in, then."

"Power," said Leon. "What kind of power?"

"Well, if I may use your words, Leon," I rolled over his question, gesturing to him, coolly, performatively, "what is it about any *particular* piece of art? The best art moves us in ways we cannot fully understand, let alone explain."

"But isn't it your job? To explain?"

In Greek, Alec cut him off. "Let's not discuss work."

In Greek, Theo said, "Why not?"

"We are not in America," Alec replied. "Leave it at home." He smiled, but I detected a building temper in his tone. Leon leaned his elbows onto the table, turned his head toward Madison. He picked up his glass of wine, threw it back, then slammed it down, and focused on Theo.

"Wants in?" said Madison. "Who wants in?"

"You don't know?" said Niko.

My cheeks warmed.

Alec grunted in frustration.

"Leon is looking to donate."

"To us? Why the largesse?" Madison asked.

"Why not?" said Leon. "What else is this money for?" He looked down at his empty glass and frowned, then turned to Theo. "Theo, darling. Let's open something else. Do you have something stronger? Tsikoudia?"

Theo rose from the table.

"Madison," Amara, said, speaking up for the first time. "You're not from Canada, are you?"

"No, no. California."

Amara clucked her tongue.

"Why drag children into a protest?" she said.

Theo returned to the table with a bottle of Mastika. "Amara. Come on."

"I saw a photo of an eight-year-old with a Molotov cocktail," said Amara. "It's not right."

Leon spoke over her. "Amara is so intelligent. A very powerful journalist. Able to look at things objectively." He reached for her hand and squeezed it. "A credit to her gender."

I took a sip of wine, and balked. "A credit to what?"

"He means no harm," Niko said.

Theo elbowed him.

"All I'm saying," said Amara, in a sincere, curious tone. "You can't fight violence with violence."

"But it's everywhere, isn't it?" Leon said. "How else do you respond?"

"Today," said Theo, "in Athens, Elizabeth and I were there when that boy got tackled—"

"That was yesterday," I interrupted.

She reddened, sat back. "Was it?" Her face looked solemn, young. "They thought he had a bomb," she said. For a moment, I pictured her as one of the student protestors, and then I pictured the policeman's knee on her spine like it'd been on that boy's, and then I glanced at Leon, who had already rolled past her comments. "Every hour, it is something new," he said. "A man ran over several people near a church in Crete. Before that, a landmine exploded at an aquarium in Malta."

"Have you ever seen what marine life does when an explosive goes off?" asked Amara.

"What do they do?" said Leon.

"I don't know," she said. "That's why I'm asking. If one goes off near you, you're supposed to open your mouth."

Under the table, I felt something brush my leg. A warm foot fondling my exposed shin. I didn't look anywhere but at my own hands, at the scraps of food clinging to my plate, trails of shining oil. I couldn't let on. By the way we were sitting, it only made sense that it was Niko. Did he think he was touching Theo? If he did, I didn't want to humiliate us all by saying something. I stared at him. His eyes fixated on his wife. I imagined him as her, and her as him. I wanted them to be one body, one body dedicated to me. His foot aimed higher and higher, edging toward my knee. I tried to relax, keep perfectly still. Amara's voice edged into focus.

"I always think of the mothers," she was saying. "Grief isn't only about loss. It's also about which parts of a person you are forced to keep."

"Yes," Madison said, sincerely. "I agree with that." I glanced at him, deeply envious of how easily he'd settled in.

And then, without warning, Niko's foot retreated, and I felt a rush of coldness. I shifted my hips away from him, though my torso continued to face forward, and for the rest of the dinner, I rooted my heels into the ground.

Eventually, when we were all but finished with the last course, I garnered Leon's attention again. "Now, Elizabeth. Is curating really as dirty as they are saying?"

Madison and I stayed silent.

Alec huffed and muttered under his breath. "No business," he said.

"Ah," Leon added. "Sensitive subject. I didn't mean to pester."

Theo swirled her wineglass and grimaced. "Absolutely you meant to pester." She and I made eye contact as she tried to take a sip of her wine, but was instead intercepted by Niko. Calmly, he touched her wrist and guided the glass back down. In return, she squinted at him, her gaze heavy and waspish.

"It's public knowledge," Leon said. "People are not happy with what's been taken from their countries. They want repatriation." He took a bite of food, napkined his chin, and looked off, with a solemn—if not rehearsed—expression.

"Madison," I said. "Care to take this one?"

He considered the question. "Who's saying it's dirty?"

"Did you not hear me?" said Leon.

"I can speak for only us," said Madison.

Leon waved his hand. "So, then. Speak."

"We have ethical standards, procedures. And if you must know," Madison began, then stopped. I shook my head, but he went on. "There are about to be some changes. A—a rearranging of positions."

Leon's eyes flashed at me, then Madison.

"Ah, and one of you?" he said. He picked up his butter knife and pointed it back and forth between us.

Madison laughed. His cheeks were flushed from the wine and liquor. He surveyed me. "Oh, wipe that look off your face, Elizabeth," he said. "No need to hide things amongst friends. New and old."

"Well, we don't know which one of us it's going to, yet, so—"

"Hide what?" said Theo, her attention like a spotlight.

"Great news," Leon said. "Elizabeth and Madison are vying for a top-tier position. That's it, right?"

Madison nodded. I remembered the discussion we'd had, the day of that meeting with William. He had cornered me in the elevator and said he was sick of the charade, that we should be on the same team, that together, knowing what we know, we could force William out entirely, take over the department together. Burn it to the ground, then start fresh.

But what did Madison know, really? Had he forged recorded donations? Handed an envelope of cash to several of the interns and secretaries who had quit under distress? Calmed them down when they cried in the bathroom stalls? I assumed we'd both been primed in our own ways, but we'd never disclosed the particulars.

Either way, I told him his plan was idealistic, shortsighted. If we ever hurt William, we'd only end up hurting ourselves.

"That's it," I said, forcing a smile. I glanced at Theo, whose face I could not read, but whose effort to appear unreadable I could not unsee.

"Congratulations," she said, though I could not tell which one of us she was speaking to. She held her glass up in cheers, before tipping her head back and swallowing the rest of her wine in a single sip.

We all went quiet for a moment—a vague but certain tension stacking inside the cavity of my chest—until Madison, once again, breathed life into the room. "Tell me, Theo," he said, coming across as annoyingly affable, cocking his head in her direction, "what is it you do out here?"

Niko was quick to interpose—too quick. "She is an artist, at work on something private. She does not like to discuss before it is finished—"

"That's not true," Theo said.

Niko shut his mouth.

"I'm working on nothing," she said. "I'm working on a ghost. Who cares. Who wants more?"

Theo got up and began refilling the table's wineglasses with Mastika. Madison whispered into my ear, "Are you mad that I said something?" I hissed back, "No." He pushed. "You are. I can see it. I'm sorry."

Soon, everyone began getting up. Theo and Niko cleared our plates; she was short with him, shaking her head and mumbling under her breath. Still mildly incensed, Alec excused himself to the restroom. Amara turned to me and asked the price I was paying for the statue. Irritated, I told her we couldn't disclose that.

"So, when will the sale be complete?"

"Should be by tomorrow," I said, then turned to Madison. "It's why you're here, isn't it?"

"We have to get some things in order first," he confirmed. "But it will be soon. If you'll forgive me for a moment." Madison shot up. "Do you know where the phone is? My wife has just paged me. We have a sick baby at home. Could be important."

I didn't see a pager on him.

I said, "Why didn't you tell me he was sick?"

"*She*," he said, to himself, mostly. He scooted his chair away and got up.

Amara said she needed a cigarette, but she'd forgotten them inside, and she left too. Leon and I now sat alone. A single fishbone glittered in the middle of the table. At the sight of it, my stomach felt heavy, regretful. He leaned back in his chair and turned his face toward the night sky, and for a moment, I felt he was harmless because I couldn't bear the idea that he wasn't.

The wind picked up and I crossed my arms. He offered me the coat he didn't have, and then laughed. He seemed nervous, desperate to lighten me up, desperate for my confirmation that he'd done nothing wrong, and that even if he had, I would never hold it against him.

"Amara is nice," I said.

He exhaled. "She is. She's too good for me."

I said I couldn't argue with that. He then stretched his arms and placed a hand deep in his pocket, as everyone came back to the table. Theo, then Alec, then Niko, followed by Madison, and lastly, Amara, grinning with those red gums and carrying a massive bowl of drunken honeyed figs and lemon mascarpone whipped cream.

"They are fantastic this time of year," she said, setting the dessert down in the center of the table. "You know what Lawrence wrote about these beauties?" She paused and looked right at me. "'Every fruit,'" she parroted. "'Has its secret.'"

We ate in silence, only the cruel clink of our spoons against porcelain, and the long, thrumming buzz of night cicadas dissolving into the dark.

26

As I walked along the water, back to the rental, wind snapped against my face, and the ground steamed from the heat and moisture of earlier rain. I was sweating and shivering, attempting to forget the arrogance of Leon, the warmth of Niko's rough foot on my shin—I even tried to forget Madison's arrival, which was challenging since I could hear him behind me, his footsteps piercing the night's quietude. I told him to hurry up, but instead of acquiescing, he stopped in the middle of the road and told me to hold on. He asked about Theo and Niko. "Are they always like that?" he said, mocking Niko's gestures and posturing, Theo's bored expressions and heavy drinking. He crossed his arms and started walking again. "They want to sleep with you," he said, and I couldn't decide if he was chiding or testing me, so to be safe, I shook my head and feigned nonchalance, though I did feel myself smiling.

Right then, I wanted to sleep with Madison in the same way I sometimes had the urge to slice my finger whenever I held a steak knife, but even before we'd left, I'd told myself I wouldn't. With a child in the picture, he'd surely turn me down, and I couldn't heal from that wound, even if I had earned it entirely.

Another few minutes in, he started to whistle, and when I pleaded for him to stop, he whistled louder, which filled me with a disproportionate amount of anguish. I plugged my ears to drown him out and suddenly felt he and I were participating in some petty and bizarre brother-sister rivalry to which I hadn't consented. He reached for my hand, then apologized, his voice lowered and serious. He told me he wanted to say something. I gestured for him to go ahead.

With an excessive amount of concern, he noted that I seemed *off*, and I wondered if he meant off in terms of mood or appearance or both, and then wondered if I'd gained weight in such a short amount of time. He said I was putting too much pressure on the deal. The amount of pressure was fine, I told him, and demanded he respect it—though in my demands I was sure I sounded unrespectable—and the more we talked, the louder our voices grew until eventually, he must have wearied, or else gotten spooked, because at some point, he cowed.

We walked in silence for a little while. Until he brought up William.

"I've heard rumblings that some of his practices are being—well, looked into."

"How so?"

"I can't reveal my sources. I just wanted to give you the—a heads-up, I guess."

"Ah," I said, "how nice of you."

We didn't discuss what would happen next. I hadn't asked Madison where he was staying; he hadn't asked where I was staying either. We made a tacit pact as we avoided eye contact, never parting ways, our clandestine feet marching straight to his rental, which was only a few blocks from mine and, I immediately noticed, significantly nicer.

It was dark in his room, and airless, and before I knew it, he was kissing—lightly biting—my neck, the void above my collarbone. He stopped and said we shouldn't, but his reticence was part of the act and we both knew it, our roles already cast long before we'd arrived here, in this moment. I said, "Having a child has made you weak." Which felt heartless, but he seemed drawn to it, more than he'd been back home. How far could I go? Could I bring him to tears? I said, "You disgust me." His eyes lit up. I wondered how many other women he'd enacted this kink with, outside of his marriage. It was idiotic to think I was the sole provider. Then again, who knew. He grabbed my hand and pulled me in for a kiss, but I didn't let him have one.

Instead, I stood back. He told me to keep the lights off, but I turned them on and then removed my shirt and watched his eyes fall to my bare skin, my breasts, my belly. I hated this part of the show, but it was the only way I knew how to subjugate him. I'd spent decades gliding by on the hands of needful men, trying to use them before they used me—and even now, all the way out here, I could not fool myself out of that desire, though I would have liked to try. I removed my pants, my underwear. Breaking character for a moment, I said we needed to be at the museum early tomorrow—seven-thirty am. He said it was a Sunday, but I told him we could get in because the guard would be there, and if she wasn't, I'd call Alec. Make him open the doors. As though I had such control. It was fine to take a day off, he said. "The statue will still be there Monday, won't it?" I didn't know why he was saying these things. To incense me, perhaps? To imply that I hadn't been acting quick enough myself?

"We leave at seven-thirty. Do you understand?" I came closer and gripped his jaw with my forefinger and thumb. "Do you understand?" I said again, and forced him to nod, before I let go and climbed onto the bed and wrapped my legs around him. All the way up to his chin, I crawled, looking down only once to gauge his reaction. He was smiling, as I lowered myself onto his tongue, but it numbed me almost instantly, and other than the humidity of his breath, I could barely feel a thing. Running my fingers through his stiff gelled locks, I pulled. A brutal sound rose from his mouth, and I pulled harder. I wanted to inflict not just emotional, but physical harm. What I liked about Madison was that he'd let me. My inner thighs pressed into the space above his ears where the bones had some give, and I wondered about the banal scribblings and machismo arcana he kept in that brain of his. I felt a phantom pain on the right, ticklish inside of my knee, where I once gashed it open.

Margaret was dead by then and my mother wasn't home, so I told Henry. "Something happened. Can you look?" He glanced at my leg, the blood crawling down toward my knee in thick, slow drips. "Go to your mother's cabinet," he said. "What you need is in there." I knew not to push—or else, understood that my options did not include disagreement. Doesn't it sound unbelievable? That, for hours, I ambled around the house with an open, gushing wound, until my mother returned and slipped on the charming remnants of my subservience? That beige tile in our home, gored with blood.

Madison's fingers moved upward and then around to my hips, where he clutched whatever flesh he could. With a hunger I secretly found horrifying, he flipped me over onto the bed so that I was now below him. I wrapped my hand around his neck and squeezed; his eyes met mine, and his face reddened, and once I enjoyed how easily I could have pressed into his windpipe, cut off his airflow, guilt overran me, and I let go. He pushed himself inside me. I stared at the white ceiling as it transmogrified into the white gauzy material of Theo's nearly see-through dress. I pictured Niko ripping it off, saw her shove him into a wall, the two of them fucking ruthlessly and flippantly on their clean floors, and afterward, depleted from the release of such symmetrical desire, sitting on their white couch in their naked apartment and listening to something classical and anachronistic, sipping on espresso in dainty cups, kissing each other on the forehead, their legs and arms, weak and worn-out, but revivified, and alive—so alive. Once I could see the full picture of this, I felt what I assumed to be pleasure. It didn't matter what Madison was doing, how seriously he was taking this, how humorous I found his austere expression. It didn't matter what dull and determined noise might have been coming from deep in his throat, exhale after exhale, what rhythm the bump of the bed frame made against this hotel wall, because when I came, my howl drowned everything out, my cry, that of an animal, passing through a wormhole, back around and into my ears.

27

A thick heat and the noiselessness of early morning woke me. Footsteps paced outside the door, the hotel's maid, I assumed, cleaning up the atrocities of some other foreigner's mess. Madison had stolen all the blankets in the night and now lay on his side, sleeping heavily. He grunted, turned over, and faced me, his cheek squished into the pillow. For a moment, I imagined him as Julian. They both slept in the same dumb, openmouthed way. Then, I remembered Madison's post-partum wife at home, likely still bleeding through her hospital pads, stitches on her perineum like teeth. My mother always liked to remind me that I'd given her a third-degree tear—twenty-five stitches—in contrast to Margaret, who was tiny and faultless and slipped right out.

The rental's telephone rang, and I answered. "Hello?" I said. But they hung up. Five minutes later, they called again. "Hello?" I said. I heard a mumble in the background, then silence and a static, like a broken television. As I listened, I had a presentiment of disaster, but I didn't let go of the phone. Could it have been Madison's wife? I tried to calculate the time in California, but in my half-asleep mind, none of the numbers made sense. I left the receiver by my ear and fell back asleep until I was woken again, hours later, by a knock at the door.

I got up and slipped Madison's dress shirt over my chilled body, then looked in the interior pocket of his suitcase to see if he had any pills. Another knock, this one more urgent. Madison groaned.

"Coming," I said. I heard feet step back.

I didn't know who I expected to be there, but it was certainly not Theo. She looked surprised to see me too as she glanced at Madison's half-nude body in the background, our clothes strewn on the floor, and then back to me, my legs, my mortified face, as she put the pieces together.

She said she'd come by my place first, but I wasn't there, and she'd tried calling here a few times but couldn't get through. She said I needed to come with her. I'd had enough of her and Niko taking me places without telling me what was happening, so I asked. She promised she didn't know. Her camera hung from her neck as it had the first day I met her, but she seemed small and unsure of herself this time. She explained that Niko had called her, unintelligible, ordering her to retrieve Madison and me. She didn't seem like the kind of person who could be ordered to do anything. I said I'd go but warned her—in what I'd thought was a light tone—that it had better be good news, though I immediately regretted how threatening they sounded as the words left my mouth. Theo seemed not to care, her eyes floating behind me once more. I told her I'd be right down, and then before she could respond, I shut the door.

Madison woke and I relayed what I knew, which was nothing. He moaned and named my retelling a "dramatization." I turned my back to him and dressed quickly, though all I had were yesterday's clothes, and in anticipation of someone else noticing this, I was preemptively ashamed. I tried to fix my hair with Madison's sticky, gel-encrusted comb, but the smell irritated me, and my arms fatigued easily from all the motion. When I saw my sallow face in the bathroom mirror, I pinched the skin, hoping life would rise to the surface. It did not. Defeated by the inability to remake myself, I gave up. Madison and I made it downstairs and slid into Niko's tiny car, me in the front, Madison in the back, Theo at the helm, rapping her fingernails on the wheel, the seats sweaty and sunbaked. I wondered why Theo was always present during these moments—why not send someone else for me? Why wouldn't Niko come himself?

Once she got going—after a few misfires with the stick shift—Madison leaned toward me and murmured something about what we were doing and why we were doing it, but I moved away, gripping onto the door's warm handle, peering out the window. Theo was an overconfident and somewhat reckless driver, almost hitting every other pedestrian. I thought she might kill someone. I tried not to let that become endearing.

The car drove up the entrance to the town square. On my left, I recognized the restaurant we'd visited my first day in town. On my right, I blinked at a stone church and realized it too was familiar, the same church where Theo had claimed to have met the quasi-suicidal nun. Theo backed up and parked alongside the building, tinting the car in shade. "Can we stop here?" I asked, but she paid me no mind. When we got out, the smell of motor oil rose from the streets and then passed, followed by the smell of flour, and fresh coffee—though the shops didn't seem open, the whole place deserted and quiet, and the day hot already, the sun menacing.

As I followed Theo—Madison behind me—I asked again where she was taking us. I made a visor with my hand and looked up to find, a few feet ahead of me, Niko and Alec. They were both standing so still, so immovable, it was as though they'd become immaterial, inhuman.

"What?" I said. "What are they looking at?"

And then, I saw.

28

The foggy plastic bag—a small grocery bag, ballooned and full of air and susurrating in the wind—came to me first, and then came the marble neck, the delicate, stretched neck, to which the bag was affixed with black tape.

My vision blurred as I tried to rearrange the details into something more comprehensible; under the milky-white plastic, I projected the shape of the statue's nose, her oneiric gaze, a crown of twisted hair, but a blink killed each mirage. Images misted, then disappeared under my lids, and soon, I understood the truth of the bag's presence as a symbol rather than a container, holding nothing but an absence: a space where a head used to be, the mere evocation of form.

The statue's decapitated body shored up against the center column of the fountain, which was carved like a goblet and burbling water out its top, lazily. The rest of the monument was simple, modern: a basin ten feet wide and hexagon shaped. From the column, clear liquid fell in braids, cascaded over the statue's clavicle, her breasts, down onto her stomach and hips, moving slowly and deliberately, almost libidinally, but making no sound, as sunlight scattered over every inch of the figure, scathing, yet softening her frame, her fleshy calves dunked six inches in water, the stoned bottom bestrewn with coins and bits of glass.

I centered myself by concentrating on the bag's movement. It bulged, then contracted, a mouth inhaling, exhaling. I could almost see a real head in there, the heat of a breath, and this image was so ugly, so horrifying, that it became excruciatingly beautiful to me, and I couldn't control what happened next. I began to cry.

I felt the warmth of my tears, as I half listened to Niko, who nervously babbled, labeling whoever did this a group of "vandalists," saying they had taken a few other minor artifacts from the museum, but the statue, the one we were on the brink of paying millions for, the one that was going to change my career and life, this was the one mutilated. Niko said the vandalists might have acted elsewhere too, as though it were a comfort to know we were not alone in our carnage. And had anyone any idea where the head was now? Had Niko and Alec looked? Of course, all over the town square, they'd searched. When I asked Niko about Melia, he said she wasn't there, and when I asked why, he appeared bewildered. "Because it is Easter?" he said, like it was strange I didn't know. I thought about the day the statue's head had been asphyxiated with tape. I thought of the protestors too—the boy at the Acropolis, the young woman speaking to Theo—and about William and his long list of enemies, but all explanations, any connections I tried to make, seemed immediately incomplete, dim-witted. Behind me, a group of pigeons hopped closer to the fountain and pecked at the ground.

Niko said we couldn't move her yet. The police were on their way. Who had called them? Alec would know not to, unless he no longer cared about the sale. I looked at the water, the dirty, chlorinated water. How harmful it might be, to her delicate materials. We needed to get her out. Now.

I turned to Madison for backup, but he was silent and useless, gaping at the statue, a hand resting loosely over his chin, another on his cocked hip. Theo remained quiet. Alec paced. At this point, I doubted all of them.

I considered the monstrosity of this production—lugging her all the way here. The statue weighed at least a few hundred pounds. The movement of her would have entailed meticulous planning—lifting slings, hoists, custom packaging. The removal of the head would have required power tools. On a logistical level, it was an extraordinary feat.

I walked around to the other side of the fountain, immediately enraptured by the shadows of the statue's spine—how the indented flesh guided the eye down to the tailbone, onto the curve of her rear. How the marble prismed under the morning sun. I needed to be closer. I slipped off my shoes, and crawled into the basin, planting my feet in the water, at which point, I noticed something flying around inside the bag, an insect moving so fast, so frightened, I could barely make it out, and I began to reach for it—

But Niko shouted not to touch.

"There's something in there," I shouted back. I turned around to find Madison, Niko, Theo, and Alec all regarding me with worry, which caused me to worry about their level of worry. I touched my cheek to see if I was still crying; my skin felt hot, but dry.

"Do you not see?" More to myself than anyone else, I said, "I think it's a cicada." I thought about the wing found in between the statue's lips, about the maggot in the fig, wriggling in my hand. I watched the bug die to get free. It would give up soon, fall to the bottom. Wouldn't it?

"Elizabeth," said Madison, as he approached and grabbed me by the elbow. "Let's get out of the water, yeah? The police are coming." When I glanced down at his hand, I remembered the statue's arm. Where was it? Niko said the vandalizers had left it in the room at the museum, which seemed like an act of derision—what was an arm without a head?

I told Madison to get off me, but his grip tightened. "Now," I said, a force in my voice, the severity of which caused the pigeons to scatter. Madison retreated, but I didn't move; the liquid felt pleasant on my skin, cooling my shaking legs. I couldn't remember the last time I'd been in any body of water, outside of a bath. As the noises around me faded, I focused back on the statue but was having a hard time reconciling her existence. Two versions of the sculpture seemed to exist at once: the one in front of me, here and now, with a bag for a head, and the other, material only in memory. I wondered which was real. And what about the others? All the past versions of what she'd been.

The police zoomed into the town square, two men on one motorcycle, and instructed me to get out of the fountain. Because I'd almost always folded around authority, I first obliged but then, in a subsequent act of defiance, I decided to sit a few feet from the basin. As the officers hovered over me, blocking out the sun, I relayed what they wanted to know about why I was here and what I was doing, trying not to let their yawns offend me.

Niko told the police all of this had happened this morning, based on one eyewitness who noticed some strange activity over by the fountain and came out to find the statue, at which point the eyewitness had called the museum, and then Alec. The convenience of this story sounded suspicious but not impossible—everyone knew everyone out here.

They asked what time, exactly, and Niko said it had been eight am, and I confirmed that time with him, making sure I heard right, and when he asked why, I did not say that I had planned to get to the museum at seven-thirty. Instead, I said nothing and tried to compose my face, tried not to look how I felt, which was, somehow, guilty, and therefore, hot with rage.

The questioning went on for a few more minutes. The police were surprisingly pleasant and unbothered. All they seemed to care about was the kokoresti they were going to make for the holiday. Niko asked me if I felt unsafe, and said if I did, I should certainly stay with him and Theo, and though the thought of this thrilled me, I was unsure if the invitation was cursory or sincere, so I said I didn't feel unsafe and thanked him.

When the police finished their queries, Madison, who had been silent this whole time, crouched down to my level. That he looked calm bothered me immensely. He asked if we could get some cold water, take a walk? I nodded as the police encircled the fountain with red and white striped tape, the result like a cheap stanchion. When done, they began wrapping the statue's headless body in a tarp—a filthy one, no less, the bag still heaving with movement. I thought I might throw up or cry again. What were they going to do with it? How would they get it back to the museum? Madison grabbed my jaw, turned my face toward his, and demanded I stop watching. I didn't flinch or move his hand away. Someone else might have witnessed this as an act of hostility, but I saw it as one of care, until I glanced back up and clocked Theo's eyes on us, at which point, I quickly changed my mind and jerked away.

Madison and I made it to the shop on the corner, the shelves of which were almost completely deserted. It was hotter in there than it was outside. The lights and refrigerators were off, and I didn't see anyone at the front register, though the door had been wide open. I strolled between aisles, sickened by their unrelenting emptiness, twists of dusty light, plaited garlic hung up on every other corner. I ran back into Madison, the two of us nearly colliding.

I told him we needed to call William. "Let's talk strategy," I said, straightening up. "What's the angle?"

He handed me a bottle of water. It was room temperature, but I put it up against my forehead anyway.

Hands on his hips, he dropped his head and looked at the ground. There was no angle, Madison said. The angle was that the acquisition was dead because someone had sawed our statue off at the neck. The angle was that we were going home. "I have a child," he said, as though this was relevant—as though I had forgotten. Which, of course, I had.

From a shelf, he grabbed a dusty bag of chips and read the label, then put them back. He reached for a different bag and put that one back too. His brows knit, his neck forward, he seemed concerned about which to choose. When I asked if he was listening to me, he nodded. I said this wasn't over. The head could be found, fixed. It could still be the focal point I—*we*— had initially imagined, the grand moment in the new opening. I leaned up against a dark and warm refrigerator and reminded Madison how, in the late eighties, the museum acquired a stunning marble rendering of a fighting Gaul—without its head. They restored it, displayed it proudly, and then by some miracle, found the head five years later in a different gallery on the other side of the country. The museum offered that gallery a lump sum of money, and the restorers welded the head back on and gave the figure a second life. I imagined all this happening to my statue, though in quicker succession. It was the kind of against-all-odds story the media would tell for a long time; it could define my career. Even more so than the statue would have alone.

Madison settled on a bag of chips, opened it, and stared at me.

"This whole thing is too bizarre," he said, lowering his eyes.

I asked him about the *Nike of Samothrace*. They never found her head, and she's arguably the most recognized Hellenistic statue the world has ever seen. She altered history. But, Madison said, she was a late-nineteenth-century find, I couldn't compare the two. I said I could do whatever I wanted and the only reason he was saying all this was because he wanted to see me lose.

He popped a chip in his mouth. "This is bigger than you, Elizabeth."

Our eyes remained locked on each other until Theo came into the store and found us, halting the conversation. Madison smiled at her, then at me, and walked out. She gave me a sympathetic, borderline pandering look, then gestured for me to follow her over to the other aisle, where she began reaching for bottles of alcohol.

Turning one over, she said, coolly, "Care for a drink?"

She unscrewed the bottle of an amber liquid, took a swig, and handed it to me. It was revolting, but strong. I gave it back, then searched my pockets for some change, before excavating a single unidentifiable coin. She stopped me, touched my hand, and said, "I'll get it. I know the owner." Of course she did. I dropped the coin and watched it fall to the floor as her hand let go. When I bent down to retrieve it, she did the same, and our foreheads slammed against each other.

"Fuck," she said, holding her palm up to skin. I apologized. She apologized. And then, in the middle of the aisle, we both gave up and sat down, pressing our backs against the sterile shelves. Our heads were facing forward.

"About this morning," I began.

She promised she wouldn't say a word. "Is that why your husband left you?"

Her tone was so sincere, I had no choice but to laugh at the audacity of the question. Light-headed, I tilted my body toward hers, pleasantly careless about boundaries, about borders, our shoulders now touching. I said my husband never knew, and I asked why she assumed *he* left *me*.

She said there was no need to speak of it anymore, and I felt shameful for bringing it up, but then she added, "No judgment here. I don't find your indiscretion sinful." I waited for her to elaborate.

"Niko and I have an agreement," she said.

I nodded with slow understanding. I asked if there were parameters. Light swept over her face in shards, and she turned closer to me, raising one eyebrow. "Parameters? No details. That's one.

"It's interesting to see what else a marriage can lean on," she continued, "once you remove the constructed pillars of monogamy." Though it had been her idea, she was worried the agreement would cause her to lose all trust, but she'd never trusted Niko more. In her opinion, this was the only honest way for them to live. Was there something in her tone that sounded compensatory? And why was she telling me this now?

We stayed quiet for a few moments, sharing the warm bottle of alcohol. Emboldened by our nearness, I rested my head on her shoulder, her dewed skin redolent of oranges and what I assumed to be photo developer. She looked down at me. I wondered how I appeared to her then, if she could see old, calcified memories clawing through my skin. If she was the one wheedling them out.

I asked if she had noticed the cicada in the bag.

She said she hadn't. "I can see you worrying about the details. You get so lost in the details."

"It's my job to get lost in the details," I said, but as soon as I heard myself, I wasn't sure if I believed that. I wanted to tell her about the first vandalization, about the wing I found—it seemed important, but I couldn't decide how.

She shook her head.

A beam of rage flared through me—fleeting but potent.

"What?" I said.

"Maybe it's a—"

"Say it," I interrupted her. My hands began to shake. "Say what you mean."

She pulled her head back, a tuft of hair sashed behind her ear. Did my anger make her nervous?

"Maybe it's a sign," she said, regaining herself. "Reason to keep things where they belong. To whom they belong."

"I see," I said. "An object of immense value has been *irreparably* harmed, and you think it's a *sign*?"

She put her hands up in mock evasion. A gesture she learned from Niko—or that he'd learned from her. "Value," she said, repeating the word a few more times—"*value value value*"—its vowels and consonants, a piece of candy, a shard of bone, stuck in her tooth. "Explain it, will you? This mystical, rootless value?"

"What is your role here? Why are you always so—so—"

She turned to me now, cocking her head in antagonistic curiosity.

"So present, for fuck's sake. Don't you have your own things to work on?"

This time, she said nothing. But her eyes deepened—two black holes, taking me in.

"And you're mistaken," I added. "I don't have the power to keep anything anywhere."

The words left me breathless, and I had to admit, a little intoxicated. To be speaking like this, and with her, of all people. I watched as she took a pull of liquor. There was a long pause, and then, slowly, she sat the bottle down, leaned over, hooked a forefinger under my jaw, pulled me toward her, and kissed me on the mouth.

Her lips were sour but sure of themselves, and I could feel the blood pumping through them. I'd never kissed a woman before. In some ways, it felt entirely nonsexual, like a mild kiss a mother might give—but then, she bit down, and my lip flushed with pain, with want. I remembered the morning after I woke from the blackout, my wounded mouth, the deep lacuna of that night. I wondered what Theo knew and why I felt so unable to ask, and why I couldn't pull away, even though she was hurting me. If there existed a tenderness without threat, had I ever known it? I watched her with awe, my eyes still open, hers closed. Purple veins thickening her lids. I thought of the veins in the statue's marble, soft and swirling and golden. For the first time, Theo appeared vulnerable to me, malleable. In my head, I dared her to break through skin, but I knew she wouldn't. She was only pretending. But for whose benefit? She let go, and in a rush, moved back from me, said nothing, and stood.

Still in shock, I stayed put, leering up at her. She reached for my hand and helped me up, and we were close again; I heard her chest rise and fall; I thought she'd lean in one more time, but she didn't. She stepped back and strolled through those barren aisles, displaying no signs of penitence or even change, touching the lonely goods on the shelves with indifference. At the register, she stopped, the back of her figure lit up dreamily, dust motes circling her head. She took a few coins from her pocket, tallied them in her palm, then dropped them on the counter, the sound of metal on glass radiating outward. A moment later, she turned right, strode toward the door, and finally, her face half shaded, said, "Aren't you coming?" She had the unreadable countenance of a Victorian portrait. I pictured her in some baroque dress, rendered in delicate brushstrokes, a stark attention to details; the dramatic width between her eyes, the eddying baby hairs at her forehead, a crooked smile containing itself under her lips.

I told her I'd be right there, but instead, I remained behind, stupefied, as I watched her disappear into the white, chalky light of the square.

29

When I left the store, instead of returning to Theo and the statue, I went right to find a phone, and felt Madison behind me, but didn't acknowledge him. A few moments later, a side street opened up and seemed promising, so I went that way and entered an enclave of stores, all of them closed, padlocks on their handles in the shape of up-turned faces. I went left into a wending, aphotic alleyway, where a trio of gangly teenagers circled one another on bikes and passed a joint around, the smell of cheap marijuana mixed with freshly caught fish and lemons. The boys had the appearance of kouros statues: broad shoulders and thin waists, the kind of body one gets from swimming and luck. Their laughter filled the space between mortared walls. They were talking boldly about a girl with whom one of them had slept—or had wanted to sleep with. I was pretty sure. "She looked older," one said, gravely. Another said something to the effect of, "I would bring her home to meet my mother," but his tone was not kind; it was depraved. He had piercings up and down his entire earlobe. The third one, the smallest of them, said quietly, "I think she's magic."

As I strode past the boys, my eyes caught on the shine of their bikes. I thought of Margaret and me rolling through town during those listless, summer days of my youth. Unfortunately, the boys noticed my attention and began taunting me with whistles, each one growing louder and louder.

In return, I offered a coy smile and subtle wave, enacting my part of the deal, but on they went, every howl more aggressive than the last, until that is, they saw Madison. At that point, they finally stopped, sheepishly resolving themselves to silence.

At the end of the alleyway, across the road, stood a phone booth. It looked like every other phone booth I'd ever seen, and the fact of its normalcy made me queasy. I forced myself inside and dialed William's number, careless about the hour back home. The air around me felt damp and balmy, like the air inside a mouth. Madison took a seat outside and as I waited for William to pick up, the boys' collective taunt still echoing in my ears, I tried to get Madison to acknolwedge me, but he kept his head down, eyes away. The phone burned in my hand.

When William answered, he wasted no time. "Congratulations, kiddo. We got it."

I thought I'd heard him wrong.

He must have sensed this because he repeated himself, this time louder.

A space below me opened, and I let myself drop into the overblown blankness of triumph. It was like entering an orb, a different spiritual plane devoid of gravity and reason. I did not listen to William's voice as it told me the board had voted to purchase the statue for eight and a half million dollars. Rather, I felt his words frenzy through me with unimaginable desperation—on his part or mine, it was impossible to tell. Nonetheless, the paperwork was done, the deal sealed. I opened my mouth to speak, but I couldn't catch a word or sound, and then, as though trying to pull one out, I touched my lip, the spot Theo had kissed, and remembered, again, everything unknowable to me—the statue, the bag, the cicada—and a coldness overcame me, and I shot up and out of the void and back into the booth. I thought of releasing the phone, watching the cord snap back with velocity, and running out. But what then? I had no other options, nowhere else to go. Did I even have a life outside of antiquities? I wondered who I would be without the imprints of terra-cotta figures, friezes, marble reliefs, contrapposto stances, without Phidias and Praxiteles. The truth lodged itself between my ribs. A sharp and stubborn ache. I looked around. This was it for me. This was everything.

So, I told him: about the probably looted arm, how gross its restitution; I told him about the tape, the hacked-off head, the fountain. Though it did pour out of me, it was horrible to verbalize, and I felt no weight lifted off my shoulders, but instead, a tunneling inside my chest. This was the point of no return. It had been said—I could not unsay it.

When I finished, I waited for his response, silence stretching between us, across whole worlds. The clouds came back together, formed one long shadow. I walked the booth in tiny circles, wondering if some part of William had been relieved. If he'd been waiting for this call, waiting for me to fuck up. Maybe he had a bet going with some colleagues. I wouldn't have put it past him. Foolish to think I'd ever been immune to his brutality.

Finally, he spoke. "In the seventies," he said, "some maniac tore out several faces in one Caravaggio, and then killed the guard. Consider yourself lucky you weren't in anyone's way."

"That's it? That's all you have to say?"

"What do you want me to say?"

I asked how we would break this news to the board.

He said he'd have to think about the next move, but to put Madison on the phone for now.

"Right now?"

"What do you mean? Fuck sake, yes."

I told him I wouldn't; I wanted him to talk to me.

He sighed. "Put Madison on."

"I asked Niko for better security, but nobody listened. You can't—"

"Niko?"

"My translator."

"Why would you ask your translator for security? Jesus. Elizabeth. Send me Madison. Now." I made a quick calculation—how much further could I push this without sacrificing my future, myself? Or had it been too late? I reminded him how many other statues were presented without heads. I reminded him of the fighting Gaul, its miraculous restoration.

"That's different," he said. "Plus, it's—"

"What?"

"It's lost its main appeal."

"If this is about price."

"It's always about price. Now for fuck sake. Put Madison on the phone, will you?"

I did not respond, hoping that he'd realize the carelessness with which he spoke to me, though I knew he wouldn't. I stuck my head out of the booth and gestured for Madison to come inside. He sullenly nodded, then took my place and shooed me out. "What?" he whispered. "We both can't stand in here; it's too cramped."

From the outside, I watched them have their conversation, and though I'd no idea what was said, I imagined the worst—likely something about how this was my fault, how *of course this happened on Elizabeth's watch*. I wanted to laugh at my own self-pity, as I stared at the back of Madison's head. He was quiet, making almost no gestures but slight, sad little nods. I turned around and pressed my forehead up to the shaded side of a building, and then noticed color—blues and yellows. I backed away, taking it all in, a mural of the sea. It was one of those three-dimensional illusion scenes, the kind you'd see chalked into a city street. I reached to touch, half expecting my hand to move through the brick and into the painted sky. A wasp crawled across the ersatz ocean, then whooshed toward the ground and fell into a stream of water.

Finally, Madison came out of the booth.

"Why'd you really come all this way?" I said.

"You don't want me to say it."

"He had doubts."

"He thought you might need help."

I felt my shoulders rise. "Huh. Then why'd it sound like he was going to give it to me? He told me, '*Congratulations*.'"

"You're clearly under a lot of stress."

I wanted to snap—but snapping would only prove his point.

He said he was going back and thought I should too. No part of me considered giving up. Not after everything I had sacrificed. Time, for instance, whole weekends and nights lost to the office. My ego, certainly. Friendships, conceivably. I couldn't remember. A marriage, definitely. Not a particularly solid one, but a partnership, nonetheless.

"No," I said. "You go back. I'll stay here and find the head." It was a ridiculous sentence, but I was way beyond the point of ridiculousness, and if William had sent Madison to Greece to check on me—or to test me, if there was a difference—I still had the chance to prove myself, didn't I? Even after everything. I'd have to—I would. Or else I'd kill myself in the process.

Madison warned me not to be a martyr. I warned him not to be a coward—an insult he took in stride. He said if I was really so hell-bent, please could I stay with Niko and Theo? And not alone?

I told him I wouldn't.

"We can work something out. Let's just go."

"No," I said.

He stepped toward me and reached out his hand. He said he was sorry, which I found more vulgar than any verbal laceration would have been.

"Be sorry for the mother of your child," I said. I needed to get far away from him, the alley, the phone booth, town square. I turned around and left. "I'll see you in California," I yelled back.

He asked when.

I refused to answer.

30

I paid little mind to where I was going, folded my arms and walked against the wind, ultimately ending up back in the alleyway where the teenage boys had been. It was desolate now, but the boys' bikes had been left behind, each one propped up against the stone wall. I looked to my left and saw them through the window of a corner store, laughing and throwing things at one another, generally menacing around. I convinced myself it was not my problem the boys hadn't locked up their property. In some ways, they were begging me to take it. But I'd never stolen anything from an individual. I wasn't a thief—was I? In certain circumstances, I supposed I was. I'd never ascribed the word to it, which seemed thoughtless now. Why not? What was I so afraid of? I touched the bike's handlebar and the electricity of opportunity spread through me, the metal smooth and warm under my fingers. I hopped on the seat and pedaled off, thinking I would return it, when I could. I did not feel guilty; or told myself I didn't have to, and really, wasn't that the same thing?

I cycled down to the water and followed its edge, listening to the rhythm of slow waves, counting all the boats with their sails tied up and rocking to sleep. The passing of time cooled the air, and I could breathe again, and I convinced myself that I would figure everything out; the right path forward would reveal itself. Whether this was optimism or capitulation did not matter. I went a little faster until the pedals and my feet disappeared, and then I floated, coasting.

I saw the cat before it saw me: a Calico with retribution in its eyes, staring at the road across. In my head, I quickly pleaded with it, realizing I wasn't sure how to brake the bike—the normal stopping mechanism was missing. *Please, don't go,* I tried to telepathize, *please, I won't be able to stop, and I don't want to hurt you,* but it didn't listen. It fled onto the street and cut me off. I overcorrected and hit a lonesome shoe. The commotion threw me from the seat, my body rigidifying as it hit the ground. The bike landed a few feet away on its side, and from it rose the unholy noise of its still-spinning pedal.

Dirt and dust now colored my clothes. I'd scraped up my hands and elbows, sharp pebbles lodged inside my palm. I watched myself bleed. The absurdity of skin had always baffled me: how much it holds, how easily it breaks. Under the sun, the scar on my thumb shone pink.

In our last fight, about a month before I arrived in Greece, Julian sat on the edge of the couch, head in his hands, crying about all the time I'd spent away from home, how little I'd been considering him. How he'd felt taken advantage of. I was holding a glass of water, sipping it slowly, listening to him moan, too exhausted to defend myself. I did feel bad. I also felt resentful. He knew what he'd gotten into when he married me. Unlike him, I'd been honest about my dreams. "Tell me something, Elizabeth," he'd said. "Tell me how I've become a man who is jealous of stone?" To picture what happened next seemed challenging now: How did I have the strength to crush the glass? It must have already been cracked by the time I picked it up, and the force of my fingers pushed it over the edge, or else it must have been cheap and manufactured incorrectly. It began with a searing pain in my thumb, followed by the sound of his dramatics. He kept threatening that he was going to faint from "all the blood." I did bleed a lot, certainly more than I would have imagined. He called the ambulance before I could stop him, and as we waited outside on the curb, he, in tears, announced he couldn't live like this anymore. "Like what?" I'd replied, woozy. I'd given him the most agreeable parts of myself, the easiest sides. I'd given him space, freedom. Now he didn't want a wife who "worked herself to death" and—as a complete surprise to me—had decided, sometime within the previous year, he'd wanted a different kind of futurity. One with kids. Three of them, in fact. Before we married, Julian had never given me any indication he'd wanted children. Sometimes, when he was in a depressed mood, I found him sitting at the kitchen table at midnight with a J. R. R. Tolkien or C. S. Lewis book, but I chalked it up to nostalgic desire or arrested development. It was not my fault he had outgrown his earlier predilections. How could I have predicted he would? But then it became clear. He hadn't changed his mind. He was waiting for me to change mine, to heel to his needs, and a child's, too. To become the selfless, bodiless mother.

The night of the glass breaking, I begged him not to come to the hospital with me. I didn't want to make a scene. At least, he respected my final request, standing dumbly in the middle of the street, still crying, as the ambulance pulled away, my blood all over his collared shirt, as I wondered if I would miss not him, but his weaknesses. How strong they made me feel. How righteous.

Trying to find my stride, I got back on the bike, but a few minutes in rolled over something sharp and punctured the bike's front tire. "Fuck," I muttered. "Fuck fuck fuck." The breeze had turned despotic by then; trash flew everywhere, a crushed melon undone on the side of the road, its open flesh lit up with flies. My feet toddled over uneven stone as I dragged the bike along, headed nowhere.

A few moments later, a cab pulled up alongside me and rolled down the window, revealing a face blown out by sun.

"I found you," the man in the cab said. Or maybe, "You found me."

I pulled myself and the bike closer. I knew I'd heard this man's voice before, but I couldn't recall if it was lived or dreamed. He said he'd taken me to the hotel on my first night in town.

"Oh," I said. "Yes." I smiled, tried to look approachable.

"Dimitri," he said.

"Elizabeth."

My name drawled out his mouth, deep and hollow. "Al-liz-ah-beth. Me, you owe money."

I wasn't sure I had enough euros on me. How would I tell him I couldn't pay? Again? Noticing my flat tire, he insisted on giving me a ride and popped the trunk for the bike, which he then secured with a mixture of twine and stretchy rope, huffing and wiping his forehead throughout. Even after all that work, its security seemed dubious, but I thanked him, my teeth chattering from adrenaline.

"I don't have your money," I said. My skin felt itchy and hot, almost sunburned. I told him I would pay once we got to the rental. I hoped I had enough cash. With the back of my hand, I brushed a speck of dirt off my cheek. His eyes fell to my scraped-up palm, and he cocked his head. He must've pitied me. From his back pocket, he slipped out a silver flask, then took my hand, and poured the liquid over my skin. He had dirt under his short fingernails; a gaudy gold watch cuffed his wrist. My eyes teared as the alcohol burned, and when he offered me a drink from the flask and I said no, he shrugged, sipped on it himself, and said, "This is very good. Made from figs." Then he went to the front of his cab, where he procured a grease-stained shirt, tore the hem off, and wrapped the strip of cloth around the abrasions. Next to his hands, I was ashamed of how small the wound looked, how inconsequential.

As he drove on, we spoke to each other in a mix of Greek and English. He asked me to remind him what I was doing here, but I didn't remember telling him in the first place. I explained about the statue, not mentioning what had happened earlier. He said he loved artwork and that his wife had been a beautiful jewelry maker—or maybe he said, she *is* a beautiful jewelry maker. The tense seemed important, but I couldn't make it out. In the rearview reflection, his eyes—huge and ancient—kept finding mine. He caught me looking at a small gold pendant hanging from the mirror; then he unlooped it and handed it over. I said I admired the craftsmanship as I traced the inscription: *Η Πότνια Θηρῶν*. It was a figure of a woman—a version of Artemis perhaps—standing with her legs and arms spread apart, holding two swans by the neck. He told me his wife made it; then he told me about his family—he had two daughters. On his dashboard, he pointed to the photograph of the girl and said she was now in her twenties. He'd said her age so quickly I couldn't figure out if she was twenty-one or twenty-nine, and though there seemed a world of difference between the two, I didn't ask for clarification.

The picture was sepia toned, and she was beautiful, maybe the most beautiful child I'd ever seen, save for Margaret.

She'd just had a baby, Dimitri said, a little boy. Her other boy, he said, had come out stillborn. He didn't know the English word for stillborn and I didn't know the Greek one, so it took us a while to arrive at this understanding. He asked if I believed in an afterlife, which he called a "death spirit." His words disarmed me, so I told him yes, probably, and gave the pendant back, but he insisted I hold on to it for a few more minutes, and I was too overwhelmed to decline. I looked out the window and pretended to think of something meaningful, though really, with the cold weight of the pendant in my hand, as he droned on and on, and the trees on the sides of the road blurred by and became one large, long tree, I couldn't think much at all.

As we crept closer to my rental, the idea of being alone preemptively haunted me. My arms and legs went rigid.

"Where else can we go?" I asked.

At first, he didn't seem to understand. I said I didn't want to go to my rental, and where was he headed? He was celebrating the holiday with his friends and cousins, up in the mountains. It sounded far enough away, so I asked if I could come. Even the day before, I would have never considered such a bold move; I would have gone straight to solitude—pills, followed by sleep.

I begged him. "Please don't take me back," I said. "I know I still owe you, but I will pay, I swear on my own life." I hoped I might be able to cry on command, but nothing came out, only the suggestion of sadness.

"I'm sorry," I said. "I just don't want to be alone."

He tapped his thumb on the wheel, and caught my eyes in the mirror again, assessing my fragility, calculating which would eat at his conscience more: leaving a sad woman alone or bringing some foreigner to his family gathering? With a soft smile, I promised him I wouldn't be any trouble. He turned the cab around and we drove inland, my stomach flipping but eventually settling down. Behind us, fireworks started to boom. Or maybe they'd been going off the whole morning and I'd only now been able to hear them.

As the incline grew and the roads became windier, I recognized some of them—from the drive up to the bar, in Theo and Niko's backseat—but what about the drive down? What had I seen then? I had the urge to flee a memory that wasn't even there to begin with.

In the background of my thoughts, Dimitri chatted on and on. He seemed enthused to have an audience, distracted by his own stories. I tried to zone out and watch the town behind me recede, but every so often, he'd pause for me to speak, waiting for validation, confirmation I was listening.

"It was a scare," he said.

"I can only imagine," I lied, utterly unaware of what he had been saying.

"It's lucky you were there," I added, pandering.

He said, "Yes. Luck." He flicked a tear from his eye and exhaled in relief, and I looked at him, coveting how freely he'd shared this emotional story with a complete stranger, as though all he'd needed was a warm body—any body—to listen.

We drove through the country, which stretched with dull green slopes, sharp rocks on either side of the byway amongst tall, wild grass, and sparse shrubs punctuated by yellow flowers, each the size of a child's fist. Every so often, a singular white home would sit atop some hill in the distance, and I would wonder who could possibly live there, and if I could've made a life somewhere like that. Elsewhere, crumbled ruins populated the landscape, along with trees missing tops. They looked out of place and incomplete, their top halves like a bird's upside down claw, their bottom halves stained a chalky white; Dimitri said the paint repelled pests.

With time, the roads steepened and narrowed, covered in dirt and detritus, and I kept worrying that the cab would slip on some debris, and roll back down and into the ocean. I craned my neck out the back window to gauge how far we'd come, and felt I could see the whole island: schematic as a blueprint. Dimitri put something on the radio, and I turned back, my forehead on the glass, my eyes flicking past the fast, unchanging landscape, my mind eventually, floating away, into a light, fitful sleep.

31

I woke at the woozy feeling of a hairpin turn.

As we drove up a gravel road, Dimitri's radio went static, then quiet. A long rectangular building, made of white stucco, one-story with a terracotta Spanish roof, and green doors and shutters, stood at the top of a hill. Dimitri rolled down the windows, and a breeze winnowed inside the cab. Picnic benches spread out along the expansive property, which was full of untended bushes and piles of rocks, knotted olive trees sprouting from patchy grass. Whatever this was seemed both establishment and home: a chalkboard sign listing several different types of honey, the costs of various farm tours, standing alongside muted toy cars, a plastic swing set.

Before anyone else, I saw the man with the bees. He didn't have one of those protective suits, only khaki shorts and no shoes, and the gray hair on his head was as unruly as his eyebrows, which swirled upward and toward the sun. He stood beside a wooden box, about the size of a filing cabinet and painted a pastel pink. With ease, he uncovered the box, extracted a board, and held it to the light. Most of the bees clung to the board in clusters, but a few bumbled around his head, inches from his skin. One of William's most prized possessions was a silver four-drachma coin—one side stamped with a honeybee— kept on his bookshelf. Once, when he caught me looking at it, he told me that male bees die after they mate, ejaculate themselves right into death. I remembered feeling like I envied them—that final pursuit of unencumbered pleasure.

A few more men lingered about—fifties, sixties—some spread out over by rusted chairs, leaning against the main building and smoking, faces cut by shade. A young girl—six or seven—sat beside a tree, labeling jars of honey, her hair frizzy and defensive, her forehead freckled.

Dimitri opened the car door for me, and when I got out, a goat appeared from behind the cab, trotting his hoofs through pebbled dirt and a narrow river of sullage. "Hello," I said, but the animal sauntered past me and toward a second goat sitting under some shade and blinking softly. On the property's rolling hillside, there were dozens more—black, white, and brown and bleating—chewing on the bases of olive trees.

Dimitri roved off and said something to a boy perched on a picnic bench, his back toward me. He was shirtless and narrow, a glisten of sweat running down his spine. He shot up and embraced Dimitri, and I saw who he was then—the kid from the rental. I called out his name.

"Baz?"

His eyes found me as he shouted some Grecian expletive. Dimitri lightly slapped the back of his head, which prompted Baz to hunch over and scowl. A few of the other men got up and walked toward us.

Baz told them he knew me. It sounded like a brag, and I worried how much it flattered me. Dimitri pinched Baz's cheek and said Baz was his nephew, that he came up here to help with the goats. Baz smiled proudly, nodding. He dusted his hands off on his cargo shorts and tripped on a dip in the grass as he ran toward me. He didn't ask why I was there, how I knew Dimitri, anything. All he wanted to know was whether or not I was ready to eat. I remembered again that it was Easter. They obviously had some festive meal planned, some grand symposium. The little girl had approached me and was now pulling at my slacks and staring up at my face, her brown eyes unyielding. Her head snapped back, and her mouth opened and closed soundlessly, like she was trying to breathe underwater.

One of the men told Baz something and then Baz left, went inside the house, and came back with an armful of pale octopi. He sat them down on a chair and then, one by one, began slamming each octopus body against the stucco wall of the farm's main building. The sound was horrifying. Flies flew around his head, and he swatted them off, but when he saw me looking, he grinned, gave a thumbs-up, and then went back to battering the spineless animal, all eight of its soft limbs thwapping against the hard wall like putty.

32

For the feast, we sat down on a decrepit picnic table, the air filled with smoked meat. Above us, through serried, cracked clouds came a dazzling but unforgiving light. There were five men at the table, and then Baz. I did not know where the little girl was. Perhaps she was napping, or they'd wanted to keep her away from adult chatter. It didn't seem right for me to inquire.

Of all the men, I only knew two names: Dimitri and that of Dimitri's friend Konstantin—a man with a permanent smile and sorrowful jowls. Konstantin had introduced himself several times, making sure to sit beside me at the table. We ate fresh bread with honey, and saganaki fried with the same cheese Baz had brought to my rental. The octopi he'd slammed were now grilled and drizzled in olive oil and lemon and flakes of salt. Every time I tried to chew off a bite, I felt the rubbery tentacles reaching inside my mouth and trying to latch on, but I knew Baz was watching, so I swallowed anyway. In time, I got used to the sensation. My hunger expanded, then contracted, expanded again. The men handed me blackened pots full of undefinable meat, and at one point, I caught eyes with a gray goat and felt an overwhelming shame that I might have been gnawing on the feathered bone of his brethren. What helped was the carafe of wine that tasted like it had gone bad from blistering under the sun too long, and of course raki, and the cruel combination of both, twisting my senses into one, so that the food began to taste yellow, and orange, and the cool shade from the trees smelled like my private idea of tranquility.

Once the eating had slowed down, Konstantin asked what I was doing in Greece. Everyone went quiet. I told them about my line of work, which they seemed to attain only the gist of, as I had to explain it in both languages.

"Today," I said, in English, "someone decapitated a statue I'd been trying to buy for eight and a half million dollars."

The men gaped at me as Dimitri translated. After a brief pause, they laughed and said I had a strange sense of humor. I was pretty certain I'd even heard one mutter the Greek word for fool.

Konstantin took a particular interest in my story. In English, he talked with pride as he told me his grandfather was an archaeologist who had found two marble funerary statues in the forties, when Konstantin was a young boy. He said that one of the statues was so lovely that he'd think about her all the time—specifically, her dress, the sensual way it fell off her shoulders.

"At evening time," he said, "I would lie awake and see her next to me in bed." His eyes veered off into the distance, romantically. "She reminded me of the most beautiful young lady on the island."

Dimitri chimed in, "Not Lia?"

They both laughed. Dimitri blushed. "Oh, we all loved Lia."

Konstantin took a handkerchief out of his pocket, blew his nose, and returned to his story. He said Lia had the face of a goddess, but devils for parents, and so, despite their obvious connection, they were never allowed to see each other. But of the statue, he said, often his father would take him to see it, and he would think of Lia, of their unconsummated love—and this, Konstantin said, pleased him.

"Did you—" At this Dimitri raised his eyebrows.

"No, no, no," Konstantin bellowed. "She was stone!"

"Sex. Desire. It makes us human," said Dimitri.

"No," said Konstantin, shaking his head. "Sex makes us God."

At the other end of the table, Baz watched on, seemingly frustrated that he could not understand the conversation.

"Oh, but those shoulders!" Konstantin said, throwing his hands up, his eyes glowing. "Smooth as . . ." He searched for a word but couldn't find one. "Old man that I am now," he continued, "I have no joy to look forward, but looking back, looking back can still be a joy."

I smiled at him. He cast his eyes toward my plate, then face. "I like your hunger," he said. He looked as though he wanted something from me, and out of old habits, I began preparing myself for the eventuality of having to give it. I shifted in my seat, noticeably uncomfortable now. Konstantin said American women hated compliments, didn't they? I asked when he'd complimented me. My pulse sped up. Konstantin didn't answer. Instead, he turned to Dimitri and said something indecipherable. Dimitri laughed, and so did Baz, which, for a moment, startled me. Baz's laugh was deep and scratchy, too adult.

Both Baz and Dimitri got up then, but only Baz returned, and with a pot of coffee, koulouria, and a set of porcelain cups. Mine was white and doll-like, a delicate blue pattern around the rim, the words *kalimera ellada* etched inside. As Baz poured coffee, I learned Konstantin and his wife owned a taverna in town and had seven grandchildren. I asked Konstantin if the little girl was one of them. He said she wasn't; then he pointed to one of the men at the end of the table and said the little girl was that man's cousin. He said that for all nine months of her pregnancy, the little girl's mother had maintained that there was no father. The mother was young—sixteen, he said—her strict Catholic family had kicked her out and sent her to the farm. She swore up and down that she was a virgin. At one point, she said a goat had impregnated her, and then, she said, it was a colony of bees. She told a tale that the bees had swarmed together, turned into a man, and raped her—at least, I thought this is what he'd said. He'd begun implanting English words that he'd pieced together such as, *unflower*, *sex threat*, *radish* instead of *ravish*.

The young woman was adamant, he'd said; she stuck to her story, hadn't once cracked, not even under ruthless questioning from every doctor in town. But after she birthed the little girl, she fled. No one had heard from her since.

I was struck by the story, disturbed and curious, but mostly worried for the little girl, the deleterious effects such fables had on the young. I wondered how deeply they'd ingrained themselves in her, if they'd already started to feel truthful, in the way absolute truth never could.

"Does she know?" I asked, and Dimitri swiveled his head toward me like some wide-eyed, prehistoric owl and said, "Does who know what?" He left and returned with a box of cigars—dark wood, tessellated with blue tiles—and I watched as each man unsheathed one, even Baz, but I wasn't offered anything. They lit up and drank more coffee, more alcohol. With every passing moment, their voices lowered, words liquified, coterminous with one another and impossible to translate. I realized how much I'd relied on Niko to clarify things for me, but I didn't want to think about him or anyone I'd left down the hill, at least for one night. I took a cookie from the stack Baz brought out, a koulouri: a braided, buttery confection, orange and vanilla. Instantly, I wanted another but was too self-conscious to ask; I had to keep reminding myself that the pleasure of taste is transient, and I opted instead for another drink. The men eyed me, seemingly impressed by my ability to keep up—unlike my coworkers, who at dinner parties and fundraisers always coddled me with half pours of champagne—and in what seemed like no time, I became significantly drunker than everyone else, downplaying my lack of coordination, when I accidentally knocked my perfect little porcelain cup off the table, and almost cried of relief as it bounced back in the grass, unbroken.

All the men got up from the table and started gathering around, leaving behind their mess of food and plates. Konstantin made a fire a few feet from us; the smoke blew into my face. In the trees, I heard the goats' collective bleat. Dimitri stayed next to me as Baz left and turned some music on—Dari Dari, Dimitri called it, before he asked about the head. He said he wouldn't be surprised if a local was responsible. "People know bad things about each person but won't say a thing. There is Greek code, and then there is island code. Understand?"

I nodded, though I was finding it hard to keep my mind on what he was saying because I could have sworn I heard noises coming from the home—trashing, banging, either maniacal laughter or tears, but it was hard to tell over the music. Still, I worried about the little girl.

I glanced at the open kitchen door. "Everything all right in there?" I said. He didn't seem to hear, or if he did, he didn't understand, or didn't care.

"It is a mistake to think here is a paradise," Dimitri went on, "with all the beauty. You come out seeking a society of peace, you are to be woken up. Me, I think many holidayers die stupid. Jumping into shallow water. Drinking too much and drown. Motorbike accidents."

"Right," I said. "But I'm not a holidayer."

He shrugged. "You are American. You are holidayer. Means, you don't belong, you want something from our home. Experience, story, something else. This is no offense, but Americans," he said, "they take; they take, take. What do they give?" I crossed my legs and squeezed them together; sweat pooled under the back of my knee, made my skin itch. I couldn't tell if he was still talking about vacationers, or if he'd meant this as a personal dig, and then I got my answer.

"Do you like it?" he said. "This work?"

Perhaps I did agree with him. We were takers—I was a taker. I got paid to take. But not for nothing. And to believe otherwise would have been—well, what, exactly? A blight on my already fragile ego? Proof I was a person incapable of discerning right and wrong? So what, I thought then, stubbornly, righteously—drunkenly. I lived in pursuit of beauty, not integrity—they were different goals, each no less political, no less valuable, than the other.

"Do you like yours?" I said, careful to make sure my tone was serious, but not critical. Threads of smoke needled at my eyes, and they began to water. I held on to my smile, nonetheless.

"Driving people around, it is fine," Dimitri said. "I hear many things. Good ones, bad ones." He paused then, and I thought he might add something, but instead, he squinted over at the group of men and shook his head, then yelled in excitement. He got up and joined them, and for a moment, I expected them all to dance, to stomp their feet in merry bacchanalia with erect cigars suspended in their mouths and smoke befogging their faces, their hands connected by blue and white handkerchiefs. The scene like a Matisse, but instead of nude, androgynous bodies, a circle of overweight men with tufts of brown chest hair and wimpled foreheads.

They did no such thing. Instead, they merely stood, and smoked in silence, tapping their feet to the music, until one of the men—the drunkest of the lot—grabbed something from his back pocket, an antique pistol.

He swung it around and shot it in the air, rupturing the fixedness of the fading night sky.

Seeing the gun sobered me, and I excused myself to use the restroom. I wandered through the open door and straight into the kitchen, cluttered with empty honey jars, cigarette butts, amber bottles lined up on dusty sills. The alcohol shot to my head, and I felt intoxicated again, possibly more so than before. I padded into the living room, where the little girl sat on the floor. She noticed me right away, as though she'd been waiting. She waved, then resumed what she'd been doing: zooming a plastic fire truck around herself. On the other side of the room stood an off-brand Barbie. The little girl revved up the fire truck twice, three times, until she let it go and watched it ram into the doll. In slow motion, the doll fell over.

I went and grabbed it for her, and as I held it in my hands, I thought about this truncated terra-cotta figure we had at the museum from the fifth century BCE, kept in one of the back cases, about the same size as a fashion doll, but missing its arms and legs, ostensibly on purpose. Scholars failed to understand the oddness of the figure and presupposed she was a doll meant for play and that perhaps she came with different pairs of clothes to which the missing limbs were sewn, and in which the children would then dress her. Several male colleagues of mine thought the figure's arms and legs unnecessary and argued children were meant to swaddle her like an infant. It took me a long time to convince them this was not the case, not with her mature figure, full breasts, and wide hips. She was the original Barbie, I told them, as seriously as I could. Was it painful—or comforting—to know that young women had an aspirational ideal, even back then? I remember my colleagues laughing at the declaration until I brought in a fashion doll of my own, something I picked up from a drugstore. We laid both figures on a long table and compared the two. They stopped laughing after that.

After retrieving the felled toy, I sat next to the girl. She was wearing a dress embellished with strawberries, and it hung around her frame, gaps between skin and fabric, like the garment was afraid of contact. She was fragile up close. I might have miscalculated her age. I'd missed her absent front tooth, the eczema patches on her cheeks, her greasy and knotted hair. She squinted at me, and I handed her the doll.

"Hi," I said.

She took it, displeased.

In Greek, I said, "Age?"

She inhaled, her expression pinched. She said, "I eat bees."

I said, "What?"

"I eat bees."

"You eat honey?"

"No. Bees."

Perhaps I was mistranslating, but she kept saying it: *mélissa*. It was the same word written on the boxes where the hives lived outside. She seemed vexed by my confused reaction, and I considered she might have been messing with me—she must have known, must have heard the lore about her mother and the bees. Did she say this to other guests? To scare them off?

She stood and motioned for me to follow, then guided me into the kitchen, where she began going through the cupboards. Was she hungry? Should I bring her food? I tried asking her what she was looking for, but she was so determined, and I didn't want to break her concentration. I stood there in a stasis, my forehead, the back of my neck, growing warm. From a drawer, the girl procured a string of amber worry beads and handed them to me. I thanked her and didn't know what to do with them, so I set them on the counter. When they made a noise, she scowled at me, and I apologized. She then returned to her search, and as I waited, I counted all the dishes stacked and drowned in the kitchen's leaky-faucet sink. There were eleven. Finally, she found what she had been seeking.

It was a nursing bra. I could tell from the way it unhooked at the top of the cup. White, milk stained, and wireless. She put it on, struggling to secure it behind her back for so long that I wanted to assist, and I took a step forward to communicate this desire, but stopped myself.

When I was young, there were times I felt tended to; times when my mother—in clear, lucid moods—would curl up on the couch beside me and tickle the inside of my arms as we fell asleep together, the television painting our limp arms and legs an unnatural blue. Other times, I'd go months without the warmth of her, when she was so distracted caring for Margaret, she'd hardly blink in my direction. Once I stopped fitting into my childhood clothes, when everything I wore projected sex, her affection disappeared, and she seemed suspicious of me—like I'd been traded out for an imposter.

Little raindrops began hitting the windows as the girl finally secured the bra, then hurried back to the bedroom. From the corner, she procured another, dirtier doll, this one an infant.

"Your baby?" I asked her in Greek, trying to lessen the gap between us, find some common ground. The rain hit harder.

She held it back from me. "I eat bees," she said again, and looked me in the eye, daring me to challenge her. She pulled the flap of her bra down, and I averted my gaze; even though I knew she was wearing a dress under the garment, it still felt wrong to look. She pressed the baby to her chest, and I imagined the doll's lips puckered against pilled fabric as the little girl rocked back and forth in silence.

33

Beyond the kitchen window, I heard a shot, then another, followed by an eruption of cheers. Before I left to walk back outside, I glanced at the girl, envious of how natural it seemed, her devotion to care.

Night had fallen now. Konstantin bent over, loaded a chamber, then wobbled upright, closed one eye, and aimed the pistol at a tree in the orchard. Another man went after him. The bullet hit an orange still on the branch; pulpy bits burst like a brain.

Konstantin hobbled over to me and tried handing me the gun. I'd never held a gun before. He presented it like a gift, cradled in both palms. Rain dotted the black steel. He was grinning wildly and mumbling. I said no, I couldn't. Was I afraid to touch it, hold it? I supposed I'd never been so close to a gun before; I'd only ever seen bronze spears, and swords, but they were dull, stuck behind glass and whirring only with the past, a safe remove from actual violence.

I shook my head, no thank you. Konstantin shrugged, and Dimitri came up behind me and said, "You, cannabis?" His head rolled around like it was having a hard time staying on his neck. I took the joint and inhaled. The rain was causing the bandage on my palm to unravel, but Konstantin grabbed my unwounded hand and tried to dance with me, pulling me close and warbling, "Marry me," still waving the gun as we swayed. The air smelled like mud and oranges; I remembered Theo, and then forgot her as the Dari Dari thrummed inside my ears and Konstantin's heavy feet thundered the ground. My blood rewilded, ringing with adrenaline. I felt furred and bared and—finally, truly—unlike myself. He'd given me the gun and I'd taken it. Or someone had. I supposed the hand belonged to me. I supposed the oddness of the night had been a fortification and I'd been beseeched to hold something lethal. I supposed I was still drunk, but it seemed dishonest to place the blame there. Sometimes I did things without knowing why, but I hardly stopped to consider whether such behavior was worrisome; if anything, it always felt uniquely human: this desire to be someone else, as though one errant move could rewire my entire personality.

The rain fell harder; the sky aflame with water. I stared at the gun, turned and aimed toward the fruit trees and pressed. When it went off, it startled me, the sound reverberated in my right ear, and my heart rate shot up; the blowback hurt my shoulder. I shrugged it in circles, rubbed the sore spot. All the men behind me laughed, which motivated me to try again. I glanced at Konstantin, whose downward gaze struck me as complicitous. The rest of them began cheering me on, and at their collective encouragement, I couldn't help but smile. I possessed no physical talent: sports, cars, outdoor activities. I'd never had men root for me so blatantly, and I wondered what Henry would think if he could see me. Or William. Even Julian. I imagined them all swelling with pride as a father might, and I felt a zap of juvenile arrogance as I went again.

This time, I hit a tree—at least, that's what it sounded like: a rapid thunk, a branch falling. I turned around, expecting congratulations, but all the men went silent. I saw the little girl to my left, over by the kitchen door. She stood breathlessly, surveying the orchards before sprinting into them. Konstantin grabbed the gun from me, and I felt myself mouth, *What happened?* All I could hear was the girl running through the trees, faster, whooshing, and suddenly stopping. A cold dread ran from my head to my feet. The little girl screamed.

Baz rushed in after her. I tried to catch their silhouettes, but my senses were too alert, everything clouded together: the evening sky, the feel of rain hitting the top of my head, the echo of the gun's shot. Who had I hurt? Baz came out first, his slight arms holding onto a squirming figure.

It was so close to his chest; he was embracing it like you might a child. I didn't recall noticing another kid on the property. As Baz came closer, I still couldn't see the details; the rain had left everything foggy—and I couldn't tell if I was imagining the musky scent of blood. Was it my own? Was it from the meat I'd eaten earlier? I wanted to throw up, but I knew my body wouldn't afford me that kind of relief.

The little girl sank to her knees and began chanting a prayer. She looked back and glared at me, snot glistening on her upper lip, and I saw what it was then. A goat. Baz laid the animal on the ground. I stepped back. Its big eyes opened and closed slowly as it whimpered. A bullet had cleaved its ear, half of it hung off like a tassel, and the blood was plentiful, fountaining down the side of the goat's face, and it was all over Baz too, his neck, his chest.

I couldn't breathe. My tongue felt swollen and heavy, engulfing all the language I needed to apologize and demand someone to take me back down the hill, where I could buy a return ticket and go home—though home to what? My hands were shaking, and I was dizzy, and I wished I could will my drunkenness away or make it more extreme. "Move," someone said, and dumbly, I stayed still, until they repeated it, and then I watched the men carry the goat through the open kitchen door. I followed them through narrow halls as they stumbled into the bathroom and placed the goat in the tub, which was peach in color, and conjured a strong memory of the bathtub in my childhood home, even though I knew that tub was white, or light gray. The little girl blew past me and knelt by the lip and continued to pray. I thought of Margaret dunking her head underwater during bath time, her limbs effervescent, and her face shooting back up to spit at me through two front teeth, her eyes squeezed shut, a halo of bubbles around her, and then, I saw her in a different tub—a clawed one, with cracks at the bottom. Was that my mother's? I saw her in the community pool, a neighbor's pool. I saw her in the river. All the images reordered themselves on top of one another, sometimes canceling the other out so there was a hole where a recollection should have been. The problem with memory is not its duplicity. The problem with memory, I thought then, is that it doesn't have the guts to look you in the eye.

The little girl glowered back at me, but I stayed motionless, watching by the doorway. *Well, this is what you get*, her body language seemed to say, *for being a reckless interloper*. The men were too busy to care about my presence. They genuflected in front of the tub, sighed with calm breaths, their calloused hands gingerly washing the goat's ear. It stood with half-open eyes, struggling to stay upright as it produced these indescribable sounds—not exactly like a bleat or a cry, more like an attempt to clear its throat. Konstantin had a cigar still hanging in his mouth; every so often, Dimitri would smack the smoke away. The beekeeper was there, and I thought I saw a bee fly around his head, but when I blinked, I realized it was an aura, and I felt a flash of dizziness, of paralysis. I had nothing on me—no pills, no promise of comfort.

When the men finished washing the goat, they wrapped it in a towel, picked it up, stomped past me as though I were invisible, and returned to the yard. "I'm so sorry," I said after them, at least I think I said it, but no one acknowledged me; I couldn't tell if this was a good or bad sign. I didn't know what they would do with it next. They seemed to have stanched the bleeding. I wanted to go with them, but I felt too overwhelmed to be back outside again, subjecting myself to their attention, or nonattention—and then I heard the tapping of someone's foot.

It seemed like it was coming from the kitchen. I thought it might be the little girl, but it was not. It was Baz. He had headphones on, music full blast, and he was chewing gum, bovine-like, while playing a handheld video game, his thumbs bobbing up and down. I motioned for him to remove his headphones, which made me feel shamefully motherly, and then recited the Greek words for head, pain, and medicine—the panic heaving inside me, a starved predator. It took Baz a moment to understand, but when he did, he seemed pleased to help, leading me back to the bathroom, now empty, though still trailed with the goat's blood and a few errant hairs; he opened a drawer and took out a prescription bottle. I hesitated, but not for long. I took what he offered me, some oblong, yellow pill that looked vaguely familiar, and though I passively wondered if it was ADHD medication, I swallowed nevertheless. I asked Baz if the goat would be all right. He furrowed his brows and nodded. The bathroom smelled of blood and dirt, and artificial cleanness. He said, "Goat. Fine."

I said, "I feel horrible," in English, then, "I am bad," in Greek because I didn't know how to say, *I did a bad thing.*

He frowned and repeated himself earnestly, though this time forlorn— "*Goat, fine*"—and I felt as though he was leaning toward me, could sense the anticipatory heat of his hand on my shoulder. I backed away.

He sat on the closed toilet seat, and I settled on the edge of the tub, which was still a little wet and sprinkled with mud and grass, but I didn't care. I wondered if Baz could sense my inebriation, if I looked flushed and disheveled. Was he drunk too? I straightened my posture, and opened my eyes wider, hopeful it would convince him that I was in the right state of mind. Almost immediately, the pose fatigued me and I relaxed. We had nothing to say to each other. The music began again outside, but inside the bathroom we were both so silent, I almost forgot I could speak. What a luxury was our divide. Perhaps this was the companionship for which I'd always been searching: someone so incapable of understanding me that I held no false aspirations about what kind of conversations we would—or would not—have. In many ways, he was the ideal audience for secrets. I couldn't hold any reactions against him. I couldn't become disappointed.

"I want to tell you something," I said in English. Then tried rephrasing the words in Greek, my speech a little slurred.

He nodded. "Goat. Fine."

I said it wasn't about the goat, and then I apologized again for almost killing it—or maybe I had killed it; maybe it would die by the end of the night. He observed me blankly; boredom rushed over his face. I feared he would get up and leave. So I said, "Wait. Just listen." And I told him what I'd done.

34

When Margaret and I went to the river that day, it was in the hundreds. Henry thought AC was a waste of money, even though we had enough money to waste. I watched him gift my mother a tennis bracelet that year: 1978. I see now that it wasn't about financial security, it was about control. I see now that for some families, these are the same thing.

During those sweltering days, I would wet washcloths with cold water and lay them over Margaret's face, the moisture evaporating within minutes. Her cheeks bright, temples and nose beaded with sweat. She was seven then; I was fourteen. Our mother and Henry hadn't been speaking to each other for days, but every so often, we'd hear their bed frame bang against the walls, after which, my mother would emerge from the room and make coffee in a robe, vacant and disposed. Was this what true love looked like? There was nothing for Margaret and me to do but overheat and wallow. We'd run out of games. No one had been to the grocery store in days because my mother was on the Sleeping Beauty Diet, which involved taking sleeping pills to avoid meals. There was an infestation of ants in the cupboard—I'd pulled out a cereal box and watched them crawl from the top corner up to my elbow before flinching. These elements are not meant to incite sympathy, but they are vital to me, and I cling to them nonetheless. They are the ébauche. The underpainting. The first layer put down on the canvas in order for colors to adhere properly. If this layer is not done correctly—too rich, too thick, for instance—the final product will crack.

I don't regret leaving home that evening. Anyone would have gone. The sky was clear, and the neighborhoods smelled like barbecue and citronella. We tried the community pool first—coasting on bikes, a veil of waning sunshine cascading over our backs. When we got to the pool, the gates were closed. We could have gone home then. Instead, we hopped over a stranger's fence, ludic and desperate, and lay waiting for the sprinklers to start. They never did. We moved on to someone else's yard, slipped into a kidney-shaped pool, artificial green lights glowed at the bottom, but a man came out and yelled at us to leave. We could have gone home then too. But we biked to the river. It was dusk by then, still triple digits. Margaret had a trail of mosquito bites growing down her calf, welts the size of limes around her ankles, where her skin met her Mary Jane shoes, her feet pedaling into a blur.

I remember thinking those were the wrong shoes, worrying they'd give her a blister. Before we left, she hadn't been able to find her bathing suit, so I let her borrow one of mine. The top was distractingly large; the cups gaped open, barely covering Margaret's small frame. I watched her in the hallway mirror between our rooms, feeling like I wanted to trap her there, not because I wanted to prolong her youth but because I wanted to prolong mine. Her hair had been baby soft, long and easily tangled at the ends. I almost made her change but stopped myself. I didn't want her to be embarrassed. Would she have been? It's complicated to lose a person who barely feels like one in the first place. In my evocation, what does she become but a godded remnant? An empty signifier of my own neuroses? I couldn't even conjure her voice, remember if she called me Sissy, Sister, if she called me by name. When I think about that time, I paint black over the parts I don't want. In those last few months, she'd become increasingly dangerous to herself. Threatening to open car doors when in motion. Holding herself underwater at the community pool, testing to see how long she could last, or else trying to get the lifeguard's attention—a boy, fourteen, dark lashed—and that night at the river, I must have thought she'd been doing the same.

I must have thought it was a cruel joke.

A performance.

She could be cruel.

I don't know.

Time has not benefited my understanding. There are gaps. I'm afraid of all the things I've let them hold. I'm afraid the picture is a chiaroscuro of all shadow and no light. Margaret withering under Henry's touch, becoming less of herself every time he hugs her a little too long, every time he prods her, tickles her, every time a cry of laughter turns into real woe. Every time I witness him treat her as a possession and don't say a word— because what words do I have, really, in the face of his? *You didn't see. You thought* you saw. For years I notice things I don't want to. For years I am a container, but not a confidant. For years, I am gone.

And somehow, still, we make it to the river. We make it to the river and then she does not come up for air. We make it to the river, and then she jumps in, and in the meantime, I do all sorts of things, whatever my cruelty can imagine. I play chess, file my nails, grind my teeth to the jaw-bone. We make it to the river and then? Do I call her name when I can't hear her? How long does it take me to notice the silence? Is the air calm? Does the sky disappear into the water? Or can I see a horizontal hem, a differentiation, keeping me company, clear as the line in my palm?

When I retold the events to the police, to my mother, to Henry, I recalled diving into the river to find her, crawling out of the water, then diving back in, crawling out, diving in, trying again and again—but later, I grew suspicious of these recollections. I must have convinced myself of them, down to the sensory details: the feeling of my feet slipping on algae-covered rocks, the sound of desperate splashing against my ears. In the years that followed, such details returned to me, and my mind latched onto them, desperate to mistake specificity for truth. In reality, I probably made no such heroic gesture. Not in my altered, blank-faced state, ruled by—what? Primal shock? However you want to spin it, know I've spun it a thousand ways before, attached to it every kind of thought, anything to make the act feel less reprehensible, feel like a mistake any-one could have made. Truthfully, I did what I'd always done. I looked the other way. I left.

I left our bikes behind and began walking out onto the path, then the highway; then I walked into a neighborhood, directionless. I'd still been in my bathing suit and the frayed denim shorts my mother forbade me from wearing out of the house. My breasts felt heavy and full of water, pulling me forward and down. The night hummed. I'd been out there for ten minutes, twenty, sixty. I'd lost track, but at some point, a car had pulled alongside me—a white sedan, low to the ground, shiny and expensive looking. The first sign of life I had seen or noticed. The driver rolled down his window and asked if I needed a ride.

My feet were tired from the walking. Had I been wearing shoes? I didn't know where to go. I wanted to be home and not home. I wanted to be nowhere; a stranger's car felt like the closest thing. He opened the front door, and I catalogued the specifics of him: a man in his twenties, shiny blond hair flipped below his ears, a simple white T-shirt and jeans. A frayed, tan leather jacket, stitched with teal thread, laid out like a corpse on his backseat. His eyes were cool gray, or blue, or neither; the color didn't matter, what mattered was how they latched onto mine, what mattered was how I couldn't bear to let them go.

"You coming?" said the man. There was no air in his voice. And so, I got in.

"Where are you headed?" He gave me a good up-and-down and, in doing so, swerved the car. I didn't know what to do with my hands, so I placed them on my thighs and looked out the side-view mirror, watching the houses become smaller and unrealistic as the missing sun washed everything dark in its absence. I told him the name of my street and pushed a canvas duffel bag out from under my feet; I wondered what was in it, where he was going, what his life was like, what he was doing here, and I thought maybe he was a college student, maybe a teacher, maybe he'd been in the war, shot another soldier in the head, maybe he knew everything I didn't. He asked how old I was and when I said fourteen he said I looked at least seventeen and then I felt found out, like I'd been lying about it, even though I hadn't. He turned up his talk radio. A woman called into some talk show to discuss the death penalty. I couldn't say if the woman was for or against it, but I could say how she sounded: fluttery—and almost, happy.

When we arrived, I lingered, and the man turned down the radio. "You don't want to go in yet, do you?" he said. I shook my head. I wanted him to beg me to stay, but he handed me a cigarette instead, the first I'd ever been offered. "I don't smoke," I said. "Take it," he said, so I did. I put the cigarette between my lips and leaned over for a light before I fumbled and accidentally dropped it between the console and seat. My distress must have been evident. He told me not to worry; he had plenty more. He smiled, and the nanoscopic gap between his two front teeth vibrated with the promise of an innocent future, and when he opened his mouth and laughed, I thought it might swallow me, and I thought I might have loved him.

He asked why I'd been down by the river all alone, and for the first time since getting in his car, I let myself remember my sister, and I saw spots and my hands vibrated, and I pressed my palms into my eye sockets and leaned over, my head between my knees, and I could not find my bearings as he said, "Whoa, hey now, you can't puke in here." My temples throbbed, the physical ache an almost pleasant respite. Was it the first migraine I recall having? Perhaps of such magnitude. Perhaps not. Pain has a way of erasing every beginning, every ending. Of making time into a loop.

The man grazed the top of my back and rubbed in slow-motion circles, almost unthinkingly. It was the kind of velvet care I'd always craved. The kind without expectation. Without motive. Or so it felt to me then. But what could I have known? My desire to stay with this stranger, to fall asleep in his car, in that soft leather seat, or in his lap, and wake inside a different world, one where Margaret was alive and inside the home, was so all-encompassing I could not see beyond its fantasy. But, at some point, he pulled his hand away, and told me, apologetically, that he had to go. Before I knew it, he was leaning over and opening the door, and I was peeling my wet thighs from his split leather seat and falling out, tripping over my own foot. I said goodbye, my tone meek and almost unkind, as I waited for him to say goodbye in return, my self-consciousness momentarily eclipsed by an adolescent eagerness for validation, an eagerness that might have explained why I stayed on the sidewalk and watched his eyes on me, trying to see what he saw as he

put the car in reverse, and instead of flipping around, kept moving backward, his face still forward, staring at me like he'd known how vile I was,
every bad thing I'd ever done, and that it was fine with him, perhaps,
even preferred, his large hand gripping the top of the passenger seat, the
strength of that hand incomprehensible as his image bruised into the
shadows, then night, as light hair turned dark, and the sound of his talk
radio momentarily trembled out the open window, and then, in a snap,
like a scream, cut off completely.

35

Baz stayed nearly motionless the whole time I spoke, only interrupting once to mutter—"Mary Jane?"—in either recognition or confusion. And even though I'd expected such a nonreaction, when the reality of what I'd said hit me, I was so discomforted that I remained, for an excruciating minute, on the precipice of laughing.

I'd never spoken so plainly about Margaret's death before, not even to Julian, whose watered-down version left out unseemly particulars and who had once, while drunk, told me he found Picasso's *The Weeping Woman* gauche—though for the record, I agreed.

I slipped off the lip of the tub, my back now against the porcelain, my bottom half on a damp, hand-woven mat. I pulled myself into a ball. I felt flayed open. I felt Baz could see my organs, and I wondered if they glistened. I swallowed audibly, remorseful that I'd forced him against his will to listen to me because I was an adult and he was a child, and typically children did what adults asked of them. He looked like he was afraid to move. Perhaps the sheer amount of force with which I spoke had startled him. He was probably concerned I would break into tears. I held back the urge to apologize, thinking it would confuse him further.

"You have goat blood on your neck," I said, to say something, because no longer could I handle the silence I'd earlier thought I wanted, and because it was true: he did, and it was all over.

I searched for a towel, and though the one I procured crunched under my fingertips, it would have to do. I stood and turned on the faucet and then ran the rag under the water and handed it to him. He stayed seated and tried to wipe the mess off, but kept missing the opaquest spots, then glanced at me for confirmation he'd done a good job. I reached for the towel to help but stopped myself. To touch Baz in any capacity felt immediately wrong. What might it look like if someone came in and saw us? At this point, the shirt Dimitri had wrapped around my palm had fallen apart. Baz picked up my hand, held it in his, crossing this threshold for us, and looked at it, and then at me with wide, supplicating eyes.

He said, "Sorry," in English, and I knew he was apologizing for the scrapes and not for my dead sister sob story, and though it was undoubtedly no absolution to my confession, it was, at least, an acknowledgment of pain.

"Bike accident," I said. I took the towel from him. "May I?" I said, my eyes watering, my mouth dry.

"Yes." He nodded.

I told him to get up and he stood with his back toward me, facing the tiny, foggy mirror above the sink. I hadn't realized our height difference until then. I was a head taller than him. I wiped the nape of his neck, where his hair was shaved down to a buzz, and shimmered every time he moved under the fluorescent light. I got into a rhythm, washing the towel, wringing it out, locating more parts of his neck to clean, before moving on to his head. Whenever I filled the towel with water, I sensed he was looking at me in the mirror, but I didn't have the heart to check, or else I didn't want to see myself from his vantage point. When I wiped over his carotid artery, I could feel his pulse.

Once he was clean, my mind cleared, and I felt if not better, certainly not worse. I asked Baz if I could lie down somewhere. He bobbed his head in excitement and I worried I'd phrased my question wrong.

I didn't want to stay the night, but all the men were too drunk to take me back down the hill safely. I'd been stupid not to think this through. Baz led me to the farthest bedroom, which had two sleeping areas, a twin bed with a wooden frame and a mattress on the floor, hardwood warped with water damage. The walls were plain white, but the ceiling had several parallel oak rafters. On one wall, there was a painting, no bigger than a six by six. I stepped closer, my face inches from it—from the texture, I could see it was encaustic, meaning, made with beeswax. It was an image of a nun. The background was the color of sand, which added depth to the nun's black habit, the stark contrast of colors—shadows on the right side of her face. A lightness touched her left eye, the pupil leaned slightly toward her nose, giving her gaze an unfocused appearance. She seemed to be looking at something beyond the spectator. The encaustic technique originated in fifth century BCE Greece but was used heavily in Egypt. When a person passed away, they were mummified, and encaustic portraits were placed over their faces—they were supposed to last forever—held in place by wrapped linen. I wondered who this nun was to the family, if she was anyone at all. I had a strong sense she was painted by a female artist—the paint strokes were delicate, devoid of vanity: an honest longing in her expression, a drooping on the sides of her mouth, a chin unflattering in its length. I assumed she was dead. If only all dead women could be remembered with such clarity—such lack of abstraction. I asked Baz about her, but he dismissed the question and threw a heavy, floral-patterned blanket at me; it smelled musky, and worst of all, unfamiliar. Once more, I asked about the goat. This time, his expression changed, a drop in temperature. "I'm sorry," I said. "No worry," he said back.

I lay down, the springs squeaking below me. The blanket was itchy and cold but molded to my skin like chain mail. Elsewhere, Baz began closing the door, which was scratched at the bottom, an animal's or human's tracks? Their presence concerned me, but I told myself I was being paranoid. "Wait," I yelled out. "The lights?" He reached his hand back in and flipped the switch. I squeezed my eyes shut. Outside, the men laughed in loops as though on a track. I felt almost entirely sober. I wondered if Baz had given me something useless like allergy medication. I started to panic, thinking about how long it might take me to fall asleep, how long I'd have to lie here with my thoughts.

Years after the night of Margaret's death, while I was out to dinner with an old love interest in Berkeley and during my last semester of undergraduate school, I saw the man who gave me a ride home. I couldn't believe it but convinced myself it was possible—Berkeley was a few hours' drive from Sacramento. I was sure it was him; I would have recognized his jacket anywhere: that fringe, and teal thread, and the scent of him: wet wood and leather. His fathomless gaze. The restaurant was one of those small establishments where patrons sit elbow to elbow. My date stopped mid-bite, looked over at the man, and then back at me, his mouth barely open as he whispered, seemingly titillated, "That gentleman can't keep his eyes off you." I kept finding myself in the company of men who paid too much attention to how others looked at me, the kind who calibrated their own worth through what they falsely believed was mine. If only they could have seen it—that gulf between how they valued me, and how I valued myself. Big enough to swallow us both.

I told my date to meet me in the men's bathroom, and though I could see he was confused by the vagaries of my mood, how it might change from quiet to carnal at the drop of nothing, he and I had sex halfheartedly in the stall. It smelled like bleach, and he called me a whore, and I resented the fact that I had no equivalent degradation for him as he made me come. My date left first, and I went after him, slinking through the tiny restaurant, slatternly and buoyant, a particular emptiness only accomplishable through sexual debasement in a tiny restaurant bathroom. As other restaurant goers eyed me, I focused on walking in a straight line and tried to make peace with my choices. We do not get redemption. Instead, we get small chances to forget our mistakes via a series of euphoric muscle contractions, and though sometimes they are worth the psychological torture, other times, they are not.

When I sat down, the man was gone, but his coat was still there, and as I swirled a glop of lukewarm mashed potatoes around on my plate, I kept waiting for him to come back and recognize me. My date didn't notice my distraction; despite the post-coital clarity men allegedly feel, he was a classic navel gazer, an archaeologist interested in chiding me about my potential trajectories. I'd been considering curation—I liked the control—but he said it was the wrong line of work for me. It was too cutthroat. "You should take some time to think about it," he said between bites. I went along with his imperious tirade, ordering the most decadent dessert, then pretending to have an allergy to it, ordering some pretentious digestif, then coffee, waiting and waiting for the man to come back. At every opportunity, I allowed my eyes to find his coat and imagined all the things he might say to me if he returned. He never did. I had a hard time keeping the coffee down; it tasted earthy and organic, like it'd been filtered with river water.

Since it happened, I hadn't planned on telling anyone about the man, how often I'd daydreamed of our slim interaction. I knew it meant nothing to him, a single chance encounter. He'd probably had so many of those. He'd probably carried on exactly as before: intact. But for all the times I tried to fade him from my history, I couldn't. He'd remained with me, or else I remained with him. I liked to think some part of me never got out of his car, never tried to puke in Henry's beloved hydrangea bushes, never walked through the front door to tell my mother what happened, never experienced the deafening yearlong shriek of her grief, never knew Margaret's borrowed bathing suit got caught on a branch underwater and caused her drowning, never blamed myself or started taking Tofranil, or Valium, or Sansert, or Dexedrine, or moved to Berkeley, or Los Angeles, or received several degrees, never became afraid of listlessness or regarded each small failure as one big death, or married the first man who looked me in the eyes while he fucked me, or tried to make a home with him, tried to find safety within us, or failed to find that safety, or flew to Greece. A part of me remained in that front seat, warmed by the summer air trembling through rolled-down windows, inhaling a strange man's scent, watching his golden hair billow with the bumps of the road, pressing my knees together until my bones began to throb. I'm still hoping he'll turn the car around and take me somewhere else.

36

Waking inside someone else's home was a shock, but only a momentary one. Baz was snoring, curled up on the floor mattress, his shoulders cloaked in a white sheet like a chlamys, as the little girl slept silently, facing away from him, covers kicked off, dirty soles exposed. That I'd been given the only bed filled me with a nauseating self-reproach, and then I remembered the events leading to sleep, though I'd have been happy to forget about the ear I shot off, and all the unloading I'd done on Baz. At least, I wasn't hungover, not yet. Perhaps I was still drunk. Either way, the pills had put me in a dreamless, deep slumber, and I felt different, not necessarily better, but different, like something in me had loosened.

Dimitri waited in the kitchen with an extra cup of lukewarm coffee, which I drank in a few gulps, despite its acridity. He sipped and read the paper until he was finished with both, and then we drove back down the hill. As we descended, the warmth and gasoline smell of his cab wombed me, and I didn't wake again until we'd reached the bottom, until I heard the noise of a small but voluble crowd. There were roughly twenty people gathering toward the center of town. I slunk farther into my seat, trying to hide my face. Dimitri shook his head. He rolled down the window, and I asked him to roll it back up, but he wouldn't.

"Maybe they get off asses and work," he said.

Had the movement from Athens reached the island? Or was it something else? I tried to read some of their signs, but I was nervous of making eye contact.

"What are they saying?"

He shrugged. "What are they always saying. Something is not fair."

At one point, the crowd crossed the busiest road on the island and blocked traffic. We were only a few blocks from the rental, and I thought about getting out and running back. Cars honked; drivers yelled in frustration. We waited for five minutes, until a few cops on motorcycles came by with plastic shields and dispersed them. It was a spectacle, but then, as though nothing happened, everyone moved on. I felt the alcohol from last night, thick in my stomach.

Dimitri pulled up to my rental, accidentally parking on top of a curb, the jolt of which caused me to almost vomit. Before I got out, I looked once more at the pendant; I'd left it on the seat beside me. I felt a sense of aching for it, for the woman etched into its metal, for the woman by whom it'd been created. I traced my finger around its edge; it was bulky, clotted with sentimentality. I pushed it away.

Dimitri popped the trunk and set the bike on the ground, its front tire still flat. I thanked him. He said, "You, be OK?" I nodded. "The money," I said. He let out an almost violent sigh. By me, he seemed exhausted. "No, no, no money," he said. For a moment, I thought we might hug each other, but then the moment passed, and he was already gone, getting back into the cab.

I hauled the bike up to my room, heaving and trying not to pass out, hopeful I wouldn't run into anyone—until I heard the soft clatter of sandaled feet. A middle-aged woman turned the corner and hurried down. I worried she'd see the bike and wonder where I'd gotten it—I imagined she knew one of those boys from the alley—but she didn't register my existence. Was it odd that I'd not seen anyone else but Baz at the rental? I watched her saunter down the stairs, her hands gripping the banister. I supposed the woman was Baz's mother—she was dressed in a blue polo. I'd noticed similar shirts hung up in the closet behind the front desk. I wondered what kind of mother she was. If she was outspoken or quiet. If she had taste. If she'd ever been redeemed.

There was a small note taped to the door, the edges peeling up with the wind: *Where did you go?* The handwriting was atrocious, chaotic and almost unreadable, but I assumed it was from Theo. I was too afraid to assume it was from anyone else.

37

When I got inside, I propped the bike against the wall. I didn't bother to shower or do anything else. My ears rang, and my entire body felt overcooked, veiled in a sudden, conspiratorial sweat. Once I fell into bed, it rained off and on, the inside of the rental aswarm with a chthonic humidity. Someone kept calling—Theo or Niko, I presumed, as international calls were still not working in my room—but I never rang back. I couldn't sleep. I thought often of the statue, the trickling fountain water, the empty bag, whipping in the wind.

In the afternoon, I woke to one of the worst migraines I'd had in a long time. I draped a cold cloth over my eyes and took two of the six pills I had left to fall asleep again. I woke every few hours. During the evening, when I opened my eyes, the corners of my vision went black. I blinked a few times, then ran and turned on the light, feeling my way through the rental, clutching onto the walls. I made my way into the bathroom and lay down on the cool floor, closed my lids, and counted to a hundred. When I opened them, I could see fine again.

Eventually, I got up. As I idled around, made coffee, I became irritated by the bike's presence, so I moved it out onto the terrace, where it barely fit, and covered it with my bed's top sheet. After that, whenever I caught sight of it, the amorphous shape spooked me. Why did it look so much like a tall body, crouched on all fours? I closed the curtains and returned to the photos of the statue. Though I couldn't see her well in the dark, I didn't feel like turning on the lights. I feared what she might have told me. Like how I had no business being here any longer.

I still wasn't sure what William and Madison had discussed the day before in the phone booth. If Madison had been given the position, I couldn't stay and work under him. It would be a constant reminder of my failure. But where else would I go? I assumed William would give me a decent letter of recommendation—if I begged, demeaned myself enough—but these positions were hard to come by, the turnover rate low. I hardly imagined I'd be able to get lucky like I had the first time, and I could not move backward, compete with people right out of graduate school, hungrier and smarter, and more equipped than I was.

It had been over thirty-six hours since I'd checked in with William. Even during my period of blindness, I called the office every other day to stay informed. What I would find in my email, I didn't want to know, but at the same time, I could no longer wait. I took the bike off the terrace and hauled it back down the stairs.

Mostly, the streets were empty and the air, muggy. A few men tried to get me to stop and eat souvlaki at their tucked-in restaurants, where spooled slabs of lamb swirled and dripped oil, but I politely declined. The smell of grilled meat made me sick, invoked the goat's mangled ear, or else some other animal, destroyed and skinless and hanging from a hook in gory, endmost nudity.

I searched several alleyways before finding the one where I'd seen the group of boys. I tied the bike to a large potted olive tree and wrote an apology note, folded it, and tucked five euros inside—it was the best I could do—and then, I left.

When I walked inside the internet café, the AC rumbled in the corner, but barely let out air. It smelled stagnant inside, the scent of a stale refrigerator. A young woman sat behind the front desk reading a magazine, bare feet propped on a stool. When she saw me, she stopped reading and used the magazine to fan her chest. I sat down in a cracked plastic chair, took a deep breath, and opened my email.

From the number of messages I had, it was clear I wasn't fired—though I was still unsure if the promotion was mine or not.

Per William, I learned that the statue's headless body lay in purgatory, still at the museum, still belonging to Alec. Once the police got involved that day of the mutilation, the Greek government had been tipped off, and they'd begun to put up a fight. They were threatening lawful retribution, claiming the statue had not been found in international waters, but had been stolen from a drug-looting ring on the southern coast, along with various other objects. That we knew of, they had no proof. Of course, we had none either—no paperwork that solidified patriation, at least not yet, but, according to William, if precedent was any indication, we still had a good chance, and perhaps this was the piece of information that startled me the most: somewhere between then and now, William had decided he still wanted the statue. Which meant that there might still be a chance for me, after all. I allowed myself to imagine it, the new Hellenistic space, opening night: a party with all the most important guests: collectors, the press, celebrities. William and I standing outside the exhibit, a bright red ribbon strung between two plinths. Seventy-eight degrees with a cool breeze, the air full of smog, but lovely in that post-apocalyptic LA way. William introducing me, rattling off my successes. *It is my pleasure to present the new antiquities curator, Doctor Elizabeth Clarke.* At the thought, I felt not happiness, but the idea of happiness. I wondered if that was enough.

Elsewhere, on a different email chain, was a message from our head lawyer, a stringent man with thick-framed glasses.

It would be reckless for you to purchase this piece right now, with every-thing going on. Lay low. We are not asking.

And one from our PR team:

We need to remain on the right side of history regarding public discourse. The issue is too hot. Too hot!!

According to the PR email, the Athenian protestors had gotten word of our vandalized statue, and they'd begun citing us as one example of how acquisitions actively destroy objects of cultural significance. They'd talked to a few small outlets about us—I wondered if I'd been named—but according to the PR team, it was only a matter of time before the story got picked up. I could picture William smiling at this news. William loved it when things were too hot. No such thing as bad press, he would say. There was a time when he might have been right. When I would have sat there in silence and nodded alongside him. But I couldn't imagine that version of me now, her face a blank wall. Had she really believed in William's leadership? Or had she been too blinded by who he was, by the validation she thought he could give her? I remembered the protestors from that morning, the ones I'd seen on the street. I opened another tab and searched but then retracted. I was too daunted by the possibilities.

I went back to my email and read another one. From Julian. *Call me*, it said. *Haven't heard from you in a while . . . need to discuss logistics.*

As I was about to sign off, I noticed one last email. It was from Theo. I'd never seen her email address before. I wondered how she'd gotten mine. The subject was blank, and in the message, she wrote a time and place in which to meet her. Some cove. Tomorrow. *I'd rather tell you this in person.*

The woman behind the counter laughed an infernal, vapid laugh. I glared back at her, wondering what could possibly be so funny, but she kept her head down, eyes focused on her magazine.

When I returned to the computer, colors infiltrated the screen, zigzags, and floaters, and then the monitor went dark. I hit the side, first delicately, then with increasing anger. For how long this went on, I could not say. I must have blacked out my escalating emotions. The last thing I remember is watching my face contort into frustration, feeling heat build in my ears, and then turning around and seeing the woman with the magazine still in her hand, staring, mouth open and asking me—painstakingly calmly—to please exit.

38

I walked down toward the water and found a phone booth. Outside, it had quieted further. Except for one car parked a few yards from the booth on the other side of the road, I was all alone. The Mediterranean splashed against the seawall, slow and lethargic, like a sleeping breath. It would be almost midnight in LA. Hot still. The air dull and windless. I dialed home. On the other end of the phone, a woman's voice crackled.

"Who is this?" it said.

I heard a shuffle, some muffled conversation.

"Who is this?" I said.

"One sec." She sounded young. Younger than me. When he got on, it was the first question I asked.

"She's sixteen."

"What the fuck, Julian?"

He laughed. "It's Clara. My niece?"

I was stunned. Last I recalled, Clara was a child.

"Where are you?" he asked.

I heard him rummaging around some boxes, the screeching of packing tape, the sound nausea-inducing. I pictured him in our deserted house, old newspapers strewn about. I imagined the place still smelled more like him than me. I'd never felt like much of a presence. Most of the furniture belonged to him in college. I was too noncommittal to buy anything of value. I had a few pieces of art—primarily gifts, or virtuous thrift store finds, some first editions of books. The rest, I didn't care much about.

"Greece."

"Still?"

"Yes," I said firmly. He asked why I called. I said, "You emailed me?"

"That's right," he said. He sounded kind, amiable.

I wanted to tell him everything that had happened, about the statue, the head, but I couldn't bring myself to say the words. To risk pressing on that bruise.

"So, how is it?"

He ripped another piece of tape: I felt as though I could smell it, the chemical adhesive.

"I met someone," I said. "Two people."

He laughed. "Two people? I guess you always had a hard time making up your mind."

I wanted to say that he was wrong, that I'd made up my mind on him, and had chosen my career—but it seemed such a dreary, antiquated sentiment, that I'd had to make a choice at all.

"I'm messing with you," I said. "It's nothing. They're married. They're young."

"How young?"

"Not as young as Clara."

"Sounds messy," he said, a hint of judgment in his voice.

"You don't understand the logistics."

"I can't tell if you're being honest," he said.

I changed the subject and asked him how packing was coming along. He said he was nearly done and almost all the way out. He had just the garage left. I thought of the snake I'd killed in there, the way its body still wiggled—just for a second—after its beheading.

He said, "So, did you get the email from our realtor?" and I told him I hadn't.

He relayed that at least one party was interested before he asked if I'd figured out where I would live next. I said he didn't need to worry about me, and thankfully, he accepted this and moved on. He wanted to know if he could take the original Volanakis painting Madison had given me.

Though he didn't use those words—he didn't know Madison had given it to me. This was before the two of us had slept together. We'd gone to an auction where Madison had procured two original Volanakis works. The painting he gave me was tiny—twelve by sixteen inches—and after I fucked Madison, I did something even more despicable, even for me. I gave the painting to Julian as a present. He never knew its original source. When he opened it, he almost cried. He said it reminded him of the beaches he'd been to as a child, which surprised me. The scene was stormy and melancholic, the tones emerald green and deep blue. I figured Julian would have visited beaches with bright water and white sand, but I never paid attention to the stories he told about his youth. They'd always felt too unreal to me; too fantastical.

"Of course you're taking that," I said. "It was a gift."

"Thank you," he said, sounding a little disappointed, almost as though he'd wanted me to fight for it back.

"Anyway," he said. "I forgive you."

I didn't know to what he was referring—it could have been a myriad of things.

"For what?" I asked, trying to sound casual.

"I believe you took my favorite pen."

I hadn't remembered taking anything of his. It was hard to recall a time when I cared about something so trivial as a pen.

"Do you know which one I'm talking about?"

"Sure," I said.

"Liar."

I paused and lowered my voice. "Right. Sorry, I don't. I can't remember," I said. "I've been feeling a bit—distracted."

"Are you all right?" he said, but I could feel he didn't really mean it, wasn't really asking.

"I'm not sure where to go from here."

"From where?" he said. "Did you get the statue?"

"Not exactly."

"Well, there'll be another."

I wanted to snap at him. There wouldn't be another. Not like this one. How did he not know that?

"My boss sent someone to come and check on me. Why would he send me all the way out here, if he didn't believe I could do it?"

Julian's voice dropped. "He gets off on seeing people squirm."

"You don't know him," I said, suddenly defensive.

Silence.

"Fuck, sorry, I—someone's knocking on my door," I said. "I should go."

"Sounds like you're outside," he said.

"The windows are open."

I paused for him to say, *Wait, don't.* I paused for him to say, *Please, stay,* even though I didn't want to stay, and he knew that too. I realized then that I'd always wanted him to need me, but I'd never been equipped to handle the reality of his needs. Or maybe I'd known this before. It was becoming hard to tell. I would apologize for my part in our downfall, take accountability, be honest, but not then. Later. When I could make it good, when I could mean it.

"Give Clara my best," I said, as though I'd ever known more than two things about Clara: one, that a plastic surgeon pierced her ears when she was still an infant, which seemed obscene on various levels, but I never said that to Julian because he was so sensitive, so protective about his family, and two, that his protectiveness of her had, at one point, filled me with a shameful, seething jealousy. Though I supposed the latter piece of information was more about me, than it was about Clara. Now I wondered if Julian had ever thought of me as family, if our mistake was not taking sex out of the question entirely. Perhaps, if we had, he might have loved me wholly, purely, like he loved his niece, like he might have loved a daughter.

In the second before he let me go, I heard Clara mumble in the background, and then I heard something shatter.

39

The next day, the rain left and, in its place, came a heat wave. I tried to sleep with the window open, but by morning time, it felt like my whole rental had filled with flies and the hot panic of reality set in, the sun beating through my window, shopkeepers filling their baskets with fruit and yelling at one another. I watched the insects make a home in my space, land on the weeping edges of my pillow. I tried not to think about where they'd come from—hot garbage, fresh manure, a dead body—but every time I heard the buzz of their wings, the thoughts cycled through me. When I finally had enough, I left.

The cove wasn't far from my rental. I must have streamed by it a hundred times without noticing. To find the shore, you had to pass a row of outdoor restrooms, and a café walled in by a white gate, the establishment currently closed and dark, chairs upside down on tables, dim blocks of refrigerated drinks. Mini palms and olive trees lined the entire cove, their shadows stretched onto the land. From the water extended a rocky headline populated with red and yellow sea poppies. In the distance, you could see another island, and beyond that, a volcano.

It was Amara I saw first, lying on a white lounge chair made of closely knit mesh, rusted metal legs halfway absorbed into the sand. An orange-striped umbrella shaded her face and an open book balanced on her navel, the pages flitting up, down. Amara was not moving at all. She looked serene. She looked serene and I could not imagine how.

Elsewhere, everything seemed too alive: the trees teemed with birds, the shrubs popped with cicadas, water fizzing against the shore. A man in a lavender-colored Speedo paced back and forth on the sand. A small child's head bobbed in the clear water. Amara glanced up at me.

"Can I help you?" she said.

I told her I was looking for Theo.

"Have we met?" she said.

"At dinner."

"That's right," she said, but her expressionless eyes betrayed her claim of recognition. She might have been drunk. Or happy, balmy in her black one-piece, the top strap wrapped around her chest instead of neck. She wore a straw hat with holes. I had on a linen, sleeveless dress I'd purchased at a kiosk; it was knee-length and delicate, but it covered me.

"Are you going to swim?" she asked.

I told her I didn't swim.

"On principle?"

"You could say."

I glanced around.

"I think she's out there," Amara said. "Somewhere in the water." She put on a pair of tortoiseshell sunglasses. "She's been," she said, then stopped and thought for a moment. "She had a few too many."

"Did something happen?"

Amara shrugged. "Something is always happening. But I can't stand these beaches like she can. Tourists, tourists, all the secrets are out, and nothing will ever be what it used to be. How is the uh—what is it again you have come here to take? Don't mind me; I'm just a dilettante. Oh, wait, there she is—Theo, do you see?" I turned and noticed a woman floating facedown on a bright orange raft. She was motionless, and not in a way that suggested sleep. One of her arms in the water, the other resting by her side. I hustled toward the shore and slipped off my shoes. Up against the sea, the texture was rough, pebbled, tiny rocks slicing at the softest parts of my soles. The waves folded on top of one another, like fabric.

Amara yelled behind me, "That's her, right? We had a spritz or two at lunch, but I—"

The woman on the raft floated out of sight, behind another group of swimmers. Should I have called for her? I was ankle-deep and stuck, too scared to go in farther, the water clinging to me like mud. Behind me, Amara rattled on about how nice the day was, and then, something else caught my attention—a curiously shaped stone looming under the water, a few yards away, about the size of a head, and white in color. A carved nose peeked through the windblown caps—or did it? Was that an intricately rendered curl of hair? I began to wade toward the object, the tide creeping at my knees, the image becoming clearer—until a splash to my right startled me. Drops hit the side of my face. A man had dived in. Ripples haloed around him, on and on, blurring my view. I tried to find it again—the head, the stone, whatever it was—but it was useless.

"Oh, never mind," Amara was saying, her voice clear again. "The princess has graced us. Darling, where've you been?" I turned.

There stood Theo, wearing a pale blue bikini, an open white shirt, flowing in the wind. Her face appeared smudged by the sunlight, as though it'd been painted with a palette knife. I recalled the easy surrender of my mouth on hers, the warmth.

"What are you so fixated on?" she said, as she approached me. She smelled of alcohol, of metal and salt. I turned back—I thought about trying to explain. But then she set her chin on my shoulder and gazed out in the direction of the object, our eyes unified in their field of vision. "What's there?" she said. "Nothing," I told her. When she moved away, I felt untethered. We both plodded back toward Amara. As Theo sighted her, she communicated with a single nod. "Right. I'm going to get some Popsicles," said Amara, rising from her lounge. "Orange. Lemon. I hear the lemon is beautiful. Sour or sweet, or both. Who wants?"

Theo asked for the lemon. "Two," she said. She pulled a second chair closer to Amara's and sat down, and then motioned for me to join her. It took me a moment to find my bearings. My body wouldn't settle in, my mind drifting back to the stone.

"Where did you go?" said Theo.

"What?"

"After."

"After?"

She nodded.

"Oh? Right. I went to a friend's."

She seemed nonplussed by the comment. "It's stifling out, God," she said, fanning herself. "Let's go in, shall we?" She'd brought an extra bikini. I'd never have agreed to wear it but wished I were the type of person who could. How rousing a thought, for my skin to brush the same fabric as hers.

"You brought that for me?"

She said she had.

"So, you knew I'd come?"

"Why wouldn't you?"

"Wait," Theo said. "What friend?"

"What?"

"Where you went to. You said a friend's."

"You don't know him."

She leaned over and reached into her bag for a cigarette. The wind smelled overripe, as it blew through her hair. How badly I wanted to slink onto her lounge, pull myself up against her back, experience the sun-soaked heat of her.

"How have you been?" she said. "Since."

"Not great. I thought I saw the statue's head just now. Out there in the water."

She nodded as she lit the tip of her cigarette with one hand and shielded the sea breeze with the other. She couldn't catch fire, so I moved a little closer to my right, toward her, and cupped my hands around hers, and we both blocked the wind, and once we were successful, I got up and moved to the other chair. She lay down, and so I did too. There were only six inches between us. She smoked with her right hand, and her left hand she dangled off the side of her lounge. I let my arm fall beside hers. Out of the corner of my eye, I watched her fingers move toward mine—or maybe I sensed it, or willed it, as simultaneously, mine began to move toward hers. We reached for each other and interlocked. Our hands hung there for a moment. She traced my palm with her thumb.

"Is it possible?" I said.

"I wouldn't say it's impossible."

Her voice was smooth, disembodied. Her touch calmed me. "That feels nice," I said. "Good," she said, and then, without taking a breath, she told me they were leaving the island. She and Niko. I waited to respond. The sun moved behind a cloud. A shadow cast itself over our faces. In my head, I practiced how to sound neutral, but when my words came out— "What?" I said. "Why?"—I knew she could hear the blueness of my tone.

"I can't really say."

"You can't or you won't?"

She didn't answer. We were still not looking at each other.

"What will you do? I mean, elsewhere?"

"Settle down. Have kids. Et cetera."

My mouth betrayed me with a laugh. "You're joking."

She shrugged. She did not seem to be joking. Could the creation of a new life be her antidote to death? The thought bothered me. It felt uncreative. Or perhaps I was envious of its simplicity.

"And your art?"

"Everything I do," she said, seriously now, "I do for art."

I asked when.

"Soon. A few days," she said.

It didn't make any sense. It was so abrupt. What would she do with all her things? The life she'd made. I felt woozy. Too hot. Hungry—I hadn't eaten a real meal since dinner on the mountain. I couldn't remember the last time I'd had water.

"Are you OK?" she asked.

I couldn't see straight. My skin burned. "I'm just a little—I'm tired I think," I said. "I should go."

"No," she said. "Nobody's going. Take a rest here."

I said I couldn't. But then she squeezed my hand and began tracing again—and it got to me, the rhythm of her touch, the whipping of the umbrellas, the soft rustling in the trees. I closed my eyes and a weightlessness spread from limb to limb. I thought of the woman floating out there in the water on the raft, and then I wondered, was I that woman? Was I in the water now?

The next thing I knew, I was woken by the noise of her and Niko in the middle of a hushed argument.

Theo was sitting up, and she and Niko were facing each other, him on the edge of the lounge, his body leaning farther with every declaration, his hair wet and slicked back; a bead of water dripping down his neck. They were speaking Greek, and I could make out only some of their words. Niko mentioned Amara—and then he mentioned Leon. He said something about Theo's drinking. How she shouldn't have been. My eyes traveled down to the towel wrapped around his waist, his hand fisting the knot, knuckles striated white.

I cleared my throat and pretended to wake up, stretching out my arms.

The sun had lowered, but shade had moved away again. The two of them spun toward me, regarded me in surprise, like they'd forgotten I was there. At their sudden attention, the space between my eyes throbbed. I pressed my fingers against the skin to absorb the looming pain, but it didn't work.

"You went out like a light," said Niko.

"Did I? What time is it?" I sat up. "I should get back." With the sun, the dehydration—I could sense the ache would be too substantial to will away or ignore.

"Where?" said Theo.

"But you did not swim," said Niko.

"I don't swim." The agony built, extending toward the sides of my skull. An aura floated around both of their heads.

They told me to stay. "Please," they said. I didn't understand what they wanted from me, what I might have wanted from them, but I realized our relationship—if that was what I could call it—had been predicated on these questions, and to answer them would have been to fracture an already fragile reverie, to answer them would have been to watch it die.

"Is it too hot?" Niko said. "We can proceed into the shade."

Theo smiled at me, dimly. I said no, it wasn't that. I said I was feeling a little unwell. The pain was coming on fast; it was hard to get the words out. I told them I appreciated the invite, and then we all stood up. Gravity rejected me. I fell backward onto the chair. I gave in, hanging my head between my legs as pressure crescendoed behind my eyes, which teared up with a brackish liquid. Blood or water? I saw an aura, and another, and another, and then, my vision fell through me like my ocular bones were a sieve. The whole world didn't go completely black as it had before; it was more that it blurred, the sand, the ocean, the sky, rippled and reflective, like a moire.

Vaguely, I heard Theo's voice. "What's happened? What's wrong?"

"It's my head," I said. "It's just a thing. It will pass."

"What thing?" said Theo.

"It's my vision. Ocular headaches. It's like—I've lost my sight. A little."

"A little?"

I said again, perhaps too harshly, I would be fine. I was fine. But every time I drew a breath, I thought of the bag taped around the statue's neck like a caul—inhaling, exhaling. The image overran my system, then left me vacant, an echo chamber of repercussive sounds. The waves roaring. Screeching children. Plastic ripping off Popsicles. The scent of sweet, frozen citrus. Had Amara come back? All I wanted was to be alone. Though for reasons I could hardly ascertain, the idea of that, too, felt wrong.

"You're not fine," said Theo.

I pleaded with them to give me a minute, but they wouldn't. They wanted me to go to the emergency room, to, at the very least, see a doctor. I refused. However ridiculous that was, I didn't care. "Then you have to come with us," said Theo. I didn't want to fight her. I couldn't. She helped me up. As we walked, the sand burned my bare feet. "Do you have my shoes?" I said to the air. We stopped and Theo slipped them on as I held her shoulder for balance. We began to move again. Niko's arm wrapped around the other side of my waist as they both guided me. He smelled of alcohol too. They called a taxi. For a second, I worried we were getting into Dimitri's cab. I was always doing that, assuming coincidences, searching for proof that the world centered around me. But the seats smelled different than Dimitri's—like talc and sun-dried laundry—and I didn't recognize the driver's voice. When we hit a corner, I leaned into Theo and then didn't move. Niko was up front, I guessed. I wished he had sat back there with us, as Theo mothered me, setting her cool palm on my tremoring thigh. "Sh," she said. "Almost there." I couldn't tell if I resented her patronization or was racked with desire for it, and then I felt a soft, casual kiss on the forehead, the texture of dry lips. I mourned the fact that I'd never be able to remember the moment visually. How would I ever conjure it again, by feeling alone?

By the time we got to their place, I was embarrassed but also grateful and I didn't know how I'd ever be able to express that, or if I'd need to. I heard the iron gate creak open, felt my feet move over those dried-up pine needles and bursts of dead leaves. We climbed the steps together and I remembered that little stone nymph I'd seen my first time here. I tried to recall its details—how the sun broke through the marble.

When I mentioned it to Theo, she said, "What nymph?"

Once inside, Theo sat me down on a bench or chair in the alcove and took off my shoes. I felt like I was on something psychoactive, acutely alert to every micromovement, every signal of touch: the blunt skin of her fingers, the soft palms, the sharp tips of her nails as they grazed my heel— and then it was done. "Were there protests yesterday?" I asked. "Like the one at the Acropolis?"

She sighed. "I don't know," she said, but she wouldn't have told me the truth. They escorted me to their couch and I lay down. Intermittently, Theo fed me small sips of water and pieces of stale bread as she and Niko argued over how much ibuprofen I could safely consume and when they should take me to the hospital. Theo sounded incredulous on my behalf. Part of me appreciated her anger, even if I knew it wasn't about me. With every passing exchange between the two of them, her fury rose. "I am post-discussion," she yelled. "It is not enough to sit around and talk." But I remained serious in my decision to stay put. "It will come back in a few hours," I said.

"Hours?" asked Theo, and I didn't know if this sounded like a long time to her, or like a little.

At some point, they both left the room; I heard a door close, but not all the way. I could still make out their voices, and in their brief pauses, I recognized a strain, the resuscitating of old wounds—and then I heard my name. It fluttered in between them quickly, the echo of it flickering in my ears. How strange to think we were all nothing to one another, only weeks ago. Was this where I should have felt guilty? For intruding on their lives?

If only an awareness of guilt could finally deliver me from it, I thought, as I tried to quiet my mind. I couldn't tell if the pain had lessened or if I'd become accustomed to it, but either way, eventually, I could sense the light in the room shifting, the sun setting. I fell asleep to the familiar tension of their silence, the white noise of a fan plugged into the corner of the room, an insect's wings fluttering somewhere close to the window, the faint beat of my own, slowing pulse.

40

A few hours passed, and then, in the early evening, I woke. The windows were open, the lights off. Boxes stacked in all corners of the living room; yellow skates pressed up against dull cardboard. The place was mainly as I'd remembered it from the dinner party: the white couch—where I'd fallen asleep—and the heirloom rug were still in place, but the stone coffee table was gone. I looked to my left—the three-legged lounge chair had remained. Even the gauzy curtains still hung. I wondered what would be left behind, and though I was not so delusional as to believe these items harbored even an ounce of consciousness, I felt a transient sadness for their impending abandonment.

Niko came into the room mussed, as though he'd walked out of an Egon Schiele, his hair wild and dried with salt water. Beside me, he sat on the couch. Our knees nearly touching.

"You are improved?"

I said I was. Mostly, I could see fine—some things were a little blurry, and I was a bit dizzy. But the pain had nearly snuffed itself out, nothing there now but a dull thrum at the plinth of my skull.

"You offered us a scare."

I nodded, said I was sorry.

He waved his hand. "No, no apologies."

"Where's Theo?"

He looked down at his wrist, as though checking the time, though he didn't have a watch. "She will return soon. Are you well enough for some water?"

I told him no. "I need to make a call," I said. "Can I make a call?" He pointed to the bedroom; his eyes stuck on me. "It is in there," he said. I hesitated. "Oh, right," I said, standing up, "OK."

Their room was bare, nothing except for the bed, the phone, and on the wall, a night-light, glowing a blunted pink. Amongst its luminance, I felt feral and unhinged. How had I received such entry to their intimate lives, such unmerited ingress? I sat on the edge of the mattress where the sheet had curled up, exposing pilled fabric underneath, years of wear. The sheet had an inactive, flattened quality to it, cloth caught in a Doric frieze. I remembered seeing Theo in here, the night of the dinner. Her twisting foot. The tension in her toes. I glanced around. The phone cradled on the floor, graven in its stone-washed color. I reached for the receiver and held it in my palm for a second before I dialed the number to William's office. He didn't pick up, so I tried again, and again, and then I tried Sandra's number. When she failed to answer, I called Madison. His voice sounded distant, but relieved. "Jesus," he said, letting out a breath. "Where have you been?" He'd been trying to reach me.

"Relax," I said.

"No. It's serious."

The night before, William had suffered a stroke.

He wasn't dead, but according to Madison, "he might as well be."

I didn't know what to say.

"Hello?"

"Sorry. I'm here. Is he on life support? Or . . . ?"

He said he didn't know.

"How do you not know?"

"He's on a ventilator," said Madison.

There was a pause. I thought of everything catching up to William, marching toward his grand office for retribution, but I could see only a row of useless, plastic soldiers, melting in the sun.

I asked what hospital he was in.

"Cedars-Sinai. Sending flowers now. I can sign your name."

At that, his tone soured. He sounded practiced, even more removed than before. He said he was in a bit of a hurry, and that he'd tell me everything once I was back. Did his wife have something to do with the rush? Perhaps she was sitting right there, monitoring. We both went silent.

"Elizabeth?" Madison said. "Did you hear me? About the sale?"

I told him no. The line had cut off.

"It's gone through."

I forced myself to say, "Has it?"

It was official, money exchanged between the museum's trust and Alec. According to Madison, though the protests had caused a slight stir in the media, and the vandalization had worried our lawyers and PR team, there wasn't much that could be done. William had already set everything in motion. By nine pm that night, my statue would be on its way to LA, without its head.

And then, I asked the question for which we'd both been waiting. I asked where I fit in.

He didn't hesitate to say it. He wanted me to work alongside him. But I didn't know if he was offering me the role out of pity or fear. Maybe he thought I'd talk about us, what we'd done, or worse, discuss the museum's indiscretions. The thought of working side by side with Madison felt depressingly complicated. I looked around the blank room, my eyes flitted toward the window, where there was nothing but stillness and light. A clip of the sea. The possibilities of a different life cut through my paranoia. What if I was finally tired of trying to make space inside a world that had not wanted me? What if I could do something else?

I wondered if the statue was packed up now, at this second. I imagined her head, stored improperly, in some dank and dark location. But what about what I'd seen in the ocean? How similar its shape. The way sunlight hit its stone.

"I thought I saw it today," I said. "The statue's head."

"What? Where?" His voice sounded both gentler, yet somehow, more on edge.

"In the water."

"What were you doing in the water? You don't swim."

I paused. "Would you be willing to right some of our wrongs?" I asked.

He took a second to think. "Would *you*?"

When I didn't answer, he sighed, exasperated. "Listen, I'm not begging. If it's about money, we can talk. Give me a number."

"Oh, fuck off," I said.

"Elizabeth—wait. If you're playing hardball, this isn't really the time or place. You getting poached elsewhere or what? What's the angle?"

"What about the arm?" I said.

"I know you've got concerns," said Madison. "But they don't really matter at this point. The arm's part of the deal. It's done. All sides are happy."

I felt a pang of irritation, of nausea.

"No," I said, "its provenance is—it showed up out of the blue in a completely different condition."

"Fly back tomorrow," he said. "We'll talk in person."

"I'm not coming back tomorrow."

"OK, so the next day."

"Not then either," I said.

"Don't be inflexible. You've got to come back and help with the opening. You owe this to yourself. What have you worked for? If not this?"

A dish or cup or something banged in the kitchen. A cupboard slammed. I tensed. Was Theo back? Could she hear me? I ran my finger over the pilling of the soft sheets, as though it were braille, as though I were searching for a message.

"I don't know," I said to Madison, quieter now. "I'm trying to figure that out." I didn't say goodbye. I watched my hand put the phone back in its cradle and waited to feel sorrow, but it did not come. Or if it did, it was too quick a cut to bleed. Too deep a wound to notice, the kind that kills you on impact.

After I hung up, the apartment quieted. I should have left the room, but I couldn't move. I heard footsteps approach and cleared my throat. "Hello?" I said.

It was Niko. He leaned his shoulder on the doorframe and tilted his head, assessing me like I was a curious interloper. He had a bottle of raki in one hand. His nose and cheeks peeled from a sunburn.

"What is funny?" he said. "I heard you laugh."

"I didn't laugh," I said, and then I wondered: Did I? "Is Theo back yet?" I asked.

He shook his head and frowned an almost comic frown. That he might have been on the precipice of tears filled me with panic, but out of instinct, some failed attempt at politeness, I said, "What's wrong?"

"It is nothing," he said, and then, he came closer, jiggling the glass in his hand; the ice babbled. I got up. He gestured for me to sit back down.

"Who was this?" he said, nodding toward the phone.

I told him my boss was in the hospital. I told him I received a promotion but turned it down.

"Why?"

"The circumstances weren't right."

He joined me on the bed. Half a foot or so to my right. I could smell his acidic, raki breath. He put his hand down beside him, so that it touched my knee, and then noticing the boundary he'd crossed, retracted.

"Oh?" he said, furrowing his brow. "So? What will you do now?"

I shrugged. Maybe I'd go to the East Coast, I told him, work for a smaller museum, where I could have more control. Maybe I'd become a private broker. But the thought of such low stakes depressed me.

"You can stay?" he said.

"On the island? No. Maybe a few more days, but not long."

He handed me the bottle and inhaled deeply.

"Why are you really leaving?" I said.

"Theo and myself. We have been. Having disagreements. She is not taking care of herself. This place, it is no good for her."

"I don't think that's true."

"Sometimes," he said, before he paused for a long while, "either you put out the fire, or the fire puts out you."

"That's not an answer," I said, exhausted, feeling like we'd both worn out our welcome.

He looked forward and held his breath and then, he leaned over so quickly I hadn't time to register his intent—the need in his eyes. I'd seen that need from so many different eyes, so many different times, and shouldn't I be strong enough, not to succumb to it now? By the time I could make any decision, he was already wrapping his arms around my waist, sliding my dress down my shoulders, watching it fall to my hips.

He slipped off the bed and got on his knees. He removed my underwear, his hands shaking. From the top of his head, I could smell the beach. And Theo. Once again, I imagined he was her. Or I was her. Or we both were. I closed my eyes and saw her everywhere. I saw her standing in the corner and taking our photograph—a whole museum she'd make of us.

Niko rose and shadowed over me, and we both fell back onto the bed. The force of our movements popped the sheets off the edges of the mattress. I tried to snap them back into place, as Niko pushed his mouth onto mine, his tongue hitting my palate. How many times had that tongue touched Theo's? How many times had they exchanged breaths? The ring of a siren filled the room, receded, and then it was so silent I could hear the neighbor across the alley watching television. I could hear the fabric of Niko's trunks coasting down the skin of his calves. The sound consumed me. His weight consumed me. His outstretched body—clean and loose and expecting. When I reached for him, I felt him soften in my hands. I held back the urge to apologize, offering instead to help, but he pushed me away, retreated as though he'd been wounded. Hunched over, he sat on the lip of the bed and stroked himself, silently. I felt both younger than him and older. Like his child and like his mother. Uninvited, I thought about William and his daughters—did they like their father? Was he warm to them? Too warm? Was their household as imperious as I imagined? I wondered how long William would stay in his catatonic state. His brain still active, but his body, neutered. For a man like him, a fate worse than death.

In the background of my thoughts, Niko kept apologizing. He apologized for everything but what he should have been apologizing for. "It's OK," I kept saying, when what I really meant was: *I can't help you, and you can't help me, but here we are.* He turned back to glance at me in reprieve. A crack in the veneer. His face distorted in the dark. The walls of the room looked elastic. His skin looked elastic. Our silence was elastic—and then, the pain came back. Worse than before, or maybe the same. He stopped touching himself. "What is it?" he said.

"No," I said. "No, no, no, no."

In my head, I heard a laugh, then static.

"What is it?" he said again. I closed my eyes and screamed in agony—and it felt so good, even if we didn't deserve the noise, even if we did. The bones in my skull experienced a sensation like that of a fracture, matter breaking off bit by bit, turning to a wild, tired silt. I rolled away from Niko and puked over the side of the bed. It tasted venomous, metallic. It tasted inhuman. I couldn't get up to help Niko clean, which he began to do—still naked—tearing the bedspread off—exposing the outline of our bodies, rutted into the sheet. The sweat, his or mine?

He crumpled the comforter and tried sopping up my mess, but his nakedness disgusted me, and I begged him to get dressed. He seemed bewildered by the suggestion, as though he'd forgotten what we'd been doing, only moments prior. He went to the other side of the room where he threw on a pair of boxers, and then he left, and came back with a glass of water and a towel. He didn't sound or look angry, and his nonanger made me irate. I tried to stand and put my dress back on, but the cloth felt breakable—like a paper gown—and I kept tripping over myself. Niko offered his hand for help, and I, instead, took the towel. I crouched on the floor and watched my hands as they moved the liquid around, the existence of my bile a shock amongst their perfect, glowing hardwood. I thought of the obsidian tape on the statue's head. I thought of the bag. I thought of a tunnel with no opening. An ending without a beginning. The pain seared. "When is she coming back?" I asked, again and again, my vision locked on to the floor.

I implored Niko for something—anything. Any sort of pill he might have had, but he said they didn't keep anything like that in the house. I said he needed to go to my place and get my medication. "What medication?" he said. He wouldn't listen. He gave me more ibuprofen. I was still on the floor. How long had I been there? I crawled out of their room and returned to their couch—it was as far as my miserly body would take me. I lay down in a crumple and shut my eyes, waiting for the fists in my head to unclench, the taste of Niko's mouth kindling my tongue. An entryway presented itself to me. One of total surrender. But I couldn't make out the face of the woman standing there. All I knew was that she'd been split in two, and that she was me, but not exactly. *You could welcome the pain,* she seemed to say, *instead of hiding from it,* but she looked like an idiot. An idiot trying to make herself whole, even after she'd knowingly spent everything she had, all her currency. Niko left the door open a crack, and all night, I kept my eyes on that woman, afraid of what she might do, of what else she might take, until finally, when the sun began to rise, he closed it shut.

41

In the morning, I heard Theo in the kitchen. The air was calm and dry, redolent of a lit match, a burnt loaf of bread. The apartment seemed smaller than the night previous. My eyes caught the bedroom door, still closed.

Theo appeared, emerging from the tiny hallway to find me sitting upright on her couch. She walked in my direction, got close, but did not sit, a yellowing light passed over the top of her head and hands, where she clutched on to a mug, steam rising from its gut. She bent over and stared at me, softening her eyes. I stared back.

"You can see?" she said.

"I can see."

She clasped her hands in enthusiasm.

"Do you feel up for a favor?"

"What kind?" I said, glancing around. I didn't have the gall to ask about Niko, or say his name, or even pretend he existed, that we'd existed together. Done what we'd done—tried to do. But what about their arrangement? How upset could Theo be, I wondered, trying to calculate how much I'd need to grovel—or if groveling was the wrong thing to do, if it would make her think less of me. Or had she been lying? Did they even have an arrangement?

"We're alone," she said. That I couldn't read the tone in her voice filled me with muted dread. She set the mug on a box, left the room, and re-turned with a camera.

"Stay on the couch," she said. She told me to lie on my side and prop my hand below my head. "What?" I said. "Why?"

She held the camera up.

"You want to," I began, "of me? I told you I don't like pictures."

"I remember."

She went around the room and turned the lights off, but the windows, she left open. Through them came a pleasant breeze.

"You can say no," she said.

I laughed. "Can I?"

"You won't," she said.

"Why is that?"

"I can sense it."

"That's arrogant of you."

"Sometimes, you've got to be."

She maneuvered something on her camera and told me to lie back. Against my better judgment, I did. The fan in the corner whirred. Through the window, I heard children in the alley, kicking a ball back and forth. I heard the camera shutter. I tensed up again, as I thought of the statue. The assailant of a million sets of eyes on her—eyes from the future, from the past. An unspeakable exposure.

I said to Theo, "There's something that's been on my mind."

"What?"

"You asked me if the statue was complicit. When we first met. That night at dinner."

"Did I?"

"Complicit in her unfreedom. *Unfreedom* was the word." I paused.

"Don't worry," she said. "I merely want to present you as you are."

"As I am to me? Or as I am to you?"

"Neither."

"But you hold the lens. You therefore have the power."

"You have something of a fascination with power."

"And you don't?"

"I didn't say that."

I felt we were finally speaking to each other—perhaps not about the things we would have liked to, but in a tongue with consequence.

"Now lay back, will you?" she said. "Try to relax."

My right leg hung off the sofa's edge, my left hand I draped around the top of my head.

"Turn a little to the side," she said. "Find the light."

"How?"

"No, other way. Chin down."

As she began, I remembered when my mother and Henry commissioned that painting of Margaret. Despite bribery, she wouldn't sit still for the artist. Eventually, he gave up, photographed her, and worked from that, but there was something uncanny about the reproduction. It had been filtered through an extra lens. I wished I had more pictures of Margaret, something truer. Instead, what I had was a memory of a painting created from the image of a photograph. And what would I have of this? A memory of a picture I would likely never see?

I watched Theo as she worked, trying to make sense of our arrangement. A few moments later, I heard footsteps in the hallway. I prayed it wasn't Niko. Though for all I knew, he'd already told her everything. Was that why she was doing this? Was she making me pay? I glanced at the door. I was not her hostage. I could have gotten up at any moment and left—and yet I didn't. I wanted to please her. Not out of compunction or self-recrimination. But because I could, by which I mean, because I was able to. And so, when she suggested I undress, my breathing did not catch on my own panic. I did not hesitate as I moved my fingers toward my dress, then let it drop, as I unhooked my bra and felt the weight of my breasts fall, for a moment embarrassed by my retracted nipples, betraying me with their shyness when I did not feel shy. Of my bareness, what did Theo see? I'd only ever experienced myself through the eyes of men. In the ensuing silence, she gave no indication. Was she pleased—displeased? Neither? And what would I do with that information, if she was to make it known? Could I endure it?

Eventually, she instructed that I move to the nook, where I positioned myself on the three-legged lounge, first sitting up, my legs crossed. "That's not right," she said. "You're doing too much."

"I don't know how to do less."

"Stop trying."

I folded over, elbows on knees—"no," she said—then leaned back, stretched my arms above my head—"not that"—then extended my neck, face toward the ceiling.

Quickly, we began relying only on physical cues, infinitesimal gestures, fleeting glances. In this language, we became fluent, and almost, equalized. But there was an accumulation too, an assemblage—and each time we stopped, to switch positions, for example, to change a lens—I became convinced that we had lost all traction, that I would resort to what I knew, until we began again, our breath quickening into a collective, as light cascaded over my neck and chest the way water had cascaded over the statue that day in the fountain. And I felt warmed by it, moved. My body a confessor, not a martyr—blood pumping, shimmering. Theo must have sensed a change too. Every so often, she'd demand that I hold my body, and without question, I would. Even if it hurt, I let the hurt build and build. Glorification by pain, by devotion. Thighs shaking. The pleasure in the anticipation of release. It seemed like the film was endless. I wondered if there was even film in the camera or if the exercise itself was some sort of perverse and private performance, some way to test the lengths I would go to accommodate her genius. Theo would do something like that. And I would be dumb enough to not notice.

The ancients believed genius to be an inherited divinity—the Greeks called them daemons—a guiding spirit, present in every one of us from birth, said to be responsible for artistic creativity, spiritual and philosophical fertility. Perhaps I had never understood the concept until then. Perhaps it was the only explanation I could come up with for how I was able to meet Theo where she was. For how I was able to satisfy her. To pose, but not pose. To become aware of my body, but only in the purest sense: the *becoming* sense. I could have spent all day coddled by her direction. Maybe I'd never tire of the thoughtlessness it afforded. Maybe time would not pass, and the air would not shift, and the room would not lose its light, and maybe she would never put down her lens, and declare, "That's it."

"That's it?"

"Yes," she said.

It took me a moment to move—to realize the fact of my own nakedness.

"So?" I said.

"So."

"What will you do with them?" I asked.

"Is there something you would like me to do with them?"

"I don't know. Will you—will other people see them?"

She wouldn't look at me.

"Not if you don't want them to."

"Would you let me see them?"

"If I like them enough."

Did I feel powerful or used? And why did those seem like the only two options from which I could choose? Unsure, I got up.

"Do you need help?" she said, not unkindly, as I rose to pick my clothes off the floor and slip them back on. I hooked my bra and peered back to see if she was watching. She was not.

All done, I returned to the lounge chair, but felt stiffer now, uncertain. Chilled by the air that had warmed me, only moments prior. Theo stood, poised in a disconcerting calmness, cleaning her camera lens.

"The sale's gone through," I said.

She froze, and lifted her eyes at me, her mouth opening an inch. She seemed genuinely surprised. "Even without?"

"Yes," I said.

"Did you take the job?"

"How did you know I'd been offered it?"

"I figured."

"My boss had a stroke," I said.

"So, you took it?"

"No."

She smiled. Was she proud of me? "That's good," she said. "You're better than any of those plundering institutions. You can do something meaningful now. Of your own accord."

"What? Like take pictures of naked women?"

She let out a little laugh.

"You have a such a—" She made a motion I couldn't understand—not quite admonishing but not quite welcoming either. "Such a limited view of things, don't you?"

"I'm sure I do," I said, leaning closer.

"These places deserve everything coming to them."

"And me?"

I studied her, waiting. She packed the camera up in its little case, set it down on one of the boxes, and turned around to approach me. The sun hit her face in miraculous ways, showing me versions of her I never knew existed. When I began to stand, she faced me fully, and walked closer, until we were inches apart, at which point she put her palm on my shoulder and softly guided me back down, but I refused to be overpowered, and this time, I kissed her, pressing my eager mouth onto hers and opening, waiting for her to open back, to let me in. Our teeth hit, but not in an unpleasant way. I tasted her tongue—it was saltless, and slick as glass. A warm and golden light passed through me, my desire gaining velocity, gaining traction, gaining claws, until—she pulled away, but not yet fully, her chin turned down, our foreheads resting on one another's. I imagined a doorway opening, our minds transferring ideas, and then our minds as two single entities, switching bodies. What a relief it could have been, to slip outside the narrow walls of my consciousness. Was that all I'd ever wanted from her? Or anyone else? I lifted my hand and brushed my fingers against her chin, traced the sharp angles of her jawline, moving by intuition only, the intoxication of contact. I touched the smooth contours of her neck; I touched her clavicle. Her windpipe. I did not feel like I was touching skin, but like I was touching *her*, if such a distinction could be made. I wanted to make it, and then tell her I had. But would she understand? Or would I sound empty, incomprehensible? Maybe we were, in her words, post-discussion. Post-language. Post-thought. I moved my hand back to her face, to her upper lip, her lower. She opened her mouth, and I pressed my thumb onto her tongue like a coin of Eucharistic bread. She smiled and grabbed my hand, escorted it down. I could see in her eyes what I felt in mine: The promise of tears. Or laughter. Or both.

"Stop," she said, moving fully away from me. The release of her weight like the draining of water. Bloodletting. Afterward, we stood there for a little while. Regarding each other the way one does after they catch their image in an unexpected reflection, eyes snagged in refractive disbe-lief, caught in a Möbius of recognition, unrecognition, recognition once more—and then, in a revelation to us both, her countenance turned from surprised, to completely unsurprised, and almost, even, unmasked. I felt physically stunned, awed, like this version of her was more real than I myself was. She had become tangible to me, and under the weight of her vision, I felt tangible too. Present in a way I hadn't in a long time, or maybe, ever. And, for a moment, I did not require a fuller explanation. For a moment, I wanted, only, to be.

42

After that day, I left the island and continued to travel. Julian and I had yet to sell the house, and I kept stoning funds from my savings account. Besides accommodation and hot meals, I tried to live simpler, smaller. I tried to be grateful, to forget about Theo, the statue's head. That I would never know its location left me with an inconsolable ache. But my wound was not exactly unwelcome. I held on to it like a penance.

I don't know how and when my colleagues found out about the raid, but I know when I did. Alone, at an airport in Albania, while reading the *LA Times*. I could not have prepared myself for the sheer amount of evidence the authorities found in both Alec's home and various independent museums across Greece. Actual, physical proof: binders of Polaroids, photographs of every kind of antiquity I could imagine, several of which I recognized as objects currently displayed at the LA museum. A Polaroid of a younger William and a brighter, thinner Alec, shaking hands and facing the camera, a whole warehouse behind them, teeming with sculptures, pottery, jewelry, and coinage, some items on packing crates, some wrapped in newspaper, most waiting to be restored and resold for millions of dollars. None of the information was necessarily shocking—I supposed how deep it went was the only shocking part, though *shocking* isn't really the right word. It's one thing to be aware of how it's done in practice, another to see sins catalogued in print. And though I'd made peace with my decision, I couldn't help but feel a little stung about William not telling me he'd known Alec. Why hadn't William brought me deeper into his inner circle? Had I not proved my loyalty? Maybe he'd known I was in over my head. In my most generous moments, I like to think he was trying to protect me, but I would never know. He was currently vegetating in some hospital, awaiting the ultimate vacancy.

I would not say I was on the run, necessarily, but I preferred that wherever I went, people did not know my name or the kinds of things with which I had been either obliquely or directly involved, depending on who you asked. I waited for William's inevitable indictment. For the Greek and Italian governments to use him—and by extension, us—as an example for the industry's bad behavior. Indisposed, he could bear much of the weight, and though I might have been safe for a little while, I was almost certain— perhaps a little hopeful—that my future held a reckoning as well. Even if I wasn't sure what good it would do. At various points, I considered reaching out to the authorities, making an agreement: immunity in exchange for testimony. I'd been contacted by several publications—even Amara reached out—but like the coward I was, I kept quiet. No one sought a dialectical conversation—they sought conflict. Condemnation sells. Not that it shouldn't. At the same time, the repatriation movement expanded. Protests intensified. Greek schoolchildren sent postcards to all the most prominent museums, asking for beloved items back. Vigils were held, one in Athens, two on the islands. I watched grainy footage on some shaky television in a roadside café in southern Serbia: a mass of forlorn faces in front of parliament grasping onto thin, dripping candles, wax threatening to burn their hopeful fingers. I ran to the restroom and tried to make myself sick, as I thought of the boy who died at the Acropolis. I wondered if I was only sorry because I felt I was supposed to be.

When I came back, the TV channel had been changed, and as time passed, as more and more tragedy yoked the world's consciousness, the protests died down, or else, were forgotten. The sins of the present, swept up once again, into the past.

43

Meanwhile, I went on with my itinerant life, never staying in one place for too long, attempting to appreciate the peculiarities of each new destination, to kneel at them with wonder, or perhaps, reverence. But to no avail. In Turkey, I stood before the volcanic rock formations, completely silent, waiting to be awed by the earth's eccentricities, but the heft of the midday sun interrupted my focus. In Macedonia, I spent twenty minutes watching a drop of honey ooze down the side of a cup, its viscosity like acrylic paint, unsure if I was bewitched, or horrifyingly bored. One evening, I wheedled a glimmering, palm-sized moth out of a window in Bulgaria. The way it fluttered—so unselfconscious of its gracelessness—could have spurred me to tears. But my cheeks remained a desert, every emotion a scam.

I was not trying to find myself so much as lose the self I thought I'd been. If I moved quickly enough, I could outpace her. Though all the while, the past tugged on me, or else I, on it. I kept the picture of Theo—naked, with the coins—folded in my wallet, and every so often, when the world quieted, I took it out and put it under a magnifier keychain I'd purchased at some kiosk. I would sit there with aching eyes and study the image as though it were a defining, rarified exemplifier of *Art*. Maybe it was. Or would become one, but I'd never be the right person to tell. I wondered if Theo ever scrutinized the photographs of me or viewed them longingly. Sometimes I imagined us both in bed, thousands of miles away, scanning each other's likeness. It seemed preposterous that she'd be doing such a thing—but also preposterous that she wouldn't be. Was I afraid to know that she'd owned my image, in its most vulnerable state? Was I afraid of seeing myself displayed in some cold exhibit while a sea of strangers quietly perused my naked form? The idea of such exposure—by her hands, and her hands alone—roused in me an irreducible desire to be ongoing, to be endless, and it was this, I think, that frightened me more than anything.

But I hadn't expected to see her work again. At least not soon. In fact, I hadn't expected to hear from her at all, not unless I reached out first, a task for which I was not brave enough. And then, on the day I flew to Albania, I stopped at an internet café to check my email, and there it was: a message.

> Dear Elizabeth,
>
> I'm working on something new. What do you think?
>
> > With love,
> > Theo.
> > P.S.: There are two in there.

Attached to the message was an image. I opened it and waited, blinking at the loading pixels in anticipation, my chest pink with heat, a pleasurable ache. The top half burst into clarity—black and white, thickly grained, with a hazy, retro quality, low contrast, dark lighting, and simple in shadows—but the rest of it halted, strayed into a vague gray. I could see them from the waist up only—Theo and Niko, sitting at a dining room table. They were both topless. She, leaning away from the camera and toward him, her face hidden behind his. My eyes glided down Theo's neck and traveled toward her sharp collarbones—all the areas I had felt with my own hands—bypassing her breasts before landing on her rounded stomach. In confusion, I stared at the change in her form. She must have been what? Only a few months along. Which means she might have been pregnant as early as that day on the beach, even before. At dinner. At the Acropolis. Had she known? Was this why she and Niko had been fighting? Was this their real reason for leaving? I held back the impulse to reach through the screen, run my palm along her belly. *There are two in there.* Twins? Was that what she meant? I wondered if they were girls.

I waited to feel devastated about the concept of their impending life, but as the rest of the photo continued to load, pixel by excruciating pixel, I thought instead of this relief votive the museum had of a mother, her child, and Hygeia, goddess of health. Fifth century BCE. Marble. In the scene, the goddess stands over the mother and her nurse; she, twice their size. The mother's body is bent, her head cocked, as though close to falling off, her arms leaden with exhaustion. Hygeia has a stern countenance, a stiff gaze directed at the mother, as she holds the baby toward her. It is hard to tell what sort of expression the mother wears, as the fragment's marble has eroded, but her body language does not mirror the miracle of birth. She offers no nurture, no sense of tenderness, upending the viewers' expectations of the mother as nothing more than her reproductive anatomy, nothing more than vessel, commodity. At the time, the delicate weakness of her splayed limbs had reminded me of my own mother, who rarely held anything heavier than a carton of milk.

When Margaret was a baby, I would pick her up out of the crib because my mother couldn't. Sometimes I'd hold her up to my mother's breast, but often, Margaret wouldn't take. *I'm sorry*, my mother would say, but I could never tell to which one of us she was apologizing. Was she embarrassed that her body refused its own utility? Or had she resented the idea of that utility in the first place? Sometimes I wondered if I'd relied on too many static facts, if I'd made of my mother not a ghost, but a myth. After Margaret's death, she started growing her hair out, not using curlers. Stopped spritzing overripe perfume and painting her nails that lithic beige. She discovered hemp. She'd sit on the porch on a plastic lawn chair at night, illuminated by a single light, an unknowable woman in a tenebrism portrait, ogling the empty summer street, her eyes checked in—on what, I couldn't know. It seemed like she was planning something—a rebellion, perhaps. But one never came.

Finally, the photo appeared whole. I looked toward Niko, whose face was faded, and offered no solace, his head down, side-eyeing the camera in torpidity. Against his chest, he held a plastic doll, a baby doll, and cupped its mouth with his hand, his body language inexorably loose. The doll's clothes gathered on the table, alongside spiraled orange peels, food wrappers, and a candelabra—three candles, lit. The objects were oddly arranged. Too spread out or too close together. One food wrapper, for instance, balanced precariously on an angle, stuck straight up in gravity-defying obedience. Immediately, I began to untangle everything's meaning, how each item pertained to the scene's collective message, its internal truth—its value—before I realized the objects were likely meaningless, and this, itself, might have been their meaning.

My eyes flitted around the rest of the frame, which was stark and blank, except for a crowded bookshelf, behind Niko and Theo, slightly out of focus, and unusually messy—based on what I'd known of their Grecian apartment. I realized then that this might not have been their home, but some set.

I got up from my chair and stepped back. I tilted my head, pulling at the threads of the photo—the smooth sheen of Theo's skin, the bloom of that soft mother inside, not yet unfurled. Theo's mouth open slightly, a drop of visible saliva on the tongue, like a small flame—and as I stood there, I began to see something more complex: a woman resplendent, not enervated but enlivened—expanded and borderless and ever-changing, navigating the boundaries—the paradoxes—between selflessness, self-ownership, choosing what can and cannot be done to her body. I knew I ought to conclude that Theo had shared this to let me know she'd decided to make her life work—as both mother, and professional—in a way I couldn't, or wouldn't, or didn't want to. But that seemed too easy. She'd never make a statement so clean. Perhaps she wasn't even pregnant. It could have been prosthetics, a trick of the light.

I wanted to stop questioning, to stop caring, but I'd become too attached to my ideas of her, too attached to admit that I mightn't have ever understood Theo or her intentions—that I'd never learned to see her in the ways she'd needed to be seen: personally, politically, professionally. Maybe I'd done that with every woman—every person—in my life. And then—a moment later, my eyes caught something on the bookshelf behind her, something odd, something out of place.

I sat back down, leaned so close I could hear the buzz of the computer screen, and from there, I could make out—but just barely—the crown of hair, the creaminess of the marble, charged with an inexplicable light, and the gaze, those weighted eyes, unfocused, yet somehow, penetrating both lens and pixelated display. A shadowed split between lips. Curls like limpets. That torqued neck.

Heat roiled through me. I began to sweat. I could not move. Minutes passed like this; my eyes fixed on the head as it floated like an orb, like a spectral being. *You must have known*, the head seemed to say, *that this had been bigger than you. That you were nothing but a cog*. But who else had played a part? No one was truly free, certainly not of each other. Was Niko bright enough to be involved? To pretend to know so little? Who held the head as Theo wrapped it in that tape? Who assisted her in the decapitation? A destruction so horrible it had surrendered me to tears. I thought of Leon—could he have helped? And then, I thought of all the gaps from that night—from my life—still unfilled. If only I could find something to hold them. A shape. A body.

Maybe Theo had acted alone—she'd chide me for suggesting anything else, for doubting her capabilities. I understood nothing with confidence—except for the fact of the head. But what would I do? Demand its return when it was never mine in the first place? How obvious it seemed now. I had underestimated her, just as she'd warned. But she was nothing if not committed. Obscene, but brilliant—the final act in her three-part production.

As I sat there, replaying it in my head—the reflective tape, the undulating bag—I felt a pang of admiration. If she'd wanted to elicit emotion, erupt institutional complacencies, she had succeeded. Even if it was brief, only a flicker in our lifetimes. And yes, perhaps no one would face real incrimination for these exploitative transactions of which I, too, was culpable, but at least, she had tried. And though her performance went against everything I had worked for, all my principles, and though she had lied to me, possibly used me for her artistic gain, and had, in the process, sacrificed one of the most—if not *the* most—stunning artifacts I'd ever encountered, I couldn't help but feel myself leaning toward the screen, toward the image of her, a prism of uncertainty, of possibility—closer, closer, as though, at any moment, she might reach back.

44

I n Albania, I stayed twenty miles from the sea, under a different name, at a hotel built with bricks, painted white and glassy, but overstuffed with mortar; cement preserved in the act of ooze. The staff was surly and did not ask to see my passport. In their courtyard restaurant, I indulged in an exquisite Fergesë e Tiranës me Piperka—a warm bowl of cheese, stewed bell peppers and tomatoes, butter and oil, served with fresh, rock-salted bread—as chickens clucked at my feet. When I ate, I imagined the careless way Theo would have consumed the dish, which made the satisfaction twofold. I must have gained ten pounds since I'd left America. I had to buy all new clothes. I did not feel comfortable with the extra weight, but I did appreciate the chance to curate a collection of light fabric and flowing linen, no more constricting slacks and blazers, or worthless skirts and heels. And every time I opted for a sandal or casual shoe, I, pleasantly, thought of her.

I cut back on medications—mainly because they were harder to ac-quire by legal means—but I'd had no plans to let go completely. I didn't know how much of my rawest self I could bear. The migraines followed me too, as they always had, though I'd not experienced blindness or any-thing more than a slight aura since that afternoon with Theo and Niko. What kind of answer this suggested, I wasn't ready to question. Still, I was hopeful that one day, I'd be able to look back at her through the hazy lens of time, and know—not just in my mind, but in my body—that what she and I shared was less an affair of love and more an arousing transgression of faith. We could have never gone on, worshipping our separate Gods. And yet—and yet she'd shown me clefts in the stone of what I'd long known to be *Truth*, to be *Art*, and I believed, at the risk of sounding self-aggrandizing, I'd had the same effect on her, and during my lowest, loneliest moments, I felt ignited by that: this primal scrap of power.

As for what I did to fill my days, I couldn't say. I told myself I was biding time to make crucial decisions about the future. The truth was I didn't feel strong enough to face such an incomprehensible blank.

When the governments indicted William, I followed his case as closely as possible, though it plodded along at a miserable pace. Past employees spoke up about William's constant indiscretions: trustee money to help fund his lavish lifestyle, his harassment of secretaries and interns and various young women with whom he'd spent an inordinate amount of time mentoring. All the while, he withered away in the hospital. I was embarrassed for him, that he'd go out like this, a whisper to nothing. Sometimes, to preclude my lingering adoration, or else my guilt, my grief—whatever it was—I'd picture him as I wanted: strong-willed, a clichéd, rattling glass of liquor in one hand, leaning back with panache, in his big, important chair. "It's a bunch of overinflated lies made to serve some political agenda," this version of him says to some intern, some sucker—someone like me, perhaps—still stuck in his orbit. "We have all the power and the money in the world to fight it, and trust me when I say, we will win."

Meanwhile, the museum lawyers spoke to media outlets, declaring William had done nothing wrong—the whistle-blowers were disgruntled and delusional—and to please, let his family grieve in peace. They filed motion after motion to delay. Hearings became petty and unproductive cockfights. It seemed like it would never end, and I wondered then if William's health problems were not divine retribution, but instead, more examples of the world bending to his needs, offering him, in the last moments of his life, a blindness from consequence.

One day, I went to a museum on the coast, a three-story geometric building south of the Byzantine walls. It was an average afternoon in mid-

June: cloudless and racked with heat. I jumped from exhibition to exhibition, saving the Hellenistic section for last. Back against the wall, behind the museum's most prized possessions, I came across a female nude: Pentelic marble, around five feet tall. The similarities stopped me.

It was not my statue's replica—nor its possible pair—but the details were so alike I believed it must have come from the same sculptor. Of course, this one was perfectly intact—all four limbs, head, and neck—but there was something about it that unsettled me, something I couldn't articulate until I stepped closer and saw that her feet, her ears, existed without texture, without blemish. Her toes uncurled, her mouth, now, balanced. The expression on her face neutral. The traces of red and gold paint, gone. She had been worked on, restored. Her idiosyncrasies—her histories—stripped. When I closed my eyes, I could conjure nothing specific about her—this figure, this woman, who appeared more like the concept of a woman, and therefore, barely like a woman at all. I tried to go back in time, to welcome the imagination of this sculpture's raw materials—what it all *was* before it became *Art*, before it had been made and remade in the eyes of others whittled down to a single, digestible representation of *Beauty*—but I was interrupted, my reverie punctured by the sound of a child's laugh fluttering through the open, lofty walls.

A woman walked up beside me, holding her daughter's hand, both dressed in T-shirts they'd purchased at the museum, the little girl wearing a beautiful blue coat over top, her hair in a high, buoyant ponytail. Her face delirious with light. She must have been seven or eight years old. While the mother peered around the rest of the exhibition, the girl approached the figure, then moved forward, leaning the tops of her thighs against its plinth, like these boundaries and thresholds existed for no purpose, like they were nothing to her, of no value, of no use.

When she rotated her face to the right, I saw the white plastic of her cochlear implant. By then, the mother had left, and there was no attendee in sight. I could have told the little girl to stop, but it wasn't my place to say anything—and she looked so certain, so captivated, pressing her fingers into the statue's too-smooth calves, running them up and down the topography of the marble without a second thought. A few others flitted in and out of the exhibit, but the little girl didn't seem to notice them. Nor did she move on to any other object, so focused was she on this one.

Until, that is, the mother came back.

When the mother witnessed her daughter's indiscretion, she rushed toward her and slapped her on the head, before yanking the little girl away by the wrist, and muttering harshly into her nonimplanted ear. The eyes of the other museumgoers passively skimmed the spectacle, and then quickly resumed their viewing of the art. But I stayed on the mother, how she bent down and fixed the girl's implant, which in the commotion, had loosened itself from her ear—though you wouldn't have been able to tell, and I wasn't sure how the mother had known either. It was a nurture so easy, so exact, it appeared to have been done by feeling alone.

As the mother and her daughter began to leave, the little girl swiveled back. She glanced at me, the statue, and then me again. Like she'd understood something, something I never would. *Tell me*, I wanted to say, *what is it?* But then, she was gone.

I did not return to the sculpture. I couldn't bear to, or perhaps, felt it futile, felt, finally, that it was my time to go, and however fleeting that feeling might have been didn't matter, because it was true to me then, and it was mine, and that was enough. As I walked out the museum's doors, my eyes adjusting back to the afternoon light, I knew there were things only art could hold, and there were things it could not hold at all. When asked to recognize either, I'm not sure I'll ever get it right. But I'm trying only to take what I need. I'm trying to take less.

Acknowledgments

To every reader, thank you.

Thank you also to my luminous agent, Kate, whose understanding of Elizabeth, and belief in her story means more than words could say. Thank you to the singular Jade, whose editorial brilliance shaped this book in ways I will always be grateful for. Thank you to the entire team at Atria for their support. Thank you to Emily, for her wisdom and kindness. Thank you to John for his acumen and encouragement. Thank you to Stephanie and Helena and the English Department at Cornell. Thank you to Michael, for the soup money and the stories. Thank you to the incredibly talented Vivian and Rogelio. I lucked out with the two of you. Thank you, also, to my peerless cohort: Alice, Elie, Zahid, Bobby, Chioma, Sol, Maz, and Arpita.

Thank you to Lauren, for her friendship and her faith in me, and for the laughs and perspective. Thank you to Caren and John, for their love and enduring support. Thank you to Laurie and Mark for housing me in a room of books. Thank you to Joyce for her bravery. And to Greg, for getting a ninety-nine, to my ninety-eight.

Thank you to Verity, whose expertise helped me sleep at night. Thank you to Jason Felch and Ralph Frammolino, whose book *Chasing Aphrodite* was invaluable to the construction of this one. Thank you to all the other authors whose words inspired me along the way. To the library at Cornell, I am especially indebted.

And thank you, above all, to Logan. You are everything, and I couldn't have done any of this without you.

About the Author

C. Michelle Lindley's writing has been featured in *The Georgia Review*, *Conjunctions*, and more. She has received support from the National Endowment for the Arts and has an MFA in Creative Writing from Cornell University and a BA from the University of Berkeley in English and Art History. *The Nude* is her first novel.